THE
TRUTH
YOU'RE
TOLD

THE TRUTH YOU'RE TOLD

a crime novel

MICHAEL J. CLARK

Published by ECW Press
665 Gerrard Street East
Toronto, Ontario, Canada M4M 1Y2
416-694-3348 / info@ecwpress.com

Cover design: Michel Vrana

LIBRARY AND ARCHIVES CANADA CATALOGUING IN
PUBLICATION

Title: The truth you're told : a crime novel /
Michael J. Clark.

Other titles: Truth you are told

Names: Clark, Michael J., 1969-

Identifiers: Canadiana (print) 2021023878X |
Canadiana (ebook) 20210238798

ISBN 978-1-77041-404-4 (softcover)
ISBN 978-1-77305-770-5 (ePub)
ISBN 978-1-77305-771-2 (PDF)
ISBN 978-1-77305-772-9 (Kindle)

Classification: LCC PS8605.L36236 T78 2021 |
DDC C813/.6—dc23

This book is funded in part by the Government of Canada. *Ce livre est financé en partie par le gouvernement du Canada.* We acknowledge the support of the Canada Council for the Arts. *Nous remercions le Conseil des arts du Canada de son soutien.* We acknowledge the support of the Ontario Arts Council (OAC), an agency of the Government of Ontario, which last year funded 1,965 individual artists and 1,152 organizations in 197 communities across Ontario for a total of $51.9 million. We also acknowledge the support of the Government of Ontario through Ontario Creates.

PRINTED AND BOUND IN CANADA

PRINTING: FRIESENS   5   4   3   2   1

MIX
Paper from
responsible sources
FSC
www.fsc.org   FSC® C016245

*For Mom and Dad,
and the gift of lake life.*

CHAPTER ONE

MAY 20, 1967
SOMEWHERE NEAR THE MANITOBA-ONTARIO BORDER

The pliers were worn out, just like everything else in the three-year-old Plymouth. Constable Jarrod Mulaney slipped, cursed, then cursed some more at the situation in front of him, a worn-out tripod stand for the radar array. The teeth in the pliers' rusty jaws were worn to the nub. The slip joint slop rivalled that of the worst junk-drawer tools. Two of the tripod's legs were seized in place, thankfully at the regulation height. The third leg slopped in and out like a well-used trombone. The eye bolt collar meant to secure it had reached the end of its cross-threading days.

The Plymouth was still presentable, with black where there should be black, white where there should be white, and cherry red on top. Mulaney knew better: Unit Four was the Kenora detachment shitbox, a rookie car if there ever was one. The driver's side of the bench seat had been bent out of shape by the beefier members, sitting a good three inches back from the seldom-used passenger side. The seat springs couldn't be seen, though Mulaney could easily pinpoint their respective pressure points of torture, especially after the third hour of his tour. The brakes. *The brakes!* Everyone warned him that they would pull during hard stops, they just failed to mention that they would switch the side of the car they pulled to without warning. Mulaney had started to avoid U-turn pursuits because of them.

Mulaney knew that this was standard rookie fare, things that he had been warned about at the Ontario Provincial Police Academy. He had been with the Kenora detachment since March. His home address in the mill and tourist town still read as the Kenricia Hotel. There was bunk space available at the detachment if you didn't mind moving a few dozen boxes off the musty beds. The living quarters made sense for a smaller outpost, like Ignace or Vermilion Bay. The only time the boxes were shuffled was when a member was having trouble at home or avoiding trouble at home. Mulaney had yet to find the one that he might eventually have trouble with. The night girl at the Kenricia seemed pleasant enough, a stormy brunette with hazel eyes and small-town hips. On a scale of one to ten, she'd score a solid seven among the stiff competition back home in Toronto and could pass for an eight, maybe eight and a half in Sunset Country. That would change when the summer girls showed up, especially the ones from Winnipeg.

The tripod continued to curtsy in front of the constable. Of all weekends, the May Long deserved better. There would be little interest in honouring Queen Victoria and far more interest in getting to a cabin or campsite during daylight hours. There was nothing worse than having to unload a long weekend's supply of Labatt's, hamburger buns, and lawn darts down a slippery staircase of moss and timbers in the dark. Something would get dropped, usually the beer, or worse: the Crown Royal. It had happened enough that most cabin dwellers were keeping their speed at a steady ten over, twenty over if the driver had sprung for the big engine on the family car. These were some of the easiest pickings that any speed cop could have if the tripod weren't aiming the radar beam into the ditch.

Mulaney went to the open trunk. He rummaged through the various bags and boxes, deciding on something that he knew he shouldn't: the thick bandage tape in the first aid kit. He hoped that he could get through his tour without using it, though the morning briefing had said otherwise. The sergeant had passed out colour glossies of previous May Longs, the blood-red aftermath of speeding cars taking on the unforgiving rock cuts. Mulaney kept his bacon and eggs below decks, though just barely. He couldn't argue with the stats—someone was going to die on Highway 17 this weekend, probably more than one. The ones on the edge would be needing that tape.

The afternoon sun shone hard on the constable's shoulders. The Plymouth hid in the shade, which gave Mulaney a welcome relief from a day that had punched into the low eighties. Plenty of campers and cottagers would take that warmth as the green light for a dip off the dock, only to find out far too late that the water still retained the chill of the recent ice melt. The screams heard upon splashdown during the May Long could rival the haunting call of the common loon.

Mulaney checked the hands of his new Timex, a graduation and twenty-first birthday gift from his parents. It was almost four. The speeders would start to throttle up closer to five. He fished his lunch box out of the back seat. He popped the cap off his warm Pepsi using the edge of the Plymouth's rain gutter. The sandwich was ham and cheese, fetched for him by the seven at the Kenricia. She had thrown in a brownie wrapped in wax paper, home baked, and not on the menu. Mulaney took a bite of the sweet. He smiled as he chewed, adjusting the baker's score to a solid Kenora nine. Whoever the missus would be, she had to know how to bake.

"Base to four, base to four. Are you receiving me? Over."

Mulaney looked at the antenna on the Plymouth. He smiled. *An antenna that big could probably chat with Wally Schirra.* He had chosen the highest radio point available on Highway 17. The call was hi-fi crisp, no buzz, no crackle. He reached in through the open passenger window for the mic. "Four to base, four to base, receiving you loud and clear, over."

"Base to four, base to four. Are you receiving me? Over."

Stupid rookie shitbox. Mulaney checked the mic connection on the two-way. The lights were strong on the Motorola unit, a new battery under the hood for juice. He grabbed the antenna, hoping that his frame would somehow enhance the signal, the way it did on the TV set in his hotel room. He clicked the mic. "This is four, am receiving this and previous transmission loud and clear, over."

The third answer from the dispatcher was staticky and garbled. It also sounded very familiar. The words that did get through sounded like a repeat of the first two requests. *They can't hear me*, Mulaney thought. He repeated his receipt. The response was pure, unadulterated static. Without warning, the static turned into a high-pitched squeal. Mulaney dropped the mic and his Pepsi. The bottle shattered on the edge of a large rock poking through the gravel. He tried to reach the volume control on the two-way, but the squeal kept him at bay. He held his hands over his ears and crouched next to the OPP lettering on the door. It stopped ten seconds later, and a low hum took its place. At first, the hum seemed to be coming from the two-way, then it started to waver, moving from the left to the right, a sound that Mulaney had heard before, on a stereo demonstration record that came with his parents' hi-fi. The sound confused him. How could he be hearing a stereo effect on a mono speaker?

Mulaney looked up above the canopy of the turkey trail, towards the source of the sound. He blinked. He blinked again, hard, hoping that punctuating the action would erase what he was seeing. It didn't. He kept an eye on the thing as he moved back to the open window. He grabbed his ticket book from the dashboard. He used his pencil to sketch what no one would believe, unless the thing decided to pay a visit to Kenora harbour during the May Long fireworks display. Keeping the object in view and sketching it proved more difficult than he had thought. His eyes dipped down to the page to add the finishing touches. He smiled, a panicked smile, but a smile nonetheless. He was still smiling when the sound ceased. He looked up at his subject. The thing was gone.

The two-way resumed its regularly scheduled squawk. "Base to four, base to four. Are you receiving me? Over."

Mulaney grabbed the mic. "This is four. Go ahead, base. I am receiving you loud and clear. Over."

"Four, are you experiencing a radio problem? Over."

"Uh, that's a negative, base, am receiving you loud and clear. Over."

There were a few seconds of silence. The announcer asked a question.

"Four, are you . . . uh, seeing anything *unusual*? Over."

Mulaney wanted to shout that he had. He felt the excitement in his bones, like when he had chased fire trucks as a youngster. *Yes!* he thought. *I saw it. I SAW IT! It was amazing!*

He stopped himself mid-thought. His excitement gave way to concern, then dread. He wanted to tell the dispatcher what he had seen. He felt the words at the back of his throat, waiting, *begging* to be released. He stopped them cold. Mulaney knew what would happen to him if he spoke them. No more gun, no more badge, no more shitbox police car with messed-up brakes. No more brownies from town girls of any number. The only thing that the truth would set him free from was the OPP. He felt the disappointment of his ten-year-old self. He could almost hear the hockey card in the spokes of his old CCM, as the youngster faded from his very adult world. He clicked the mic.

"Four to base, four to base. Unusual how? Over."

Mulaney heard another voice through the static, not enough to identify. The dispatcher must have been cupping the open microphone, forgetting to release the Talk switch. Then, a new communiqué.

"Base to four, base to four. Disregard request. Received advise from Pinetree line: weather balloon is in the area, repeat, weather balloon is in the area. Over."

Mulaney smirked. *Weather balloon?* He looked at the sketch. It wasn't balloon-like in any way. It was pure science fiction, the kind of spacecraft you'd expect to see giving the crew of the *Enterprise* a hard time on *Star Trek. Something experimental?* The supersonic jet interceptors were fast enough to make an appearance from a military base on either side of the border, so fast that a blink could easily miss them. *Pinetree.* Whatever it was, the Pinetree radar stations were tracking it. *The hovering.* Anything that could do that was loud, Mulaney thought, not to mention windy. No wind, no sand in his eyes, and the slightest of hums. *Weather balloon my ass!* Mulaney knew it would be his ass if he said one word about it. He composed himself, as if a superior were watching him from the turkey trail. He clicked the mic. "Four to base. Acknowledged, over and out."

Mulaney put the mic back on the two-way. He turned to see a late model Chrysler station wagon speed past at about twenty over. He tore the sketch from his ticket book, stuffing it in his shirt pocket.

It was time to get back to work.

The Rabbit was dead. Sam Hutchings wasn't happy about it. She had been hoping to "take herself out to lunch" before making breakfast, the code phrase that her friends had been using for self-gratification since the late eighties. She looked over at the Rabbit's charger. It was plugged firmly into the wall, below the ancient night light that guided her way to the washroom at three in the morning, one of the many perks they forgot to mention in Late Forties class. The night light was off. The night light was never off; the miniature coach light had guided her way at

Bird Lake for as long as she could remember. It had to be a tripped breaker, or maybe a fuse, depending on which part of the cabin you were in. She stuffed the dead Rabbit under the unused pillow next to her. "Lunch" would have to wait.

Sam peeked over the side of the bed at the tiles, a pink and grey 1950s checkerboard that her late father must have bought at a garage sale. It wasn't the colour she was worried about; it was the cold. The temperature of the floor tiles on any Bird Lake morning was best measured in units of Kelvin. She couldn't remember how the temperature scale worked when it came to cold, only that anything less than a thermal sock underfoot provided the same protection as a paper towel for an oven mitt. She squinted for her slippers. She found them, outside the door, next to the wood stove, where she had left them around three in the morning. This was going to hurt.

The tiles kept their promise. The shock lasted throughout each of the eight steps it took to plunge her toes into the fuzzy pink. The cabin was cold. A quick peek inside the wood stove confirmed little in the way of ember glow. She had used the last of the firewood the night before. She grabbed an ancient afghan off the couch. It helped warm her shoulders, though it wasn't long enough to dip past her knees. The hot flashes that had reduced her to an oversized T-shirt for sleepwear were long gone. She shivered as she retrieved the electric heater from behind the recliner. They were both old, battered, and avocado green in colour. She plugged the heater into the extension cord that hung off the coffee table. She placed the heater on the tabletop, a surface that had been modified years before into a cribbage board. The heater dial advertised a high setting of six. Sam cranked it to the max. The scent of baking dust filled the cabin as she huddled herself and the afghan around the heater.

It took about ten minutes for the impromptu dry sauna to generate enough heat that Sam was able to ditch the afghan entirely. She walked to the front of the cabin. Bird Lake presented itself without a ripple. It had rained heavy the night before—strange for late June. May was usually reserved for the wet. The entire month was all about opening up the cabin. She remembered how slippery the trail was from the road, plotting her steps as carefully as possible on the smooth rocks and greasy timbers of the homemade steps carved into the hillside. This wasn't just a problem at the Hutchings' cabin; every cottage on Block Fifteen had a similar slip-and-slide entry. The rain gear never seemed to make it into the trunk of the family car for the first trip. That was when her father, Gerry Hutchings, would pull out his pocket-knife and punch holes through the bottoms of black plastic garbage bags, crafting homemade ponchos for Sam, her younger brother, Chris, and her mother, Lena. She preferred to call Gerry "Dad." So did Gerry.

After forty-eight years on the planet, Sam was sure of one thing: the coffee wasn't going to make itself. She found the glass Pyrex percolator in the cupboard, almost hearing her mother's warning as she lifted it out. *Don't break the stem. They don't make them anymore.* The cabin was full of Don't Make Them Anymore, from brands to build quality. She rinsed out a Canada Centennial cup for the morning jolt. She let the coffee cool as she checked her face in the camping mirror on the windowsill. The baggage had arrived right on time beneath her blue-grey eyes, steamer trunks, if she was being honest. The laugh lines kept gaining prominence, though she couldn't remember the last time that she had helped them along with such an emotion. Her preference to squint hadn't helped with the crow's feet. Her strawberry-blond hair was on the frizz, with plenty of grey roots in need of attention. For now, that's what ball caps were for.

Sam brought the steaming cup to the kitchen table, a sturdy chrome relic from the 1950s. She fumbled through the mail, still adorned with the yellow change-of-address stickers. There was another explainer from the human resources department at the *Winnipeg Sentinel*. "Dear Ms. Hutchings," Sam read aloud. "Please be advised that your severance package, blah-blah-blah, must report if you are working in a contract or temporary position, blah-blah-something-something." She flung the letter onto the table. "Sincerely, go fuck yourself," she said to the page. She flipped the letter the bird just to be sure it heard her. With the severance, her savings, the miniscule profit on her condo, and the cheque from selling her Toyota Corolla to a park ranger at Tulabi Falls, she figured she could hide away at the cabin until next spring and put it on the market then. Her brother had been hinting in that direction from Vancouver. Sam knew it was for the best. The cabin needed a roof, a new septic system, and probably a timber or two at the back, where an ant colony had been clawing away for the last decade. It could probably net about two hundred thousand dollars as it stood. She knew full well that most of the interested parties would mow it down to plop a lakeside McMansion on the site. She had been in such a cabin three doors down. *Who puts drywall in a cabin?*

The morning breeze had started to remove the glass covering from the lake surface. It was still calm, with polite ripples doing little to disturb a family of mallards at the water's edge. Sam noticed a magenta Post-It note on the fridge. *Magenta*, she thought. *Must be important.* She squinted at the scrawl. *Burn out the gunk.* She secretly hoped it was the gunk that was gumming up the works of her life, but she knew better. The gunk that needed burning out was in the lake car, a '76 Chevy Caprice four-door hardtop. *The lake car.* Gerry Hutchings had picked it up cheap in the early eighties, as a backup for Lena when he had to run into the city for work during the week. Sam looked through the kitchen window at the sap-covered beast. Stan Buckmaster at the Oiseau Garage couldn't shut up about how amazing it was that it was still in one piece. Sam couldn't believe how low the repair bill was to bring it back to life, or the insurance.

"Just make sure you take it for a good drive to burn out the gunk," said Stan. "And I wouldn't take those tires over sixty." Sam couldn't remember if Stan meant kilometres or miles per hour. She checked her phone. It was getting close to ten. Her daughter Megan would be arriving in about an hour and a half. Sam exhaled deep at the thought. She grabbed the keys to the Chevy and tossed them in the air but missed the catch. She fished the keys out of the tepid dishwater in the kitchen sink.

"Burning out the gunk," she said, as she wiped the keys on the dishtowel. "Burning out the gunk."

CHAPTER
THREE

The old Chevy took the bumps surprisingly well. *Not bad for a road-going living room,* Sam thought. She headed east for the gunk burn, to the end of Manitoba Provincial Road 315. The gravel strip had been vastly improved over the years, thanks to plenty of retirees choosing to live at the area lakes year-round. The elevation continued to rise as she drove towards the Ontario border. She hit the power window switches to take in the incredible scent from the trees. Three of the four windows agreed to participate.

Sam slowed as she approached Davidson Lake. It was much smaller than Bird Lake, shared by Manitoba and Ontario. The next rise signaled the end of PR 315 and the start of Werner Lake Road, which was anything but maintained. The Manitoba terminus had been widened for easier returns, as well as ample parking for ATV enthusiasts and snowmobilers, with plenty of room for unloading their trailers. Sam pointed the Chevy west, back to Block Fifteen. She stopped at the public well near Tulabi Falls, ignoring the warning sign for the water quality as she pumped and drank. She had drunk from the spring for years without ever getting sick.

Sam drove another mile before pulling over to the side. She turned off the ignition, genuinely hopeful that the old Chevy would start again. The tree cover shielded what she wanted to see. She used the front bumper as a step, planting her feet on the hood. It still wasn't high enough. She walked to the front of the windshield, then steadied a foot on the top of the driver's door to climb up on the roof. The sap-stained steel oil-canned beneath her as she rose to stand. She could see it now, the cedar-shake peak of the Whiskey Jack Lodge. It had been built in the fifties during the logging boom, though it wasn't built with logging money. The Whiskey Jack was the brainchild of Edgar Van Cleef, an American financier with interests in mining operations in what was then known as Crown Lands. It also explained the *e* in the spelling of the spirit. It had been more of a private fish and game camp for Van Cleef's posse. Van Cleef had died in the fall of '89, his skull crushed when he fell off his Honda three-wheeler near the water's edge. He had left the lodge to his longtime personal secretary, a man by the name of Norman Peale. Peale had improved the lodge where needed, adding a few more cabins, renovating the main lodge, even restoring a pair of vintage wooden speedboats for his personal use. The lodge was still a destination for the rich, the famous, and the private. Stan had said that he was pretty sure he saw Jennifer Aniston on one of the speedboats, after her first divorce. Sam figured that it was just someone rocking a Rachel hairdo, though the rumours persisted about global heavyweights. Bezos, Branson, even Elon Musk had reportedly spent a long weekend with the reclusive Peale.

The private lodge saw little in the way of road traffic, except for delivery vans, with no roadside signage. Most guests seemed to prefer the fly-in charm, regardless of its easy road access. Sam remembered the road in. There was a large gate behind the canopy of trees, probably still equipped with the security camera and intercom system that she remembered pulling up to almost thirty years before. The Whiskey Jack Lodge made a point of employing the local summer youth, if you were pursuing higher education at the university level. Sam worked there the summer of '88. She was called back for the summer season in '89 but left in late July. It was because of the fire at neighbouring Eastland Lake, the one that had threatened to take out Bird Lake with it. The one that had evacuated the whole area, from Bird River to the Ontario border.

The one that had killed her dad.

CHAPTER
FOUR

The Chevy didn't protest when Sam turned the key. She took a slow pass through the campground, wondering if a summer playmate she had met years before had returned with their family. The campground couldn't have been more than a quarter full. Most of the trailers screamed money, with comforts that still hadn't made it into the Hutchings' cabin. One couple took more interest in their RV's exterior-mounted flat-screen TV than the slow-moving vintage hardtop. She headed back to the cabin.

As Sam approached the right turn to Block Fifteen, she noticed the newer station wagon with Alberta plates waiting to turn left. *Shit*, thought Sam, as she made the turn. *Time to smile for the asshole.* The asshole was her ex, Cooper Goodman, a star reporter–turned–editor with the *Edmonton Journal.* They were coming up on the seven-year anniversary of their divorce, including three years of separation from her daughter, Megan, not including holidays and school breaks. Sam couldn't tell if the new Mrs. Goodman was in the passenger seat. She'd find out soon enough.

Sam returned the Chevy to its spot in the oversized garage. It dieseled as she shut it off, just in time for her ex to hear it as he exited his car. "Sounds like you need a tune-up," said Cooper, as he closed the door on his new Volvo. He stood about six-foot-two, fifty-six, thin, with a hundred-dollar haircut on what had to be fresh brown plugs. He was dressy, even for a most casual outing. Megan and the new Mrs. Goodman were at the back of the wagon, unloading what appeared to be everything a seventeen-year-old could own.

"It just needs the gunk burnt out of it," said Sam, remembering Stan's advice as she closed the driver's door. "But it's like most older things. You never know when they're going flake out on you."

Cooper caught the dig. He acknowledged with a smug smirk that Sam had seen many times before. He kept his words civil. "So, how's the great Canadian novel coming?"

"Epic," said Sam. She kept an eye on the passenger side of the car, waiting for her daughter. "How's Edmonton?"

"About the same. That commuter gondola nonsense has been taking up a lot of ink."

"Gondola?"

Cooper smiled. "You know, just because the *Sentinel* screwed you over doesn't mean you never have to read a paper again."

"So, instead of taking the bus . . ."

"You'd take the gondola."

Sam rolled her eyes. "Fucking Alberta. They've been losing their minds ever since oil tanked."

Cooper moved in close. "Hey, Sam, can you flush the toilet mouth till I get out of here? Bree's not a fan."

Sam moved in closer, keeping her voice low but forceful. "A fan? And I'm supposed to be one of hers? What is she, twenty-fucking-seven?"

"She'll be thirty-three in September," Cooper whispered. "C'mon, we'll be out of your hair soon."

Sam bit her lip, just in time to turn it into a smile for her daughter. Megan was the spitting image of 1980s' Sam, with the addition of a small nose stud, poker-straight hair, and earbud headphones that were seldom out of use. She was carrying too many bags for a proper hug. It didn't stop Sam. "Hey, Meggles."

Megan rolled her eyes as she endured the squeeze. "Hey, Mom."

"Did you have a good trip?"

"Where can I put all this?"

Sam released her choke hold. It looked like quite a load in the duffle bags. She grabbed the largest one from her daughter, almost dropping it. "What's in here? Bowling balls?"

Megan replied with the family eye-roll and a glass of whine. "Mom, I'm tired."

Sam lowered the heavy bag to the ground. "OK, head on in. The cabin's open. I did up the room on the far right for you. And watch your step on the, uh, steps."

Megan let out a classic teenaged exhale as she took the path to the cabin. Sam watched her go. She turned to find the new Mrs. Goodman launching a full-on hug around her frame. There was nowhere to run. "Hello, Samantha! It's sooooo good to see you again!"

Sam took the ex-hug like a champ. "Hi, Bree."

Bree Goodman released. She was everything an ex-wife would hate: young, blond, tight as a drum, and tits till Tuesday. Like most of the classic other women, Bree clearly had no idea how badly Sam wanted to lay her out flat on the gravel. *Not a clue*, thought Sam. *Not a single fucking clue.*

"Coop told me all about your novel," said Bree, exchanging the hug episode for an awkward double wrist clamp with the first Mrs. Goodman. "How many chapters have you written?"

Coop? "Uh, just crested ten," said Sam. It was a lie, unless you counted aimless doodles in her Moleskine while emptying a box of bargain Merlot on the dock. "Going to start pitching to a publisher soon." Sam wondered if her nose had grown an inch with that second falsehood.

"Oh, my goodness! That's incredible!" Bree threw in another unwanted hug to confirm her approval. Sam looked at Cooper with her best *what the fuck?* He knew the look well; it was time to motor.

"Hey, uh, Bree? We should get going if we want to get to that bistro at Seddon's Corner."

Bree released Sam. "Lazy Tuesdays! They've got four stars on Zomato!"

"Zomato?" Sam had no idea what that was.

"It's like a restaurant rating," said Bree. "You know, like Open Table or GrubHub?"

"Oh, yeah," said Sam. "I think I've used that grub one before." She felt her nose grow another inch.

"There's just one thing," said Cooper.

Sam turned to her ex. "What's that, *Coop?*"

Bree completed the thing for her husband. "We're eating vegan now. Megan just loves it!"

Sam blinked. "Does she now?"

Bree continued. "Oh, my goodness, it's the best thing I've ever done for my body, and my *soul*! I could never eat another animal again!"

"So, fish is OK?"

Sam hadn't meant it as a joke, but Bree took it that way. "Oh, Samantha!" She went in for Hug Number Three. Sam blocked her with Megan's duffle bag.

"So, we'll see you guys in August?"

"Around the twenty-fourth," said Cooper. "Get her back in time for school."

Sam nodded. "Well, drive safe, in . . . what is that thing, anyway?"

"It's a Volvo," said Cooper. "Top of the line, the Inscription."

"Yeah," said Sam, as she eyed the car, then the new Mrs. Goodman. "You always had a thing for the latest and the greatest." She smiled at the pair, then turned and walked down the trail to the cabin.

Cooper caught the dig, again. Bree didn't. "I really like her," she said, as she got back in the car.

"Yeah," said Cooper, as he opened his door. "She's one of a kind."

The sound of old dresser drawers being opened, closed, then opened again were a familiar vignette in Sam's memories of the cabin. She doubted that half of her daughter's things would make their way into the limited space. The first thing Megan had asked for was the Wi-Fi password. Sam figured it would take another five minutes for her daughter to ask the second question. It occurred just before the three-minute mark.

"Mom! Where are the other plugs in here?"

Sam smiled broadly before she answered. "I think there's only *one* in there, Meggles."

"I'm not seven anymore, you know."

Sam took her smile down a few notches before she turned. "Uh, of course you're not." Her daughter was standing in the doorway, looking at her with the eyes of indignation. Sam wasn't sure which part of what she said was a problem, until she said it again.

"Meggles, I—"

"I'd *prefer* Meg, if you don't mind."

Sam had hoped that these events weren't going to be the first steps into renewing the mother/daughter relationship, though she wasn't exactly surprised by the request. The sweetness that had once skipped more than walked was becoming a woman: a strong, opinionated, don't-call-me-Meggles-anymore kind of woman. It had been three years since she had left Winnipeg to live with her dad. Sam thought about dropping the proverbial parent foot on the smart mouth. She also thought about the three lost years. She decided to let it slide, for now.

"So, Dad says you're vegetarian now?"

"Vegetarian? Ewww! Gross!"

"Gross? What, I thought that was good?"

Megan decided to multitask as she explained, moving the old blankets and towels out of the dresser drawers. "Vegan is better than vegetarian, because you don't take *anything* from an animal."

"So, no eggs?"

"No eggs."

"Cheese?"

"Only if it's soy."

"So, that's a thing?"

"Really, Mom?"

Sam thought about what was in the fridge, with emphasis on the wasn't. "Well, I guess we'll figure it out then." She looked over at the buzzing relic. She could have sworn she heard it laughing at her.

Megan returned to her unpacking. She dropped the drawers' contents on the green fold-out couch against the wall, which had already become Sam's dumping ground of sorts, since no one in their right mind would sit on it. The cushions were thin, misshapen rectangles that spoke of zero comfort. The bedding below had similar squashing. It looked as though the inner part of the couch had found a black hole to slowly seep into. On Megan's fourth trip, Sam saw something stuffed between the stack of sandpaper towels she had dropped on the couch. She retrieved it while Megan headed back to the room.

Sam brought the spiral sketchbook over to the kitchen table as Megan kept unpacking. Her dad had taken up sketching after "some time off," which is what they called a nervous breakdown in the mid-seventies. It was never really talked about, not by her brother, who was too busy filling his diaper and charming the nurses on the psych ward during their father's stay, or by her mother, currently in the home stretch of Alzheimer's at the Whispering Pines Nursing Home in Pinawa. Dad was no Tom Thomson, though he truly enjoyed the times when the weather was less than perfect at Bird Lake. One of his favourite vantage points in his earlier work was the screen house by the water. He sketched the birds that visited the bird feeder and the squirrels and chipmunks that raided it. As his confidence grew, the colours of the finch, the blue jay, even the bushy-tailed thieves appeared, from the large cookie tin of Laurentian coloured pencils on the bookshelf. He used an old schoolhouse pencil sharpener without a basket to sharpen them. There were still bits of his rainbow shavings in the corners of the screen house.

The smile on Sam's face grew warmer as her eyes moistened with the slow flips of the pages. Gerry Hutchings would take the canoe out during calm water evenings, hoping to freeze the sunsets. There were encounters with nature, some gentle and others that could have gone either way. She knew she had seen his sketch of the moose standing in the morning mist on the opposite shore of Eastland Lake before. The family of bears were probably culled from the rearview mirror of the Chevy, a common sighting at the dump on Osis Road. The last page of the book seemed new. Perhaps it was the subject matter, something that wasn't native to the average lakeside cottage. She remembered the year it happened: 1980. *Or was it '81?* She was lost in thought when Megan snapped her back with a strange noise. Sam turned to see her daughter shaking a bottle of nail polish. *Periwinkle. Still her favourite colour.*

Megan kept shaking the bottle. "Did you draw that?"

"This?" Sam moved to the side to let her daughter see the detail. "No, these are your grandpa's. Did you see any more of them in the drawers?"

"Just the one." Megan forgot about the nail polish. She picked up the sketchbook, flipping slowly through the selections, then returning to the image that Sam had been looking at. "Was he, like, in the air force or something?"

"Nope, just the exciting world of chartered accountancy. This was a plane that flew down the lake one summer."

Megan's expression changed, from general curiosity to intrigue. "Cool. Do they still fly down the lake?"

"That was the only time I remember seeing something like that, other than the water bombers that came to—"

Sam stopped herself. *The fire.* Sam knew that she had told Megan that her grandfather had passed away around her kindergarten age, never explaining the circumstances surrounding it. *He's in Heaven now, Meggles.* She didn't know how to dig into those memories. Right now, she didn't want to.

Megan leaned in. "So, what kind of plane is that?"

Sam looked down at the script that her father had written, beneath the blended blue waves that the plane had flown over low at a few hundred miles per hour. Her smile returned.

"The Canuck," said Sam, as she used her index finger to underline her father's handwriting. "That's a Canuck."

CHAPTER
SIX

Everyone on Bird Lake remembered the Canuck, or at least everyone who was at the lake that mid-July weekend in 1981. Or was it 1980? June? Sam couldn't remember. Her father had signed his sketches, even attached notations when he felt the need, as was the case with the Canuck. No dates had been recorded, not a one. She flipped through the rest of the sketches to make sure. Megan looked through the rest of the towels and blankets on the couch for more sketch books, shelving her teenaged boredom for the time being. She continued her inquiries as she searched.

"So, where did that plane come from?"

"I don't really know for sure," said Sam. She looked out the window at the dock. "I remember it, though. It was really fu—, I mean, it was really loud."

"You can swear around me, Mom. I won't tell."

Sam looked at Megan. "Are you sure?"

"Fuck yeah!" The two looked at each other in silent surprise, then burst out laughing.

"Yeah, it was *fucking* loud! We were just swimming around the dock when we heard the noise."

"We?"

Sam realized that Megan had no idea who the "we" was. "My lake buddies. You know, the kids at the other cabins, sometimes the campgrounds, if they were staying long enough."

"What, you mean like, *strangers*?"

Sam thought for a moment about what the world had become, how *friend* had turned into friended, or unfriended, how hanging out was more about FaceTime than playtime. The only screen time she could remember at the lake would occur when the Stanley Cup playoffs were on, with a portable black-and-white TV and a homemade antenna that her dad kept moving around to keep the snowstorm on the screen down to a light flurry.

"That's how we did it back then," said Sam. "The lake was never about TV or watching movies. If it was raining, you made a puzzle, played cards. You actually *did* stuff." She pointed up at the open ceiling rafters. "Your Uncle Chris made those."

Megan looked up. A dozen scale models of fighter aircraft hung from the beams, supported by strands of fishing line. The dogfight was anything but historically accurate, with propeller-driven bi-planes from the Great War directly in the sights of a Hawker Hurricane and a Mitsubishi Zero. Something caught her eye in the collection.

"Mom! There's a Canuck!"

Sam looked up at the dusty models. The Canuck was there, wearing the Royal Canadian Air Force decals that her brother had applied over thirty years before on the kitchen table. She remembered how the tablecloth had to be removed, no exceptions, and the surface treated to a layer of newspaper before the painting and glue sniffing could begin. She was still looking up at the plastic plane when the glow of Megan's tablet came into view.

"I found it, the CF-100." She recited the Wikipedia text on the screen. "The Avro Canada CF-100 Canuck was an all-weather Canadian jet interceptor fighter serving during the cold war . . . Mom, what's NATO?"

"That's the North Atlantic Treaty, uhm, Tactical . . ." Sam couldn't remember. She faked it as best she could. "I know they were really worried about the Russians back then."

"What, like hacking Facebook and stuff?"

"No, more like launching missiles and stuff."

Megan kept reading. "Wow, they used it right up to 1981." She swept and dragged her fingers on the tablet, bringing up the Canuck in its prime, with different squadrons, paint schemes, and official markings. Sam watched with pride at how well she manipulated the tablet. *Maybe she could teach me how to use my stupid phone.* She was just about to say as much when Megan noticed something.

"Hey, Mom, what's wrong with this picture?"

Sam leaned in closer. "Which picture?"

"The sketch," said Megan. She looked at her tablet, then back to her grandfather's rendering. "What's different about them?"

Sam looked at the Google search, then the sketch. "Well, he wasn't exactly Tom Thomson, but—"

"Tom who?"

A lesson for another time. Sam rubbed her eyes, then looked again. "I dunno, Meggles. What do you see?"

Megan didn't catch the nickname or had chosen not to care. "Mom, you don't see it?"

Sam looked again. "See what? What am I supposed to see?"

"It's not there."

"What's not there?"

"The markings. There's nothing on the Canuck. It doesn't even say Canada on it. No maple leafs." She pointed up at the model.

Sam looked up, then back to the two images. Megan was right. The sketch of the fighter jet that tore down the length of the lake in '81, '80, or maybe '79 carried no markings on its fuselage. No squadron number, no maple leaf insignia, no nothing.

Sam noticed the differences with little concern. "Well, I guess Gramps forgot to fill that stuff in, and we weren't all carrying Hasselblads on our hips like you kids are today."

"Hassle-brad? Mom, are you having a stroke?"

Sam rolled her eyes. She bent forward into a mock hunch, then changed her vocal cadence to the lilt of a woman twice her age. "When I was your age, we had phones bolted to the walls and cameras that captured magic monochrome images that took three weeks to develop."

Megan rolled her eyes. "Mom, stop fucking around."

"My stars," Sam mocked. "I've heard sailors on leave with cleaner mouths!"

"MOM!" The abrupt tone snapped Sam out of her parody. She looked at the tablet once more, then the sketch, then the model above. She smiled, first at the sketch, then at her daughter. *Good*, Sam thought. *She's found something to keep her busy, for now.* She flipped through the rest of the sketches, looking at Megan as she went.

"I'm sure it was just a goof," Sam said, stopping at the image of the blue jay. She walked over to the bookcase, retrieving a weathered copy of the Audubon *Guide to North American Birds*. She flipped to the very proper rendition of the *Cyanocitta cristata*. She put the image from the book next to the sketch.

"Well, I'd say your gramps got it about half right, most of the time."

Megan looked at the comparison. The differences were beyond obvious, from the colours to the shape of the bird's beak. Gerry Hutchings's rendering of the jay was passable at best.

"So, Gramps was . . ."

"No Tom Thomson."

"Who *is* that, anyway?"

Sam gave Megan's shoulder a squeeze. "Why don't you Google that while I figure out what to make for dinner?" She moved over to the buzzing fridge while Megan tapped her tablet. Sam opened the door and scanned the contents. "Hey, *Meg*?"

"Yeah?"

"So, chicken's not a vegetable, right?"

Megan let out a slow groan of frustration. "Whatever."

Sam grabbed the package from the fridge. "Don't worry, I've got salad too." She put the container of creamy coleslaw on top.

CHAPTER
SEVEN

Sam was pleased to learn that Megan was a fair-weather vegan at best. Meg tore into the barbequed chicken with little concern for the blackened grill marks from the Weber kettle, an imprint that probably had a touch of rust from the ancient grill added for flavour. Megan had forgotten about being tired. She talked about school, boys, the meanest of the mean girls that she had blocked from her social media. Sam fell back into her most important role. It felt good.

The breeze outside had yet to dissipate, nature's preferred solution for mosquito abatement. Mother and daughter made their way to the floating dock. There was enough Merlot left in the wine box for a fat glass for Sam and a junior for Megan that was still big enough to clinch a Cool Mom nod. They clunked the plastic wine glasses together as they watched the sunset from the weathered Muskoka deck chairs. The light was almost gone when the sound of a dog's chain and tags came down the gangplank. By the time Megan had turned to see, her hand was being sniffed and licked. It didn't take long for the Jack Russell Terrier to properly introduce herself to Megan, on her lap and in her face. She endured the greeting as Sam laughed.

"Megan, meet Rusty. Rusty, meet Megan."

"Hi, Rusty," said Megan, trying to keep her wine glass from mixing with the lake. The dog jumped from Megan, then stood in front of mother and daughter. The Jack Russell did her best downward dog, hoping that the display would result in a treat. When it didn't, she threw in a bark, then a whimper. Sam dug into her pockets, trying to show the terrier that she wasn't holding.

"I got nothing, Rusty. Don't they feed you next door?"

"Not enough, apparently." Sam and Megan turned towards the voice. A short, heavy-ish woman was slowly making her way down the gangplank. Megan looked at Sam, saw her smile, then relaxed. The woman had grabbed one of the folding canvas chairs from the shore, balancing the load with a soft-sided cooler bag in her other hand. She was blond—the bold, brash, and bottled kind. The woman snapped her chair open like she had been its engineer. As if on cue, an unseen loon trumpeted its evening song. The woman listened. She looked at Sam and Megan with a mischievous grin as the call reached its crescendo, then faded. The woman zipped open her cooler, retrieving a can of Labatt 50. She opened the can, raising it above her head.

"Now that's what I call a fucking entrance!"

"I swear you've got those loons trained," said Sam, taking a sip of her wine before turning to Megan. "Megs, meet one of my lake buddies I was telling you about, the incomparable Lisa Janzen."

"Welcome to Block Fifteen," said Lisa, as she tapped her can against Megan's junior goblet. "And don't listen to what the other kids say, this is the coolest block on the lake."

Sam leaned in to tap Lisa's can. "So Leese, how's married life treating you?"

"I think this one's gonna stick. Third time's a charm, right? And it helps that he's up north with Hydro right now, but he gave me a sound thrashing before he left."

Megan wasn't ready for that. She snorted her Merlot straight up her nose. Lisa leaned over, patting Megan's back to help her through her fit of cough and laughter.

"Oh, you little lightweight. That's it, that's it, just cough it out. There you go. See? Good as new."

Sam rose from her Muskoka to help, quickly enough that her own Merlot hit the deck. The plastic goblet bounced before hitting the water. Lisa retrieved a beer from her cooler to replace the spilled wine as she comforted Megan.

"A moment of silence for that frou-frou wine of yours," said Lisa.

Sam grabbed the can. "It's not that frou-frou. It came out of a box, for Christ's sake."

"Box, bottle—nothing beats a can. Why do you think they fit so nice in all those cup holders? Let's see a box of wine do that!"

Sam sipped on the cheap ale. "Yick. It's like I'm fif—" Sam caught herself. She looked at Megan. "I mean, it's like I'm twenty-three all over again."

"Your mom's a liar," said Lisa. "I know, I was there." She pointed over to the screen house. "I think your mom's yack is still feeding the weeds by the screen door. Your grandpa made her move rocks on the beach the next day, said she'd feel better if she sweat it out."

"Ugh," said Sam. She pointed behind her chair to the pile of rocks next to the beach. "I think I yacked on those too."

The two old friends laughed as Megan watched, smiling at the tales of her mother's youth. She took a moment in between the laughter to get some background. "So, how long have you guys known each other?"

"How long?" Lisa looked skywards, rubbing her chin. "Let's see. First, the earth cooled. Then I met your mom on the beach right behind us there. I had a plastic pail, a shovel, a hat with built-in sunglasses, and not much else on, as I remember."

"We couldn't have been older than two or three," said Sam.

"That sounds about right," said Lisa. She took another gulp of her beer, then continued to tell Megan the tale. "Most of the other kids on the block were older, so we'd go down to the campground, steal the ones our age, and bring them back here to play." Lisa sipped her beer, then looked at Sam, eyes wide. "Sam! Remember the time the cops showed up?"

"I think her name was Janet," said Sam. "Or was it Jane? Jennifer?"

Lisa looked over at a wide-eyed Megan to continue the story. "All's I know is that there were three Mounties out front, and Jane, Janet, or whatever her name was—Momma was throwing a shit fit. And here's the best part!"

"What's that?" Megan leaned in for the answer. She had a feeling it would be a good one.

Lisa leaned in to deliver. "We kidnapped her again the next day!"

The dock erupted in laughter, loud enough to spark a barking fit from Rusty and a faint "Shut the hell up" from somewhere on the lake. Lisa calmed her dog. The terrier lay back down at her feet. Sam smiled.

"Of all the Rustys, I think this one's my favourite."

"Careful how loud you say that," said Lisa. "Their ghosts are all here, you know. Hell, we buried them all behind the cabin."

Megan looked confused. "Rustys?"

Sam explained. "Lisa's family has always had Jack Russell Terriers, and they named them all Rusty. When one would die, they'd get another puppy, and name it Rusty."

"So, they were all boys?"

"You'd think that," said Lisa. "It was fifty-fifty for a while, but now we're back to girl power again." She looked down at Rusty the Fifth. "Isn't that right, Rusty? Isn't that right?"

The talk of the dogs jogged a memory for Sam. "Hey, Leese, which Rusty did you have when the plane went tearing down the lake?"

"The jet fighter? That was Rusty the Second. He went absolutely ape-shit!"

"What did he do?" said Megan.

"We hadn't even heard it, let alone seen it yet," said Lisa. "Then, outta nowhere, Rusty Two starts going nuts. He's barking his brains out, running up and down the dock, pawing at his head. We thought he might have caught rabies or something. Then he tears off into the bush. About a minute later, that jet tore down the lake like a bat outta hell. Rusty didn't come back for almost three hours."

"Did the plane have any markings?" Megan was intrigued, and maybe a little tipsy, thanks to a can of 50 that had somehow made it into her hands when Sam wasn't looking.

"All I remember is that it was silver, really shiny," said Lisa. "It was fast as fuck, and then it was gone." She took a swig, then emphasized her recollection. "It was gone in the blink of an eye."

Sam took another sip of her unwanted beer. The three women leaned back in their respective chairs. A shooting star cut through the tapestry of stars and Milky Way haze. Megan pointed to it with her can.

"Did you see that? That was *fucking* awesome!"

Sam silently agreed. She hoped she had some Tylenol in the medicine cabinet. Something told her Megan might be needing it.

CHAPTER
EIGHT

The shooting star drew many an admirer that evening in the Nopiming. Norman Peale was one of them. He cradled the ivory wheel of his 1951 Chris-Craft Riviera, parked in a custom-made slip with ample padding and expert tethering to protect the glossy lacquer. The classic runabout bobbed next to another wooden cousin in the opposite slip, a '53 Custom Sedan. Peale preferred that hardtop Chris-Craft for the hot sun of late July and early August, when the freckles would start to wreak havoc on his wispy scalp. It set him back about fifty thousand, though he much preferred it over wearing a hat.

The moonless night and cloudless sky ticked two of Peale's key boxes for successful star gazing at the Whiskey Jack Lodge. The third, a fine crystal lowball glass sitting on a red felt coaster directly above the Riviera's instrument panel. The glass held a fat double of Glen Grant scotch, single malt, the same vintage as the mahogany vessel floating beneath it. Peale brought the glass to his lips and sipped the senior offering from the Speyside region, hoping to hear additional encores from the lovesick evening loon. He did hear some loons, the very common beer-drinking variety that polluted his weekends, especially the July Long. Peale leaned back in the thick burgundy leather, hoping for a shower of shooting stars, perhaps a screening of a very busy aurora borealis event. He closed his eyes for a moment to collect his thoughts, his glass perched on the edge of the boat.

"Mr. Peale, sir?"

Peale's eyes startled open, his right hand sending the crystal glass and about three hundred dollars' worth of scotch to the bottom of the cove. He leaned back, looking up at the face of the man responsible for his current prohibition, a man dressed in a light green windbreaker emblazoned with the logo of the lodge. "Yes, McMasters?"

"How are you enjoying your evening, Mr. Peale?"

Peale looked over the side of the boat, then back at his secretary. "A little parched right about now. And you?"

The secretary stepped around the slight with more pressing news. "Mr. Peale, I have Mr. Kinsey on the secure line. Shall I bring you the scrambler?"

Kinsey. Shit. "No, McMasters, I'll attend to it inside." He lifted himself from the seat. McMasters extended his hand to allow for a steady exit. Peale wore a colourful wool Pendleton jacket, a hand-me-down from his former employer. His jeans and boots were of similar American-made pedigrees. Peale was born, bred, and educated in Winnipeg, though smart enough to know which side of the border his bread was buttered on. That meant looking the part for his guests from the States. He walked a brisk pace ahead of his secretary, towards the rear deck of the lodge. The light from within came from subdued sources, a half-dozen rustic accent lamps of varying size, each one overshadowed by the glow from the free-standing mid-century fireplace. Thick leather couches surrounded the crackling fire of seasoned pine, their deep brown hides draped with vintage Pendleton blankets. The only guests present were the permanent ones, Master Angler pike, walleye, and trout, with a few white-tail bucks staring at the scene from their taxidermy mounts. Peale checked his gold Hamilton Jazzmaster. The witching hour was upon him.

Peale pushed the door open to his office of tongue-and-groove pine. A smaller fire crackled in a corner fireplace of smooth river stone. Peale moved quickly to his custom mahogany desk, its top inlaid to mimic the planking of a classic wooden boat. What looked like a red rotary phone upon approach revealed itself to have no dial, just a flashing red light in the centre. The light served another function: the connection switch for the waiting call. Peale picked up the receiver. He went to press the button, then realized that McMasters hadn't left yet. He looked at his secretary for a few seconds before he spoke.

"Will there be anything else, McMasters?"

"Uh, no sir. I'll leave you now."

"Thank you, McMasters. Good night."

"Good night, sir. Sleep well."

Peale waited a few more seconds after the door had closed to engage the flashing red switch. He preferred to stand for these calls. He could swear that the retired United States Air Force general on the other end of the line could tell the difference.

"Good evening, Mr. Kinsey."

A jovial American accent answered, Southern, though not specific to a region, the harsh reality of moving often in the service of the military. "Norman! How are things up in that Great White North of yours?"

"Spring has been kind to us here at the lodge, Mr. Kinsey. Mother Nature appears to have had no quarrels with us over the winter."

"Well, I'm just pleased as punch to hear that, Norman." There was some paper shuffling and receiver muffling for a few seconds before Kinsey spoke again.

"Norman, I've been going over all this puffed-up paper here, and, well . . ."

"Yes, Mr. Kinsey? What seems to be the problem?"

"Well, Norman, you can start by calling me Jake. All my friends do. You should know that by now."

Peale complied. "I'm pleased to hear I am your friend, Jake."

"And that's the thing," said Kinsey. "Friends are supposed to be *friendly* to one another, catch my drift?"

"I do, Mr.— I mean Jake."

The shuffling of long-distance papers continued. "Which is why I don't understand why you're trying to fuck your old pal. I like getting fucked, Norman, I like it so much that I'm still fucking the only woman I've fucked for the last forty-six years, catch my drift?"

"I do, *Jake*."

"Well, that's right neighbourly of you, Norman. I *really* like hearing that. The only problem is that we both know it ain't true. Here's where that fucking part comes into play, catch my drift?"

Peale had caught it, again. He knew what Kinsey was driving at. "Mr., I mean, Jake, how long have we been working together?"

"You and me personally? Well, let's see now. I retired twelve years ago this August. I first made your acquaintance around 1980-something. So that would be, let's see now . . . Well, it's been a long damn time, not counting the time with our predecessors and all."

"And have you always known our dealings to be honest and forthright?"

"Honest? I would say so, for the most part. *Greedy?*"

"I assure you, sir, that—"

"Call me Jake, Norman. All my friends do."

"I assure you, *Jake*. All expenses are legitimate, above board, and provable to the last decimal point. This has been the case for the entire term of our relationship, and the ones before it."

"Well, Norman, I hear what you're sayin' and all. When I had two stars on my shoulder, I wouldn't have ever picked up the phone. Shit, the only papers I was reading in those days had Garfield the cat and Opus the penguin on 'em. Remember, Norman, hammers at the Pentagon cost more than my first car. But this, this is *private sector* money. If they want it explained, and I can't explain it, I end up being the unlucky participant in a turkey shoot. Catch my drift?"

Peale decided to appeal to something the former general would understand. "Jake, would you agree that these activities fall under what you would call in the military *clandestine* services?"

"I would answer affirmative, Norman."

"And Jake, how many clandestine operations did you oversee during your time at the Pentagon?"

"Well, let me see now. Too many to count, Norman. Too many to count."

"So, it would be safe to say that you know how to get these things done, even when committees, representatives, and the senators from the great state of wherever start poking into your files, correct?"

Kinsey let out a laboured exhale. "Norman, it all comes down to return on investment. As of right now, and if these new glasses the missus talked me into are correct, that dog don't hunt. Couldn't catch a blind raccoon with a fresh waffle, if you catch my drift."

"I understand," said Peale, knowing full well he didn't. Peale did get the Kentucky-fried gist: Kinsey thought he was full of shit. It had always been a struggle for him to earn the trust of the Americans, even with Van Cleef's grooming him as the organization's apparent heir. *The Organization.* The cloak and dagger references, the calculated vagueness of the telephone conversations that were so encrypted that no amount of digital reassembly could decipher them. *The bullshit.*

The receiver at the American end was muffled again. Peale thought he could hear Kinsey swearing under his breath.

"Jake? Are you still there?"

The general had returned, along with his composure. "I'm here, Norman."

"Are we still friends, Jake?"

"We is, Norman. Come hell or high water."

"Will you be coming to the lodge soon?"

There was a slight chuckle on the American end of the line. "Well, I don't suppose all them northern pike of yours are gonna catch themselves now, catch my drift?"

"We'll have your regular cabin ready at a moment's notice, Jake. Give my best to Myrna."

Kinsey exhaled with a hint of laughter. "Norman, that's what I love about all you Canadians."

"What's that, Jake?"

"Y'all are sweeter than a Georgia peach. G'night, Mr. Peale."

"Goodnight, Mr. Kinsey."

Peale returned the receiver to the cradle. He looked out the window of his office, seeing more of his seventy-two-year-old reflection than the nightscape of Bird Lake. He turned out the offending light to get a better look.

CHAPTER
NINE

Saturday morning streamed bright and strong through the curtains in Sam's room. She had turned in around one, steadying her daughter as she went, with plenty of beer-fed insults for doing so lobbed by her lake buddy Lisa as she walked up the gangplank of the dock. Megan wasn't drunk, just a little tipsy. Sam advised a glass of water before bed to knock any morning headaches down to manageable. She wondered if Stan Buckmaster's tiny inconvenience store still sold the ultimate hangover remedy of her youth: Beep orange drink. *The Canadian Tang.*

Sam heard her phone sound and grabbed it from the windowsill, an overstretch that she knew she'd feel later, though it was better than putting her bare feet on the floor to retrieve her slippers. It was just after nine. Cooper had texted to make sure everything was all right. *Of course, it's all right*, Sam thought, as she sent a thumbs-up emoji. *I'm her mother, for Christ's sake.* She scrolled though the emojis to see if one had been created to express that feeling. It appeared that the good people at Android had yet to table it.

Megan was starting to stir. Sam smiled at the sounds. She heard her feet as they hit the floor.

"HOLY SHIT! THE FLOOR IS FREEZING!"

Sam laughed out loud. "Welcome to the lake, oh daughter of mine!" She continued to chuckle as she heard Megan rummage through the drawers. She appeared at the doorway to Sam's room. Her feet were covered with two T-shirts, hastily tied. Sam snorted. Megan wasn't laughing.

"Those are some *nice* slippers you got there, Megs."

"Why's the floor so cold? It's July!"

"It's the lake, Megs, the floor is always cold, even in the summer. Wakes you up better than coffee." Sam swung her legs over the side of the bed. "It's like taking swimming lessons. You just have to jump right in." Sam did. Her years of Bird Lake frigid floor experience were of little help.

"Fuck," she said, as she looked at her daughter. "That *is* cold!"

"That's what I'm telling you! Mom, that cold is *wrong*!"

Sam grabbed her fleece at the end of the bed. Her slippers were AWOL. "We'll see if they have some slippers at the store when we go to see your grandma today in Pinawa." Sam made a mental note to buy back-up pairs.

Megan groaned. She used her hands to push her hair off

her forehead. "Mom, Grandma doesn't even know who I am. The last time I saw her, she thought I was you. One time she thought I was Uncle Chris."

Sam headed towards the kitchen as she spoke. "Well, he is a pretty attractive man, though I don't think you've got the legs to pull it off." She rinsed the previous day's coffee out of the Pyrex as she continued. "It's all part of life, Megs. And I know, this part sucks. In fact, it can really hurt sometimes."

"Mom! She should go vegan! I saw it on a documentary on Netflix!"

Sam turned to look at her daughter. "What's going vegan got to do with it?"

"Something about, what's it called? Oh yeah, early-onset dementia. I think going vegan is supposed to help reverse it."

Sam dumped the wet coffee grounds into the garbage. "Well, you're welcome to try. We can ask if they know anything about it at Whispering Pines."

"I just want her to know me, Mom." Megan's eyes were getting moist. Sam moved over to hug her.

"I know, Megs, I know. I want her to know you too."

The pair hugged a little while longer. Megan broke the silence.

"Mom?"

"Yes, Megs?"

"You shouldn't throw out the coffee grounds. Bree uses them for compost."

Sam rolled her eyes, knowing they couldn't be seen. "Yeah, we'll have to look into that."

It took a little over an hour to drive to Pinawa. The old Chevy had power to spare, though Sam still heard Stan Buckmaster's caution about the tires, as the needle quivered just under fifty. After getting passed by the third honking truck and boat trailer, she parked the needle at a steady sixty.

The town of Pinawa still had what Sam referred to as *the look*. She tried to explain the history to Megan, as she knew it. "This is actually Pinawa two-point-oh. The first town is where they built the first hydro dam. They closed that in the early fifties, and the town pretty much died with it."

"So, which Pinawa are we going to? One or two?"

"Two," said Sam, as she turned left onto PR 520. "The second Pinawa was created with the nuclear research facility, the Whiteshell Laboratories."

"*Research* facility? What is this place anyway, a *secret government operation*?" Megan threw in the sarcastic finger quotes for free.

Sam smiled at her, her left arm straddling the windowsill as she steered with her right. "Yeah, we might have to call Mulder and Scully in on this one."

"Who's Mulder and Scully?"

Sam thought about explaining it, *The X-Files*, the reboot, Gillian Anderson's Benjamin Button–style aging process. She got back to what she knew. "So anyway, they needed a new town, so they built it."

Megan's right arm had moved to her doorsill, mimicking her mother. "They built a whole town. For the lab?"

"And that's where it gets weird, Megan," Sam said, as they approached the second Pinawa. "You'll swear you've gone back in time. Way back."

Sam did notice one advantage to the look of the old Chevy as she turned into the Pinawa townsite: the car finally didn't look out of place. Pinawa the Second sprang up in 1963. Like most communities of the era, Pinawa was planned, a suburbia-styled mix of tract houses and community buildings, with the primary difference being the wild location. The waterfront parcels were reserved as public space for the residents to enjoy. In the winter, the deer wandering through the streets could outnumber the human inhabitants. Most of the houses had seen typical upgrades, like newer windows and siding. And yet, the town still appeared to be frozen in time.

Sam and Megan still attracted attention, receiving quizzical looks and friendly waves from the townspeople as they rolled past. Many of them were lifers, choosing to retire where they had raised their families and worked their careers. The nuclear laboratory had been experiencing a slow but inevitable shutdown since the late nineties. Sam wondered if the lab, and the town it gave birth to, would eventually resemble the ruins of the hydro dam up the road in the next thirty years. She offered a silent hope that the town would survive. She knew it was wishful thinking.

The Whispering Pines Nursing Home stood near the town centre, still wearing its original brick façade on precast concrete. It had started life as the first hospital for the second version of the town. Some of the windows were 1963 originals, which made it plenty cold in certain rooms come winter. The building had been converted in the late seventies to its current role, with a total complement of twenty-four rooms. The occupancy rate stood at a hundred percent, with a sizable waiting list. The town residents were entering the twilight of their years at practically the same time, with no way to house and care for them all. For Sale signs were starting to pop up, especially for those who needed constant home care. For many, it meant moving to the big city, with all the Winnipeg problems that came with it.

Sam turned the Chevy off while still in Drive, a trick that she remembered her father doing when the car dieseled for him back in the day. Once in Park, they headed into the nursing home. The strong odour of industrial cleaning supplies took centre stage in the olfactory, followed by sweat, urine, and far worse. Sam hoped that her mother was in good spirits, and in good scent. Remembering who Sam was, as well as Megan, would be icing on the cake.

Sam gave a quick nod at the reception desk, as she veered left down the hallway. She reached behind her with an open hand. Megan took it. Her mother's room was at the far end of the hall, a placement that continued to concern her. *Why would you put an Alzheimer's resident next to an exit door?* Sam often worried about the two calls that would probably accompany that placement. The first: her mother was missing. The second: her mother had been found, dead, in the Pinawa Channel. *No vacancy,* Sam thought. *Nowhere else to put her.*

The door to Room Twelve was open, the sound of a vintage *Let's Make a Deal* episode from within. Sam had paid for the better TV subscription about three months before, after a few trying episodes that threatened to move her mother out of the Pines completely. The retro channels seemed to calm her, though she did tend to think that most of the game show contestants could hear her. Sam and Megan listened at the doorway to Lena's coaching.

"It's door number two, you idiot. *Door number two!* Were your parents cousins? Door number two, door number two, door number—oh for crying in the sink, three is the zonk!"

Sam reminded Megan to call Lena by her name and not what she was to her in the familial sense. Megan nodded. They stepped in as the zonk was confirmed. Lena threw up her hands.

"See? I *told* you it was number two! You could have been staying at the bloody Kahala Hilton in Hawaii, but nooooo! You had to take number three! Now, what are you going to do with a baby elephant? Like Monty says, its going to eat you out of house and home!"

"Hi Lena," said Sam. "How are you doing today?"

Lena looked up at her daughter. She thought she was a nurse. "Is it time for my lunch yet? It feels like it should be lunch time. I probably won't like it anyway, but it feels like it should be lunchtime. It's always cold." She looked over at Megan. "Is it corn again? I told them I don't like corn—makes me gassy."

Megan didn't know how to answer that. Sam kept the conversation going. "Lena? Can we watch your game shows with you?"

Lena pointed at the TV. "As long as you don't mind helping with these idiot contestants. I've eaten toast with a higher IQ than these ten-watt lightbulbs."

Megan snorted at that one. It caught Lena's attention. "Do you like Monty Hall? He's from Winnipeg, you know, North End boy. Maybe you can be a contestant one day. I can help you pick the right door."

"Uh, that would be great, Lena," said Megan. "Thanks, I'll see if I can get in as a contestant."

"Oh, I have the address written down," said Lena. She shuffled through some papers on the folding table next to her chair. "Let me see, let me see. Oh, here it is. CBS Television City, Los Angeles, California. Do you need to write it down, dear?"

"No, that's OK," said Megan. "I'll remember."

Lena returned the paper to the pile. "Monty Hall is very nice. I hope you get to meet him."

Sam knew that would be a neat trick. She had written the cover story about him for the *Sentinel's* entertainment section when he died.

The three watched the rest of *Deal*, then the first ten minutes of a newer *Family Feud* before lunch arrived. Sam offered to feed her mother, an offer that the orderly quickly obliged. The segmented portions of the tray were filled with varying colours of mushy things. The consensus among the three was unanimous: the brown mush had to be the meat.

"The food at this restaurant is horrible," said Lena, her mouth full of the green mush that Megan had just fed her. "They can't even bake a proper peach cobbler." Lena pointed at what she thought was the dessert. Sam smiled.

"I think that's the corn, Lena."

"It's not much of a corn," said Lena, still working the green. "It's got a better chance of being a peach cobbler than a corn."

After lunch, the orderly stepped in to mention that a bath was in order. Sam and the orderly then stepped into the hallway to discuss her mother's current state. She discovered the bath had been in order for about three days. "If she doesn't want it, we not want to force it on her," said the orderly. "Not after the last time."

"Is she still getting aggressive?" said Sam.

"She's not bad as some," said the orderly. "Spending time always helps, even if they do not know who you are."

Sam nodded. She noticed that the orderly didn't have a name tag. His features were darker than the typical Pinawa local. "Uhm, I'm sorry. What's your name again?"

"Milad," said the orderly. Sam figured he was in his early thirties, maybe late twenties. His orderly togs were anything but flattering, but he had plenty of muscle tone from what could be seen. There was a bit of a nervous tick that Sam picked up on: Milad smiled *a lot*, the kind of smiling that most people make around locals when the country, customs, and language are new and frightening.

"Where are you from, Milad?" Sam knew from the accent it wasn't Winnipeg.

Milad smiled broadly. "My family, we come from Syria."

"Have you been here long?"

"Three years. Canada has been good. Winter colder than home, but good."

Sam remembered what Megan had told her about Netflix. "Milad, about the food here."

"Yes, very bad. Very sorry."

"Is there anything we can do to, I mean, can we get her better food?"

"You would have to bring it. It's OK, others do."

"Does my moth—does Lena eat a lot?"

"Very little. As you see, very bad, the food here."

Sam thanked Milad, then headed back inside. Her mother had hardly made a dent in the tray. She moved it over to the bed. Sam put her hand on her mother's shoulder, the way a caregiver would. "Lena, it was so nice seeing you today. Can we visit you again?"

Lena looked into her daughter's eyes. "Do you bake?"

Sam smiled. "Blueberry pie?"

"With wild blueberries?"

"Of course! And Cool Whip on top?"

"That would be so nice."

Sam got up. Megan mimicked her mother's touch as she said her goodbye.

"I'll see you later, Lena."

"Thank you for coming, dear."

Megan got up. As she turned, Lena spoke. "And Samantha?"

Sam and Megan froze. Sam nudged Megan to answer, since it was Megan Lena had addressed.

"Yes, Lena?"

"I don't care for that thing poking out of your nose. And I'm your mother, not Lena."

Megan looked at her actual mother before she answered. Sam nodded that it was OK.

"I'll, I'll take it out. Uhm, goodbye, Mom."

"Bye-bye."

CHAPTER
TEN

The ride back stayed quiet, up to the gravel stretch. Megan leaned up against her door, trying to find the best position to keep from chafing on the weathered shoulder belt. She leaned over to the radio to turn it on, quickly realizing she didn't know how. Sam noticed her confusion as Megan turned the volume switch, filling the old Chevy with static. Megan pressed the preset switches. Sam realized that she wasn't pressing hard enough and punched the middle one for her daughter. It responded with an interview on CBC Radio One. Megan pushed the rest of the switches the way her mother had shown. Talk, talk, and more talk. She exhaled.

"Where's the music on this thing?"

"There is none," said Sam. "It's AM. Unless you want country."

"Ick. Country."

Sam switched off the radio. "How you doing, Megs?"

"OK, I guess. It was just . . ."

"Kind of weird?"

"Yeah. I mean, she thought I was *you*."

Sam chuckled. "You say that like it's a bad thing."

"Whatever." Megan turned back to the trees.

"Grandma said she wanted a pie, remember?"

Megan perked up. "Yeah. Blueberry, right?"

Sam slowed to ready herself for the left turn to the cabin. "Not just any blueberry, Megs. *Wild* blueberry."

"Wild blueberries? What, they sell them at the store?"

"Better," said Sam. "They're free."

"Mom, can you start making sense, like, today?"

"We'll go pick 'em. We used to do it when I was a kid, the whole family. There's usually a whole pile of them off old Osis Road. Maybe we can get Leese to tag along."

"Really? Lisa picks blueberries? I have a hard time believing that."

Sam had reached the bottom of the Block Fifteen hill. She slowed to a stop at Lisa Janzen's driveway. Her feet were sticking out from underneath Mongo, a weathered mid-eighties Jeep Grand Wagoneer, sitting much taller than had been originally specified at the factory. The tires looked like they would beat the road into submission instead of rolling over it. A custom brush guard took up the front, along with a winch, and plenty of off-road lighting. Sam gave her horn a tap. Lisa shimmied out from underneath, then walked over to the Chevy. She had enough grease on her forehead to qualify as a close relation of Stan Buckmaster. The Oiseau Garage trucker cap atop her head practically confirmed it.

Lisa dispensed with the pleasantries. "Did you go to town? And, more importantly, did you get beer?"

"Yes," said Sam. "And maybe, if you're good."

"I'm not good," said Lisa. "I'm GRRRRRRRREAT!"

Megan laughed, a little harder than Sam did. She was still laughing when Sam spoke. "Leese, have you taken Mongo down Osis Road this year?"

"Most of it," said Lisa. "It's a little sloppy in places." She poked her head in the window to send Megan over the edge. "Just like me!"

"So, it's not great for the Chevy?"

"Aw, hell no! You'd get crazy stuck. And what's down Osis Road? No beer vendor, the last time I checked."

Sam shifted in her seat, crossing her arms on the top of the Chevy's driver door. "I want to take Megs out for some berry-picking. Her grandma wants a blueberry pie."

"A blueberry pie?" Lisa tipped her cap up. "You're sure it's not *cherry* pie?" Sam watched as Lisa rang off the chorus from the Warrant hit. Megan was starting to have trouble breathing. Sam tried to reel Lisa in.

"No cherries, you nutbar, just blueberries."

"Sure," said Lisa, adjusting her hat brim. "There's plenty out there, came in kinda early this year. I'll bring some bear spray and my noisemakers, just in case."

Megan became serious then, and excited. "Bears? Holy shit, are you serious?"

"Just don't get between the momma and the cub," said Lisa. "She'll cut you right in half."

It took a few minutes to find the ice cream pails, the rubber boots, and the ancient bottles of Muskol that held an illegal concentration of DEET. Lisa idled in front of the cabin, fast-forwarding through a mix tape. Megan called shotgun. Lisa let go of the fast-forward button as her passengers clambered in. Unseen speakers on the left side of the Jeep started humming with the opening guitar licks of Van Halen's "Unchained." Lisa turned to Megan as she turned up the volume.

"HEY, MEGS! YOU LIKE VAN HALEN?"

"VAN-*WHO*?"

Lisa answered by mashing the throttle as David Lee Roth gave a mighty all right out of the right-hand speakers. They headed towards Osis Road.

Sam was glad that Lisa had offered her goober Uber for the Osis Road adventure. The road had last received provincial maintenance when the area dump had operated. The dump site had been closed in the late nineties, though its footprint, a grey moonscape of buried trash where even the hardiest of weeds had given up their attempts at reclamation, could still be seen from the road. The current road grooming came courtesy of quads, side-by-sides, and extreme off-roaders like Lisa and Mongo. The ruts were deep, with plenty of mud splashing on the Jeep and its occupants. Lisa knew the road well, especially where the biggest splash events would occur. Sam watched as Megan enjoyed the Jeep jostle with the biggest of grins.

The gumbo became greasier as the three approached the outer edges of Osis Lake. Lisa found a stable patch just off the road, one that had been favoured by previous visitors, judging by the crisscross of tire tracks. The first thing that greeted them were the horseflies, attracted to the heat rolling off the Jeep's hood. Megan let out a yelp with the first bite.

"OW!" She smacked the horsefly hard, dropping its carcass to the ground. "Do those assholes have teeth?"

"Feels like it, don't it?" said Sam. She collected the pails from the Jeep. Megan winced at the stench of the classic Muskol, until she remembered the recent bite. Lisa slathered it on everywhere her hands could reach. She lowered the tailgate, pulling a large bin to the edge. "Make sure everyone's got their noisemakers."

Megan looked in the bin, then at Lisa with concern. "Pots and pans?"

"Works like a charm," said Lisa. She attached the pots to loops on her vest. "You want 'em to bang together as you move around, sends Smokey running."

Megan pointed at the bear spray. "So, what's that for?"

Lisa tossed her one of the cans. "In case they start running *towards* you."

The pinging pots did the trick, as far as they knew. The noise did raise the head of a nearby doe, her fawn drinking its fill from the edge of Osis Lake. The bears had visited the patch recently; Megan's rubber boots just missed a fresh pile of mother bear-sized scat next to one of the blueberry bushes. She was making sure that she hadn't filled the treads of the boots when she saw the glimmer in the trees. She turned to Sam, then to Lisa. If anyone knew what secrets were hidden in the tall grass, it would be Block Fifteen's official outdoorswoman.

"Hey, Leese. What's that over there?"

Lisa looked up from her ice cream pail, chewing on a mouthful of blueberries. "What, in the bush?"

"Yeah, what is it?" Sam rose up from her crouched position, both to stretch and see what piqued her daughter's interest.

Lisa swallowed the last of her snack. "That? I think it's an old radar station. From the fifties or sixties, I think."

Sam looked at the overgrowth. The outline of a building could be seen, not too large, with brick that must have come from the same supplier as half the structures in Pinawa. A casement of flaking white paint held the cause of the reflection, a broken shard of glass hanging on for dear life at the top of the window frame. A trembling aspen stood in front of the door opening, almost obscuring the entrance from view.

Megan looked at Sam. "Can we go check it out?"

Sam amped up her Mom voice. "It's a busted-up building. Lots of things to hurt yourself on in there, and whatever's living in there may not be expecting any company."

Megan exhaled, then looked at Lisa. "Do you think it's safe?"

"It will be in a minute," said Lisa. She banged a pair of pots as the doorbell. The warning sent a chattering squirrel out of the open door to the top floor of the aspen. She tapped the pots again for good measure as she peeked inside.

"All clear! It's a bit of a fixer-upper! Watch out for the glass! And the wood, and the nails . . ."

Sam and Megan ventured inside. The building had seen plenty of visitors since being decommissioned, of feather, fur, and Jim, if the graffiti on the battered walls proved accurate. The building couldn't have been more than three hundred square feet, with the steel remnants of equipment racks still attached to the rear walls. A metal bunk bed frame had fallen over, resting on a dented putty-grey desk. Most of the drawers had been removed, resting in various spots throughout the space.

Lisa peeked out a broken rear window. "They had a generator shack out back," she said. Sam and Megan took turns at the window to see. The shack had fallen over on what was left of the generator, which appeared to have been stripped of its most important parts to run.

Megan looked out the front window. She turned back to Sam and Lisa. "Isn't there supposed to be an antenna or something?"

"They probably took that out when they turned off the lights," said Lisa. "Or some scrap dealer cut it up." She looked out the front window, scanning the tall grass. "See? There's the base they attached it to."

Megan looked at the swaying weeds. It took her eyes a moment to find the base, a mass of concrete with a half-dozen rusty threaded rods pointing skyward, standing about a foot above the surface. The nuts that held the antenna to the base must have ended up in the back of the scrap dealer's truck.

Sam looked at the desk. One drawer remained, the thin centre unit. A quick tug confirmed that it was either locked or jammed. Her tugging got the attention of her lake buddy.

"Find something?" said Lisa. "If its money, we split it fifty-fifty."

"Hey," said Megan. "What about me?"

Lisa pointed at Sam. "Take it up with her. Age before beauty, Megs, and your mom and I are almost fifty, so it makes perfect sense."

"But how are you going to open it?" Megan asked.

Lisa pulled a survival knife from its sheath. "With the key, of course." She jammed the knife in the drawer's gap. After a little bit of leverage and foul mouth, the drawer slid open. Something had made the space a nest of sorts, then decided to die and decay to a vole-sized skeleton.

Megan recoiled. "Eww, gross!"

Lisa flicked the tiny skull aside. "It's not gross, there's no meat left."

Sam pulled out what was left of the paper. If there had been a letterhead, it must have been where the vole had started building its dream house. Some of the remnants were blank, probably for limited correspondence on a long-lost typewriter. The text that did exist had a few jumbled words, in between the damage of rodents and environment. There was one line that looked clear enough to read. Sam underlined it as she recited it.

"'Advise all stations to monitor for unscheduled traffic, as first recorded by Pillow, Naples, Sharecrop, and Boxfile on 23 November, 1953. All PINETREE stations to report any activity to' . . . shit. I can't make that out."

Lisa looked at the script. "Mouse piss, eats through everything."

Megan squinted at the illegible part. "Is that an S?"

"Maybe," said Sam. She handed it to Megan. "Wanna keep it?"

Megan carefully accepted. "I'll see what that pine tree is all about. Capital letters sounds important. Or maybe they were yelling."

CHAPTER
ELEVEN

The summer regulars at Bird Lake preferred the long weekends that fell on actual weekends. Canada Day had fallen on a Sunday. The dust clouds from the gravel roads on the holiday Monday started to settle around three in the afternoon. Sam didn't want to attempt the varnish job on the canoe until the exit traffic had died down.

Canada Day meant fireworks, and the Janzens' cabin next door never failed to disappoint. Lisa's parents had started the tradition around the same time as the Rustys, launching the festive colours from their swimming platform anchored off the main dock. After her parents had passed, Lisa's displays had grown to semi-professional levels. The latest improvement was a wireless launching system, synced to an elongated cut of "The Final Countdown." There were other Canada Day fireworks displays on Bird Lake, but Lisa's celebration would always attract at least a dozen boats.

Sam's brush glided across the hull. There were plenty of petrified drips in the coatings of years past, the years that she and her brother, Chris, had insisted on helping their father with the maintenance. Gerry Hutchings had tried to guide them accordingly, eventually realizing that every pass of their sloppy brushes was preserving the cedar strips far beyond their intended life expectancy. The 1974 Winnipeg Centennial stickers on the bow were starting to take on the look of a prehistoric bird trapped in amber. Gerry had built the canoe for the centennial Red River run. It survived the fire that took him in '89. One of the Sykes brothers from Block Three had found the canoe floating near the Dean Islands. Gerry's remains weren't found until a week later, in the smoldering ash of the Eastland Lake fire. A positive ID was out of the question, though Sam often wondered if Dad knew what was coming; his red Carling Black Label trucker cap had been found hanging on a nearby tree. The plastic mesh on the back of the cap had melted, but the front of the cap was surprisingly intact. It still hung above the garage's workbench window.

Sam's phone started to ring on the edge of the sawhorse that held the rear of the canoe. She'd planned on moving it when her brush strokes got close enough to void its warranty. She threw off one of her gloves for a clean finger to accept the call. It was her brother.

"Hey," Sam said, her glove retrieved and back to the task at hand. "Can you hear me OK?"

"Not bad for a speakerphone," said Chris. "I can even hear the birds, but what's that other sound?"

"Time to goo the canoe," said Sam. "It's the only boat left."

"What about the Hobie Cat under the cabin?"

Sam rubbed the sweat from her brow. "I'm a paddler, not a sailor, remember? When Dad told me, 'prepare to come about?'"

Chris laughed out loud. "Yeah, that was some goose egg on your forehead, almost Looney Tunes quality."

"That could also explain my marks in the fifth grade."

"So, how's the book going?"

Sam thought about soaking the answer in a positive marinade. She knew her brother would see right through it. "Well, between you, me, and the canoe, it's been a slow start. It's so slow it doesn't even look like I've started."

"But, you're still on track, right? Getting the cabin ready to sell?"

Sam tried to stop time before she answered her brother's question. She had been given power of attorney when her mother had started slipping, a role that was more about location than preference. She had pitched the book-writing sabbatical more out of necessity than want. As much as her share of a sale would be a welcome cushion, she had hoped to never sell the cabin. For that to happen, she'd need to write her brother a six-figure cheque. *Advances like that were certainly possible*, Sam thought, *if you had a last name like King or Patterson.*

"I'm taking the A-train," said Sam, trying to be clever.

"Which means what, exactly?"

"Chris, whether I keep it or whether I sell it doesn't really matter, right? As long as you get your half of the place next spring, then we're good."

The phone went muffled for a moment. Chris returned. "Well, what if you sold it now, as-is?"

Shit, Sam thought. *He's broke, again.* Her brother's business dealings had done as well as the cedar strip canoe would have done over rocky rapids, especially within the past three years. It didn't help that his second wife had expensive tastes, just like the first one. The latest venture took its business plan from the expected green rush of Canadian marijuana legalization. The money would come, and lots of it, Chris promised, when Sam wrote him the cheque for twenty-five grand. That was a year ago, an outlay that she was sure her day job would cover, until the day job went poof. Updates on the venture became more about the hurdles that Chris faced to open a brick-and-mortar location than a repayment schedule. Sam was pissed. She tried her best to keep it to herself.

"No sense in a fire sale," said Sam. "It's too late in the season. I've got the rest of the fall for the outside, and I can tidy up inside over the winter. Anyone selling now looks like they're in a panic."

"Yeah, right, we don't want to panic," said Chris. Sam could tell that he was doing just that. She decided not to care about it, for now. She changed the subject.

"I saw Mom the other day."

Chris exhaled. "I guess the better question is: did Mom see you?"

"Well, she thinks Megan is me, so that's a start. We're trying her on a new diet. Megan seems to think that going vegan is going to cure her."

"Fuck," said Chris. "A life without a T-bone isn't a life, in my humble opinion."

Maybe if you switched to veggie burgers, you'd have a pot to piss in, Sam thought. She changed the subject again, saying as much. "So, totally off topic, but do you remember when the plane went screaming down the lake?"

"Hell yeah," said Chris. "That was pretty wicked. Park Pontiac Brother Jake–wicked."

"That was a Canuck, right?"

"Yeah, the one hanging from the rafters. Wow, I haven't thought of that in years. Is the plane still up there? I should get it back before you sell the place. Can you ship it?"

Sam steered the conversation back to her intended question. "Do you remember what it looked like?"

"Well, pretty much like what you see hanging from the rafters. It didn't have any symbols or numbers on it or anything, but I put the decals on it anyway. I was just starting to get good at them back then."

"You know that Dad did a sketch of it, right? Of the Canuck?"

"Yeah, is that there too? I'd like to—"

Sam interrupted. "So, the picture he did, without the markings, that's how it looked, right?"

"Yeah, Dad was right on that. I remember him saying something about it."

"Saying something? What do you mean?" Sam asked.

"Well, it's not like he was pissed about it or anything. I just remember him looking at me as I was putting the decals on. He didn't tell me to stop or anything. When it was done, he was stringing it up in the rafters for me. He said I did a good job on it, and . . ."

"And what?"

"I'm just trying to remember what he said. I think I was eight or nine, so it's a little foggy."

Sam didn't interrupt. She listened to her brother thinking to himself out loud on the west coast. It finally came to him.

"I think he said . . . shit, trying to remember here. He said . . . *Just remember, son, even the smallest truth demands accuracy.* Yeah, that's how he said it, even the smallest truth *demands* accuracy. He really emphasized the demands part. 'Course, I was eight or nine at the time—kinda went over my head."

Sam wondered if the advice had flown over her head too, maybe faster than the Canuck had. She agreed in principle, certainly in the sense of her previous career. Sam felt the gravity of the words. It was a powerful statement, whether you were eight or eighty. *There was only one problem*, Sam thought. *Dad never said that to me.* He certainly had his Gerry-isms, gems like, "It's the heat that's so hot" and "These pants are looser than Joey Heatherton." Sam chose to keep these thoughts to herself, for now. She offered an indifferent theory to her brother.

"Maybe it was something he heard in accounting school."

"Maybe," said Chris. "I think I just nodded at him, maybe an OK, or an 'I got it, Dad'—whatever it took to get the fishing line on the plane."

Sam logged the information in her mind as she dipped her brush. She looked over at the pair of grimy Honda Trail 70's. "Hey, Chris, one more thing."

"What's that?"

"Where are the parts for the dirt bikes?"

CHAPTER
TWELVE

Norman Peale heard the massive radial engine before he saw what it was attached to. The bright yellow Noorduyn Norseman made a low pass over the Whiskey Jack Lodge, then made the necessary climb to allow for a sweeping turn over Bird Lake before making its final approach. The landings of the Whiskey Jack Norseman would always attract a few pleasure boats with amateur videographers, eager to catch the expert landings of Hap Anderson for their social media posts.

Peale first added the veteran bush pilot to the summer payroll in the early nineties, soon after acquiring the vintage float plane. There were more twists in his scotch-soaked tales than in his curly blond hair. His favourite yarn spoke of his supposed rescue of Ken Leishman, better known as the mastermind behind the gold heist at the Winnipeg International Airport in March 1966. According to Anderson, the reformed Leishman had survived a plane crash near Thunder Bay in December 1979, while at the controls of an air ambulance flight. Through a series of phone calls, off-road vehicles, seedy motels, and a night flight to Duluth in an open-cockpit Piper Cub float plane, Anderson maintained that he had helped Leishman embark on the next chapter of his life. Investigators thought otherwise, declaring Leishman legally dead a year later, his remains most likely eaten by scavenging wolves.

Peale watched as his dock hands readied themselves for the approaching Norseman, on a custom-made slip next to the gleaming Chris-Craft hardtop. Anderson shut the growling radial down at the perfect moment, with just enough rudder from the plane's tail and floats to avoid any jarring bumps to the precious cargo. Anderson opened the main door on the port side, steadying himself on the float ladder. He reached inside, retrieving the wooden crate of Glen Grant, a crate that had lost its top at some point during transport. He handed it to one of the dock hands, then steadied himself as he walked to the back of the float, using a half-empty bottle of the pricey scotch for balance. He unzipped his cargo shorts, relieving himself in the lake. None of the staff laughed or pointed. There was no reason to; Anderson would always relieve himself in this manner after a cargo-only flight, when the lodge was clear of any guests. He tapped, zipped, then made his way to the dock. His stagger spoke of a high-functioning drunkard. Peale checked his clipboard as Anderson stumbled towards him. The pilot's Whiskey Jack T-shirt told part of the tale of the half-empty bottle, with fresh spillage stains. Peale gave Anderson a proper sniff when he came to a teetering stop in front of him; the rest of the drink had made its way into the pilot's stomach, about fifteen hundred dollars' worth.

Peale slapped the clipboard against Anderson's chest before showing it to him. "Let me guess, Hap. Did one of the bottles 'pop the crate open again,' as you climbed up out of Kenora Harbour?"

Anderson squinted at the clipboard. The numbers were moving, slowly at first, then picked up speed. He pushed the clipboard back, falling to his knees, though still managing to keep the bottle from tipping over. He made it to the side of the dock just in time to feed the massive pike that cruised the cove for discarded bait, twice. Anderson pushed the floating vomit out of the way, scooping up a handful of water laced with a fuel slick rainbow. He gargled, spat, then stood. Peale waited patiently as Anderson took a pull from the bottle. He pointed to his clipboard.

"Hap, do you know how much a bottle of Glen Grant '51 costs?"

Anderson didn't miss a beat. "Retail or wholesale?" His slur came straight from the Foster Brooks cocktail napkin library.

Peale adjusted the number on the invoice, scrawling *lost in transit* next to it. "Either way, it's plenty. Didn't you get the bottle of Blue Label I left for you in the Norseman?"

Anderson looked at Peale with one-eyed indignation. *"Blue Label?* I can't fly this crate with a fucking *blend*. Let's see you pull out of a stall at six-thousand feet while drinking a *blend*.

They'd find pinecones bigger than what was left of me and your *vintage* fucking plane. When are you gonna turbo-prop this ancient piece of shit? It should be in a fucking museum, right next to the Silver Dart."

"Not in this lifetime," said Peale. "The guests at the Whiskey Jack demand the true Canadian wilderness experience. I won't sanitize that out of convenience." Peale handed the pen to Anderson for his initials. The pen's motion appeared to be bringing about another case of the queasy for the pilot. Peale clicked the pen. "Why don't I initial this for you?"

"Aye-aye, captain-my-captain." Anderson threw in something resembling a salute with the bottle. He weaved his way up the dock to the lodge. McMasters weaved his way around him on his way to Peale. He carried a similar clipboard in his right hand. Peale turned to greet him.

"McMasters, could you make sure that Mr. Anderson is sufficiently dried out for the guest flights on Wednesday?"

McMasters nodded. "Yes sir, Mr. Peale. I also have the updated guest list for you." He held his clipboard at a comfortable reading angle for his superior.

Peale squinted, nodding column by column. He smiled as he looked up at his secretary. "That's excellent work, McMasters. Not one cancellation."

"That's correct, Mr. Peale. Everyone is accounted for."

"And, speaking of accounting . . ." Peale's smile had grown more Cheshire.

McMasters smiled, as much as he thought a subordinate could. "Payments have been received and confirmed, Mr. Peale."

"Splendid," said Peale. "Our guests should all have arrived by three o'clock on the fourth of July. Did the fireworks arrive from Red Bomb in Selkirk?"

"Yes, Mr. Peale. Plenty of red, white, and blue, as you requested."

"Excellent work, McMasters. And the cabins?"

"New linens, pressed, highest thread counts with military corners, as you requested, Mr. Peale."

Peale flipped to the next page. He frowned. McMasters caught it. "Mister Peale?"

Peale pointed at the page. "Right at home, McMasters. Make them feel right at home."

McMasters saw the omission. He gulped. "The pictures."

Peale nodded. "All branches, McMasters. As well as the Pinetree candid shots." He handed back the clipboard to his Number Two. He headed up the stairs to the lodge.

Sam pulled a dusty coffee can from the garage shelf. A few taps on the concrete floor evicted the spider tenant. She filled the can with pungent Varsol, dunking the curled brushes into the solvent. As she did, she heard the sound of a camera shutter. She turned to see Megan holding her tablet. She flipped the tablet around to show off her candid technique. Sam was impressed at her composition. She also hoped it would never see the light of day.

"So, you haven't posted that already, have you?"

Megan looked at the picture. "Why not? Is it too dark?"

Sam pointed at her white roots in the snapshot. "Not dark enough. You can see my Grandma Winters."

"Oh, that's easy." Sam watched as her daughter swiped, pinched, dragged, then swiped some more. She turned it back to Sam for her approval. The white roots were gone. She looked up at her daughter with a smile.

"Lemme guess, there's an app for that."

"There's an app for *everything*, Mom. Can I post it now?"

"Post away," said Sam. "Hashtag find me a tall, dark, age-appropriate stranger while you're at it."

"Yeah, Mom, I don't think I want old guys creeping on my Instagram."

On her what-a-gram? Sam chose to swish her brushes in the Varsol instead of confirming how lame she was. "So, I was talking to your Uncle Chris about the plane, and he said—"

"Pinetree, Mom. I found a ton of stuff. Take a look at this!"

Sam looked up from her brush cleaning. Megan had thrust the tablet screen into her view. The Wiki script was small, though she did see that the page was all about the Pinetree line. She figured it would be easier to get an explanation from Megan, especially with all the varnish fumes.

"So, what is it, Megs? What was it used for?"

"It was military, just like Leese said. Looking for enemy bombers and missiles and stuff. There's even a map of all the stations."

Sam watched as Megan swiped her screen. She brought up a map of the Pinetree locations. Sam watched as her daughter filled in the blanks. "So, most of these stations were automated by the 1960s." She pointed at a location in eastern Manitoba. "This one was near Beausejour." She moved her finger to the Ontario side. "And this one is Sioux Lookout."

Sam looked at the map. The sites were spread from coast to coast. They appeared to mimic the line of an international boundary.

Megan continued. "All these places had code names, and most of them were run by the American military during the fifties." She gave the screen another swipe, pulling up some form of digital notepad. "Let's see, Beausejour was the Boxfile one, Sioux Lookout was Sharecrop. I couldn't find the Pillow and the Naples ones at first, until I punched in the date from the paper we found."

Sam noticed that her daughter's voice had been getting more animated as her story continued. Megan pulled up another page, clicked on a link, and expanded the image. She turned it towards Sam as she spoke.

"Ever heard of the Kinross Incident?"

Sam hadn't. She looked at the screen. She had seen plenty of pages like it in her previous career, the websites that screamed of both free build and shoddy creativity. Then came the content, the misguided machinations of the common loon conspiracy theorist, devoid of anything resembling fact-checking or editorial input. None of these website admins were writers; one paragraph would be all that she could stomach before she dismissed the page as a credible source. And yet, there was an attraction, a guilty pleasure of sorts. Whatever it was, the theory, the scenario, or the conspiracy, these guys *believed* it. The possibility, however remote, that this particular Johnny Whacknut could have the answers to a question that no one ever wanted answered, especially those in the towers of power.

Sam had never heard of the Kinross Incident, an alleged UFO encounter over the Great Lakes in November 1953. She looked at her daughter. A blind woman could see how excited Megan was at her discovery. It reminded Sam of her early days as an intrepid cub reporter at the *Sentinel*, before she learned that her Woodward/Bernstein aspirations would eventually be replaced by shill pieces for the special advertising sections, the ones that truly kept the lights on. Part of her wanted to tell her daughter that it wasn't worth the effort, even for a distraction from summer boredom. That's when she remembered how long summer could be for a bored teenager. *What harm could possibly come from it?*

Sam handed the tablet to Megan. "Tell me all about it, Megs. What else did you find out?"

Megan smiled even harder as she swept back to the page of the Pinetree sites. "Did you notice something on the map, Mom? Anything *kinda* strange?"

Sam looked again at the page. The varnish was still working its wonders. "Strange? Strange how?"

"It's not there, Mom. It's nowhere on the maps, on any of the ones I found. And believe me, there's a lot of them."

Sam still wasn't seeing it. "I don't, I mean, I'm not seeing it, Megs. What is it?"

Megan pointed to the spot that wasn't more than fifteen minutes from Block Fifteen, the site of the decommissioned radar station. "Osis Lake, Mom. It's not there. It's not *anywhere!*"

CHAPTER
THIRTEEN

Wednesday morning roused Sam just before sun-up. She had remembered to plop her slippers within stretching distance the night before. A westerly breeze had stolen the glass-like reflection on the water, the resulting ripples already entering the adolescence of playful waves. If things kept up, it would be perfect sailing weather. If only Sam knew how.

She checked in on Megan while the coffee bubbled on the stove. The items around her daughter's slumber spoke of the summer project. Her tablet leaned against one of the pillows. A

Moleskine notebook lay next to it, cracked open slightly by an off-brand rollerball pen. Sam had donated the writing supplies from her self-assembled novel kit, an impulse purchase that occurred on the day she cleaned out her desk at the *Sentinel*. She wondered if she would ever fill the first Moleskine she had unravelled out of its cellophane, let alone the four she had bought. Sam decided to write her notes smaller and tighter to allow Megan to have one. Sam looked at the floor. She moved her daughter's new slippers into a better position for her feet to slip into.

The morning air felt colder than usual for July, even with fleece and flannel. Sam had noted that the celebration of American independence was upon them, thanks to the oversized calendar stuck to the fridge. It would be a big deal down at the Whiskey Jack Lodge. Lisa's fireworks always gave Canada Day its proper due, but the Whiskey Jack's performances could make anyone on Bird Lake question if they were still in Canada. A lot of red, a lot of white, and plenty of blue. Sam remembered how everything had to be just right for the guests when she worked there, especially on July the fourth. Mr. Van Cleef would make a point of overseeing the touches throughout the property, aided by his Honda trike. It made for a better walker on the uneven terrain, though Van Cleef never achieved mastery behind the handlebars. Sam was still in the throes of grief over her father when she had heard the news about her former employer's death. She wasn't surprised when she learned that Van Cleef had managed to roll the trike on top of himself near the water's edge. The trike had plenty of scrapes and bent parts on it during her time at the lodge. *If only he'd had a quad.*

Old Hondas had been on Sam's mind as of late. Chris had told her where the parts for the dirt bikes were. The bucket spoke of gummed-up carburetors and cracked rubber fuel lines. On the plus side was the removal of the fuel lines from the gas tanks, according to her brother. "Dad always made me drain the tanks out in the fall," said Chris. "Kept the insides from rusting out." After a few YouTube videos, Sam had figured out what would be needed to make them run. Two made-in-China knock-off carburetors, new fuel lines, and a bag of clamps were heading her way via Amazon. For less than a hundred dollars, mother and daughter would have additional modes of transport, ones that could go places the Chevy couldn't, and for a lot less gas.

The lodge. Sam wondered if her alumni status at the Whiskey Jack could land Megan a summer job as a legacy. In Sam's day, the minimum qualifications were geared towards university students. Exams would be done by the end of April, making for an easy May start at the lodge. The fall traffic would die down considerably, allowing the student employees to make it home in time for the start of classes. The current distraction project could only last so long until teenage boredom set in. Sam had also found out why Megan had been using her tablet so much: her iPhone screen had been cracked to the point that pieces of the glass were falling out, with only six months of a two-year contract completed. She had waived the phone replacement insurance. A replacement phone cost more than Sam's first used car, a rusty Bobcat that she had purchased from her lodge earnings. It may not have been pretty, but the transaction was empowering. Gerry Hutchings still kicked the tires for her and negotiated the price down to six hundred dollars from seven. The money was Sam's hard-earned. She still remembered how amazing that felt, even with the holes in the floorboards letting in the gravel dust.

There was another reason, one that Sam felt a smidge of shame for. *The Great Canadian Novel.* The days of newsprint deadline were behind her, though Sam had realized that she truly missed them. The structure had driven her, excited her to the point of awards and recognition. That changed when the deadline became hers to impose. She had yet to dedicate a writing space, a writing time, even a daily writing goal. The Moleskines weren't the only things waiting. A new laptop gathered dust in its box. A stack of yellow legal pads, the kind that the late Elmore Leonard had favoured, poked out of their Staples bag in the corner of the living room. The most ridiculous tool was the vintage Smith-Corona typewriter, a powder blue Electra 220 portable that had been refurbished for more than she paid for it. Hitting a key felt like a firing a gun. The mighty bell tolls, as the carriage reached its end. Almost two-thousand dollars' worth of inspiring things waited for Sam patiently in the cabin. Entertaining her daughter all summer would keep them there.

Sam pulled her phone out of her fleece. She still felt weird about using the voice assistant, preferring to type in her searches. The Whiskey Jack Lodge came up quickly, with five-star reviews and a link to its website. Scrolling text at the top of the page informed would-be guests that the lodge was booked for the season. There was an Employment tab, but the page came up blank. Sam clicked on the Contact Us tab. She highlighted the number. The line picked up on the second ring.

"Thank you for calling the Whiskey Jack Lodge, located in the heart of the Nopiming Provincial Park . . ."

Doesn't anyone answer the phone anymore? Sam listened to the rest of the message, the lack of vacancies, the email address. The voice spoke of a general mailbox, though once it connected, Sam heard a message that the mailbox had not been set up. The email address was simple enough to recall. She composed her inquiry.

From: shutchings1970@gmail.com
To: info@whiskeyjacklodge.com
Subject: Summer employment for students

Greetings,
I would like to inquire as to the availability of summer employment for students. I was employed by the lodge in this regard in the late 1980s. My daughter would be interested in any position that may be available. Accommodations would not be required, as we have a family cabin in the area. Please let me know if any positions are available.

Regards,
Samantha Hutchings

Sam hit Send. She knew she should have asked Megan first, though it was likely that all of the positions were sewn up for the season. She didn't expect the message that landed in her inbox ten minutes later.

From: vmcmasters@whiskeyjacklodge.com
To: shutchings1970@gmail.com
Subject: Current openings

Dear Samantha,
Thank you for your inquiry and thank you for your previous service at the Whiskey Jack Lodge. As you

know, the majority of our full-time summer positions
are secured in advance by those attending university. In
1997, we initiated the hiring of part-time employees as
required. Currently, we require additional support staff
for our dining room. If this position would be of interest
to your daughter, please advise her to forward her
resume to my attention.

Sincerely,
Vance McMasters
Whiskey Jack Lodge

Sam smiled at the message. She hoped Megan would be smiling about it too, whenever she decided to roll out of bed.

CHAPTER
FOURTEEN

Megan Hutchings chafed from two things on Thursday morning: the Chevy's seat belt, and a crisply ironed white dress shirt. Sam had told her about the opportunity and the interview time that had landed in her inbox while they baked the blueberry pie for her grandmother on Wednesday. Sam didn't mention the résumé that she had sent in for her daughter, easily the simplest résumé she had ever written. The Whiskey Jack Lodge would be Megan's first job. Sam had told her that she "knew a guy" and that she had "pulled some strings." Megan had perked up a little when Sam told her she could spend the money earned as she saw fit. She went back to full frown when her mother suggested that it be used to replace her smartphone.

"Mom, all my friends' parents bought them their phones. It's like, a *safety* thing. Why should I have to pay for that?"

Sam clicked the turn signal lever for the service road to the lodge. "Well, Megs, if you had sprung for the insurance on your phone, you wouldn't have to get another one now, would you? And, contrary to popular belief, most adults don't have an extra eight hundred dollars falling out of their pocket to spend on their children's mistakes."

"Dad would buy me a phone."

Sam looked at her daughter. "Then you should call him. Oh wait, you can't call him. Your phone is dead."

Megan crossed her arms. "So, what does this place pay anyway?"

"Oh, I'm sure it's at least five dollars an hour."

Megan looked at her mother with disgust. "FIVE DOLLARS? ISN'T THAT ILLEGAL?"

Sam smiled at Megan as she slowed to a stop at the intercom, about five feet back from a wall of tongue-and-groove cedar. "Yes, Megan. Minimum wage is more than twice that these days. You might even get a share of the tips. I know I did when I was bussing tables here."

The thought of a raise before even starting her job quelled Megan's anger. Sam pressed the large red button on the speaker box. A man's voice answered, free of static.

"Hello, and welcome to the Whiskey Jack Lodge. How can I help you?"

Sam pressed the white Talk button. "Hello, my daughter, Megan Goodman, is here for an interview with Mr. McMasters, for one o'clock."

"Yes," said the voice. "This is Mr. McMasters. I'll open the gate for you. You may park your vehicle in the employee section. Do you know where that is?"

Sam answered. "Is it still next to the housekeeping cabin?"

"Correct," said McMasters. "I'll meet you in the main lodge. Just a moment for the gate, please."

The speaker went quiet, quickly followed by the sound of the gate motors. The wall slowly split into two sections, sliding effortlessly into the trees. Sam drove slowly down the winding drive, a ribbon of cobblestone that probably cost more than the paved section of PR 315. The tree-lined driveway wound for about two hundred feet before opening to reveal the front of the Whiskey Jack Lodge. Megan's reaction had little chance of being contained.

"Holy shit! This place is nicer than Banff!"

"It is," said Sam. "And watch your mouth here. Most of the guests swear like sailors, but you've got to keep it classy, not trashy. Capiche?"

"Yeah, no problem, Mom." Megan continued to gaze in awe as Sam drove to the employee lot, the surrounding air still thick with the remnants of black powder from the previous night's fireworks. She had dressed up as much as she could for the occasion, a colourful floral-print blouse atop black slacks that required a pass on breakfast to fit. The wash-in for her roots wasn't quite the age-reversal potion she thought it would be. She checked her reflection in the side window of the car parked next to her. More mother than grandmother. Close enough.

The Whiskey Jack Lodge had changed little in appearance since Sam's time. If anything, the main lodge looked as though the rustic had been treated to a high polish. The washed Riverstone accents wore new mortar. The windows were the same style as the originals, now with PVC construction that would never rot. The grand double doors had seen a similar upgrade. They didn't need much shove to enter, feeling more high-end home than creaky cottage.

The interior remained intact with Sam's memory. The cheesy free-standing open fireplace in the centre wouldn't be lit until the evening chill required it. The stone accents, the lacquered pine, all as Sam remembered, including the trophy mounts that required expert care and a sizable ladder to dust and vacuum. The front desk area had seen an eco-friendly upgrade, a half wall of deadfall tree slices encased in more coats of varnish than the Hutchings' family canoe. Sam knew the trees were deadfall, thanks to the plaque that said as much on the desktop, a surface composed of reclaimed dock planking. A heavy chrome bell tempted her fingertips. It was all hands on deck when Sam had to respond to the crisp ding in the eighties. She wanted to know if anything had changed.

The sound of the bell had yet to complete its ricochet off the interior walls when the rear door to the desk area opened. A clean-shaven, trim, red-headed man wearing the type of horn-rimmed glasses one would expect to see on the likes of a Depp or a Damon stepped up to the desk. The male uniform had changed little from Sam's days: indigo jeans, a thick black belt, and the light green button-down short-sleeve shirt, with the Whiskey Jack logo embroidered on the single breast pocket, custom sewn with compartments for two pens. *Must be an homage to Mr. Van Cleef*, Sam thought. All staffers were required to carry two pens in her day, in case one ran out.

"Welcome to the Whiskey Jack Lodge," said the man. "I'm Vance McMasters, the manager." He extended his hand to Sam. "You must be Samantha."

Sam shook the hand offered. "Yes, and thank you, Mr. McMasters, for granting an interview for my daughter."

"Call me Vance," said McMasters. He extended his hand to Megan. "Thank you for coming in today, Megan. I'm sure your mother has told you all about her time at the Whiskey Jack."

As far as Sam knew, Megan had never been interviewed before, and it showed. Sam wondered if something else might be contributing to her daughter's nerves: McMasters bore a striking resemblance to a nearsighted, beardless Prince Harry. The rest of him was built like something out of the Marvel Comics franchise. *Maybe he bench presses outboard motors in his spare time*, Sam thought. She figured he was somewhere in his thirties, hard to nail down with the ginger topping. *A sound thrashing.* Sam heard Lisa's unfiltered voice in her head. She hoped it hadn't translated onto her face as a rise in colour.

Megan started, then fumbled. "Uhm, yeah, I mean yes, she really, uh, liked it. I mean—"

McMasters smiled. "Is this your first interview, Megan?"

The smile brought on the blush in Megan's cheeks. "Uhm, yes. I'm sorry."

"Don't be," said McMasters. He motioned to an empty table near one of the couches. "I'll meet the two of you over there."

"Uhm, OK." Megan watched as McMasters headed to the door. Sam noticed her do something. She whispered it to her as they walked to the table.

"Megs, did you just *curtsy*?" Sam whispered.

"*Mom . . .*"

Sam backed off, hoping her daughter's cheeks would dim to half power during the interview. The chat saw little in the way of qualification queries. McMasters asked her about school, her senior year plans, and her aspirations for higher education. Sam watched her daughter doing well, noticing a level of confidence that she didn't know she had. The job offer involved bussing duties for the dining room, as well as house-keeping for the cabins, about three shifts a week. *Excellent*, Sam thought. *She might actually learn to clean up her room.* Fifteen minutes later, Megan shook hands with her new boss.

"We'll get you set up with a uniform," said McMasters. "And I'll need your social insurance number."

Megan gave her mother a look. It clearly said, *I don't know what that is.* Sam had made a point of recording it. They were getting ready to leave when Sam noticed something. McMasters caught it.

"Did you have a question, Samantha?"

Sam kept looking around the room, through the windows, down the corridors. "I was just wondering. Is the lodge full right now?"

"Till the mid-2020s," said McMasters.

Sam kept looking around. "So, if you don't mind my asking . . ."

"Yes?"

Sam stepped closer to McMasters, almost whispering. "So, *where is everybody?*"

McMasters chuckled. "Oh, don't be alarmed. The majority of our guests at the Whiskey Jack are here for conferences. You know, corporate retreats." McMasters pointed to the large cabin near the water's edge, on the opposite side of the cove. "They're meeting in Cabin Four."

Sam looked out the window. The bungalow cabin looked newer than the lodge, only slightly smaller in footprint, with a covered wraparound porch. It wasn't there during her time: the area had been home to the fish-cleaning shack. The cabin appeared to be split down the middle, with a privacy wall separating the porch at the roof's peak. The left side of the porch must have been the spa portion, judging by the white-robed ladies reclining on their respective chaises. On the right side, three men were outside, two seated in Muskoka chairs, with the third leaning up against the railing. The French door nearest the men opened. Sam couldn't see the person, but it must have been an advisement that their meeting would be starting up again soon. The men moved at a relaxed speed back into the cabin. They all had a certain look about them. Sam couldn't quite place it.

"So, Megan," said McMasters. "If I could have you here tomorrow? Around three o'clock?"

Sam turned as Megan looked at her, hoping for the yes signal. Sam gave it.

"Yes, Mr. McMasters," said Megan. She extended her hand with confidence. Sam smiled.

"Call me Vance," said McMasters, shaking Megan's hand. "All the staff does."

Sam shook McMasters' hand to wrap things up. She walked out the door with her daughter as a regal car, a grey and silver 1984 Rolls-Royce Silver Spirit, rolled past towards the gate. It had a personalized Manitoba collector plate on the rear. Sam couldn't make out what it said on the bright yellow plate. It wore different plates when she knew it, the personal car of Edgar Van Cleef. EVC II. The second.

Megan watched in awe as the car passed. "Wow, a Rolls-Royce! Who's that, Mom?"

"That's Norman Peale," said Sam. "And make sure you call *him* Mister."

CHAPTER

Constable Jarrod Mulaney pushed the throttle
hard on the new unmarked brown OPP Ford
as he approached the Kenora harbour. He had
been working a speed trap near the Manitoba
border when the radio crackled the unbelievable,
an armed robbery in progress at the Canadian
Imperial Bank of Commerce downtown. He
had been hoping to take his dinner break early, a
brown bagger that would take him to the hospital
to visit Peggy during visiting hours. The doctor
had ordered bed rest for the final weeks of her
pregnancy. The night girl at the Kenricia Hotel

had said yes to his proposal three years before. A miscarriage in '71 ensured that no chances would be taken with the good news in late October of '72. They had followed the doctor's orders to the letter.

Mulaney checked his battered Timex: it was coming up on a quarter to four. Main Street had been blocked off. One of the OPP officers pointed to a pair of marked cars parked near the harbour. Mulaney grabbed his shotgun and headed towards the command post. He heard the tail end of the latest orders as he approached. "I need the crowds on both sides pushed back now! If you have to grab them by the scruff of their necks and drag them out one by one, then do it!" The superior noticed Mulaney's arrival. He didn't address him by name. "I need you up there across the street from the bank with the rest of them. We've got Milliard from Kenora Police going in."

Mulaney nodded. He moved as quickly as he could through the throng of onlookers. *These people are way too close*, he thought, as he kept reciting that he was OPP and that he was coming through. He crouched down behind a red Maverick with Manitoba plates. A familiar face occupied the front fender position. It was Freddie Besant, a year behind Mulaney at the academy. Besant gave him a quick nod, then went back to his eagle-eyed scans of the front of the bank, his service revolver at the ready. Mulaney noticed the rifle barrel pointing out of a rolled-down window on one of the cruisers. *They're going to nail him when he comes out the door!*

Mulaney kept his eyes on the door as he called out to Besant. "Any hostages?"

"Just one," said Besant, his eyes straight ahead. "The bank manager is still in there. He let everybody else go."

"Let them go? Why the hell would he do that? Is he asking to be shot?"

Besant cut the conversation short. "Here they come!"

Mulaney saw the movement at the entrance. Kenora Police Constable Don Milliard was dressed in plainclothes and carrying a large duffle bag on his back. The robber was behind him, a small calibre automatic pistol in his left hand. The getup made Mulaney blink. The robber wore a heavy flannel jacket. His head was completely concealed with what looked like a black balaclava, topped with a summer-weight fedora. He heard the ongoing commentary from the local radio station, a tag team of a reporter on the street relaying the happenings to the broadcaster who was repeating his words of the event over the radio. From a distance, the mistake made by the reporter was reasonable enough. He had said that the robber was black.

Mulaney noticed the rest of the getup. He saw the clothespin in his mouth. Then he noticed the bulk around him. *A bomb?* He moved closer between the parked cars. The vantage point wasn't great. The truck that the robber had requested for his getaway blocked the view of the scene. Mulaney's shotgun would be of little use, unless the robber tried to escape on foot towards him.

That's when he heard the crack of the rifle. A second later, he knew what the clothespin was: a dead man's trigger.

Mulaney felt the concussion from the explosion, not enough to knock him down. The radioman on the street said the first thing that popped into his head. "Bloody hell, the bomb's gone off!" Mulaney ran towards the smoke. The street was littered with broken glass, twenty-dollar bills, and chunks of robber. Milliard was on his knees, dazed. Mulaney ran to him. He was hurt, but miraculously in one piece. The remnants of the duffle bag of cash were scattered around him. Mulaney tried to tell him he was OK, but it didn't seem to register. *The bomb must have blown out his ear drums.*

The scene was chaotic. The blast had knocked at least a dozen onlookers onto the ground. There were plenty of cuts from the shattered glass, from the bank's windows, the pickup truck, and the totaled cars in front of the bank. Mulaney looked down at Milliard. He was pointing at Mulaney's left leg. Mulaney followed the finger. Three shards of glass were stuck in his leg, his dark pants hiding the blood that had soaked them. He felt the pain then. He eased himself and the shotgun to the ground. He waited with Milliard for the ambulance to come.

The occupants of the Hutchings' cabin rose early on Friday morning. Sam found her mother's ancient Tupperware cake carrier, a little big for the blueberry pie, though the only container in the cabinets that could keep the road dust off the dessert bound for Pinawa. Megan cradled the carrier in her lap, proud of her assistance in preparing the pie. She had removed her nose stud, honouring her grandmother's request.

Sam steadied the Chevy as the gravel made the transition to asphalt. Megan's tablet swiping and the maiden browsing voyage of Sam's new laptop the night before had discovered the Congregate Meals Program, a nutritional meals service for seniors in Pinawa. The program had an informal Meals on Wheels arrangement, one that serviced a few of the residents at the Whispering Pines. The vegan request wasn't met with a scoff or confusion; three of the residents had been on the meal plan for the last six months. The first meal for Lena Hutchings had been scheduled for Friday evening. Sam had decided to ease the transition with a pie for lunch.

Sam and Megan listened to Lena, in between bites of the pie and Cool Whip topping. "I used to pick wild blueberries, up at Bird Lake. Do you nurses know where that is?"

Megan played along. "I've heard of it. They say it's very pretty there."

Sam nodded, swallowing her bite before answering. "I used to work at a lodge there, when I was going to university."

Lena smiled. "The Whiskey Jack Lodge. I had a daughter who worked there. Maybe you remember her, Samantha Hutchings?"

Sam felt the awkwardness wash over her. Her mother hadn't placed her, and she hadn't confused Megan as her younger self, at least not yet. Still, it was a memory remembered, right down to her name. She decided to change the subject.

"How's your pie, Lena? Do you have enough Cool Whip?"

"It's very good," said Lena. She took another bite, answering with a full mouth that she would have scolded Samantha for as a child. "These blueberries taste just like the ones on Osis Road. That's where . . ."

Sam and Megan watched as Lena's train of thought ground to a halt. A minute passed, enough time for the bite of pie on Lena's fork to fall back to the plate. She looked down at the pie as if she were seeing it for the first time. She did the same to the fork. She looked at her daughter and granddaughter. There was a look of recognition forming in her eyes. Sam and Megan leaned in. Lena looked at her plate.

"Gerry's gone to work in the city. He'll be back on Friday."

Sam leaned forward. Her hand reached out instinctively to her mother. "Gerry . . ."

"Yes, Gerry. He's not here right now. He'll be back on Friday." Lena looked at Megan. "Dear, what day is today?"

Megan looked at her mother, then her grandmother. "It's, it's Friday, Lena. Today is Friday."

Lena smiled. She looked at her granddaughter. "You'll like Gerry. He had to go to work in the city. I stay at the cabin with the kids during the week in the summer. He's an accountant."

"Yes, Lena. Gerry's an accountant. He, uh, he works with numbers."

"Important numbers," said Lena. "Very important . . ."

Lena started to trail off again. She looked down at the pie plate. She looked up at her daughter.

"Dear, are these wild blueberries?"

Sam smiled. "Yes, Lena, wild blueberries."

Lena took another bite. "I love wild blueberries."

Sam pushed the shopping cart through the Solo market. Like most small-town stores, the Pinawa Solo included a liquor section. She added a box of cheap white wine to Lisa's beer request. She was starting to run out of cart.

Megan returned from the opposite aisle, her hands full of the food that most seventeen-year-olds devour with little thought to future consequences. Sam held up a tube of Pringles. "Do you know how much sodium is in these things?"

Megan looked at the nutritional label. "Is that what makes them taste so good?"

"Probably," said Sam. She pushed the cart past the meat section. She reached out to cover her daughter's eyes. "I guess you probably don't want to look at that."

"Can we get some ground round?"

"What's ground round?"

Megan had already found a package, placed very close to the actual ground beef in the cooler. "It's plant-based, and you use it like you'd use ground beef. We could make tacos."

"Sounds heavenly."

"C'mon, Mom. Beats killing another cow, right?"

Sam looked at the package, then at Megan. "Tacos, huh?"

Megan smiled. "I'll get the taco shells."

Sam had dropped Megan off at the Whiskey Jack just before three o'clock. Her first shift would end at ten, typical of the Whiskey Jack's dining room hours. Many of the guests wouldn't even sit down for dinner till eight. Sam put a reminder alarm on her phone to wrap things up around nine-thirty. She was convinced that she'd need an alarm to snap her out of her impending writing frenzy, though she couldn't remember the last time her keystrokes could be translated into words per minute. By six, she had started on the taco mixture. Megan was right; with chopped onions, salsa, and a sachet of taco seasoning, she couldn't tell it wasn't meat.

Sam put the leftovers aside to cool. Megan's Pringles snarf on the ride back from Pinawa had been enough of a filler for her to request a late dinner after her shift. Sam brought her laptop over to the kitchen table. She used a fork to scoop up the leftovers of her taco that escaped the hard shell. She flipped through a few emails, confirming that the dirt bike parts were scheduled to arrive on Tuesday. She felt little in the way of creative spurt. The talk of her father during the visit with Lena steered her search window to the past. The massive 1989 smoke plume over Bird Lake on the front page of the *Sentinel* was the first stop on her tour of reminiscence. Sam ended the journey with her father's obituary. The picture looked ridiculous, a 1970s mutton-chopped, pixelated rendering of Gerry Hutchings, with a period tie, width to match. The obituary went through the usual bits, the predeceased parents, his schooling at the University of Manitoba, marriage, and the kids. There was no mention of the accounting firm he worked for, just that he worked at one. Sam knew he had to have worked *somewhere*. He left the house in the morning. He came home at night, unless he was out of town on business. He made enough that Mom didn't have to work, that Sam and her brother had money for school, plus a new family car every couple of years. He had also made the proper arrangements to ensure that his family encountered little in the way of hardships after he died.

An accountant. Sam thought back to her earliest memories of her father. She remembered briefcases, short-sleeved dress shirts and ties, a pocket protector when that was a thing. There was his panelled office in the basement, off-limits, like most dads' offices. Sam wondered if there might be a record of where her dad had worked, or if it was self-employment. Sam felt embarrassed that she didn't know her father's story. She knew there had to be some sort of association for CGAs, or maybe it was CPAs. Chartered? Certified? *Creative? Maybe someone out there has a better picture.* She found the website for the Chartered Professional Accountants of Manitoba. This was the second slice of writing that Sam had rattled off at

Bird Lake, the first being Megan's summer job inquiry. *At least I'm writing again.*

> From: shutchings1970@gmail.com
> To: info@cpamb.org
> Subject: Archives related to Gerald (Gerry) Hutchings
>
> Greetings,
>
> I am inquiring as to the existence of any archival photos or correspondence that involve my father, Gerald (Gerry) Hutchings. He was employed as an accountant in Winnipeg from 1965 until his death in 1989, though I am unsure as to the firm(s) he may have worked for, or if he was self-employed. Any information that you can provide would be greatly appreciated.
>
> Sincerely,
> Samantha Hutchings

Sam hit Send and went back to her blank Word document.

CHAPTER SEVENTEEN

Megan Goodman didn't realize how much of a workout clearing tables would be. The plates, the drinkware, even the cutlery felt dense. The arms of the Whiskey Jack serving staff were muscular, defined in places that no gym equipment could duplicate. The food looked as thick as the plates. She smiled to herself at the potential looks of horror that would have fallen on the face of her stepmother in Edmonton. At the Whiskey Jack Lodge, the main courses had previously worn one of two things: feet or fins.

The dining room jutted out from the main lodge, as if it had been trying to make a break for the water since its original construction. Floor-to-ceiling windows alternated with French doors, the type where one door tipped open for the night air to filter through the screens. Two massive ceiling fans turned at a comfortable pace overhead. Megan wondered if the blades had been culled from some massive propeller-driven airliner, like those black-and-white movies that her parents had forced her to watch for the cultural references.

The guests were American, *really* American, right down to their thick accents and waistbands. Megan had heard accents like these before, the kind that always seemed so over-the-top on the big screen. She pegged the median age around seventy. The men wore one of two haircuts: tightly cropped silver-grey or high-polished bald. The women were still hanging on to their original hair colours, though just barely. The dress appeared casual, though Megan noticed that most of the casual shirts and khaki pants of the men were without wrinkles—the ironed pleats looked like they could cut through one of the steaks.

The bartender worked a steady pace, with separate serving personnel carrying lowball glasses with plenty of brown liquors. The glasses still stank of the pungent drink as Megan cleared them away. After a dirty look from one of the silver-haired men, she quickly learned that a glass with a thin layer remaining wasn't empty until the very last drop. The man's wife came to her rescue, punctuating her point with a large glass of red wine without spilling a drop.

"Sugar, taking a glass of fancy-pants liquor away from a man before he's done is like taking a momma's teat outta the mouth of a newborn calf," said the woman, as she brought the glass of scotch back down from Megan's tray. "Best not to get 'em riled, unless you're good at ropin', and I mean Amarillo-good."

Megan nodded, not quite understanding, though still managing a smile. "I'm sorry about that, sir, and ma'am."

The woman gave Megan a playful wrist flick tap on her arm. "Well now, a sir *and* a ma'am!" She looked over at her husband. "Jake, honey, when's the last time our grandkids called us sir and ma'am?"

The man finished the last drop in his glass, then carefully placed it on Megan's tray. "It's like I'm always saying, Myrna. These Canadians are all sweeter than a Georgia peach." He smiled at Megan, giving her a grandfatherly wink. "In fact, I reckon they're so sweet they don't even gots a pit inside!"

Megan smiled some more, as the couple chuckled. She backed away in time for the waiter carrying a drink tray to deposit a new glass of scotch in front of the man she now knew as Jake but would continue to address as sir. That had been made clear during her training. Megan quickly realized that the patrons would toss all sorts of requests and questions her way. She did her best to delegate, though it wasn't long until she found herself carrying full glasses to the tables. No one had asked her if she was eighteen, the legal drinking age in Manitoba. Judging by the gate outside, a liquor licence inspector wouldn't be dropping in anytime soon.

The serving staff seemed friendly enough. Megan soon realized that most of them were better than halfway through university. The kitchen staff seemed a little posh, though it probably had something to do with the executive chef, a short, spiky-haired blond who kept up a frantic pace. He was French, though Megan couldn't tell if he was Quebecois or Parisian. Judging from the side glances she caught from the line cooks between his barks, he was at least eighty percent asshole.

The steady flow of drinks in the dining room meant plenty of trips to the dishwasher station. The commercial system used a single operator, a girl from Lac du Bonnet named Rhiannon Koshelanyk, Rhee for short, with red, curly hair attempting to escape her hairnet. "Only my mom calls me Rhiannon," said Rhee, during one of their quick conversations. "And only when she's *really* mad." Her name had come from her mother's love of Stevie Nicks. "Apparently, I'm named after a Welsh witch or something," Rhee said, as the steam rolled out from the opening dishwasher hood. "So you better not piss me off."

Megan's expected laugh was interrupted by the executive chef, who had come up quickly from behind. "The only ones off-pissing will be the guests tonight from these!" He tossed one of the dessert plates at Rhee, a toss that Megan figured she must have caught many times before. The chef pointed to the stack of dessert plates on the order counter. "Wash them again! And hand drying! *Vite! Vite!*"

"Yes, Chef Henri." Rhee retrieved the stack of plates while Megan cleared the tray of lowball glasses. She waited till the chef had moved to the opposite end of the kitchen before whispering to Rhee. "What's *his* problem?"

"He's French," whispered Rhee, giving the plates a quick scour before putting them in the rack. "Isn't that enough?"

The girls chuckled. There was no way for the chef to hear them, but he must have had a hint about the conversation.

"You're not being paid to social-wise," said Henri. "And chill the plates in the walk-in cool air!"

The girls stifled their laughs and did as they were told.

Sam had a feeling that Megan's shift would run a little late, just like hers did in the late eighties. She hadn't left the cabin until almost ten. It took almost a minute for someone to respond to her gate buzz. She parked the Chevy just outside of the floodlight glare from the main entrance to the lodge. She turned off the ignition in Drive.

The guests had moved outside, judging by the snippets of elevated conversation and laughter that wafted into the hardtop's three open windows. Sam knew the drill. The bartending staff would stay until the last guest staggered to their cabin, sometimes assisting for safety. Guests who were into them would partake in the lodge's cigar collection, at the oversized stone firepit near the water's edge. Sam sniffed at the night air. The cigars were underway, along with some logs of aromatic cedar and some oil drippings burning off the Chevy from underneath.

The pathways to the cabins had been updated with ground-level lighting, with the glow of the respective porch lights visible through the trees. Sam flipped the key to Accessory to try to find some music on the AM radio that wasn't country. As she turned the dial, she saw the head-lights coming down the driveway. She winced at the high beams as they swung past her. It was Norman Peale in his dusty Rolls-Royce. Sam hadn't noticed the garage in the trees until the automatic door began to rise. The garage had decent lighting, which showcased the usual lake things, such as chaises, fishing gear, a pile of cast iron frying pans for shore lunches, and a beat-up Honda trike with a flat front tire. Peale went to the rear of the Rolls. He opened the trunk, removing a large yellow Pelican case. He put the case on a clean workbench next to the car, removing a padlock from the front. He opened the case, looking inside at the contents for about a minute. Sam wondered what it could be that would require such secure containment. She thought back to her days at the Whiskey Jack. The only two answers she could think of were custom wonder lures to coax the Master Anglers from the cold depths or a bottle of scotch that was worth more than Peale's Rolls. He closed the case, secured the padlock, and returned it to the trunk. He keyed in a code on an exterior keypad to close the door. The lighting at the rear of the car wasn't very good. Sam still couldn't make out the plate. Peale walked briskly across the lawn towards the firepit. Someone yelled out "Norman!" as he approached, quickly followed by cheering and laughter.

The garage door closed shut.

CHAPTER EIGHTEEN

If yawns were gasoline, Megan Goodman was using as much as the Hutchings' Chevy. Sam counted six well-earned yawns from her daughter during the short trip back to Block Fifteen. Megan mentioned a Rhee, her new dishwashing friend, during the drive, one that let her in on the fact that Chef Henri had a habit of instructing the dishwashing staff to toss food that wasn't up to his Michelin three-star guidebook standards. Most of it made its way into the staff's stomachs on the back steps of the Whiskey Jack Lodge, thanks to empty food service containers that Rhee would fill and stow when Chef Henri wasn't looking. Megan didn't need any vegan tacos. She needed bed, and right soon.

After a grunt from her daughter that may or may not have meant good night, Sam went back to her laptop. She found herself digging deeper into the Kinross Incident that Megan had uncovered. The tattered communiqué tied in perfectly to the date of the incident: November 23, 1953. The websites were rife with theories, from the plausible—a crash caused by the generation of a phantom radar image for training purposes—to the fantastical—the absorption of the interceptor by an alien craft. The incident supposedly took two lives with it: the pilot, First Lieutenant Felix Eugene Moncla, and the radar operator, Second Lieutenant Robert L. Wilson. There had been reports of wreckage found on the shores of Lake Superior in the late sixties, though the pieces had never been officially identified. The interest level in the story was high enough that an elaborate hoax was hatched in 2006 by a fake diving company that claimed to have found the wreckage on the floor of Lake Superior, along with the flying saucer it had collided with.

Sam found her cursor finger wandering into the choppy waters of UFO sightings and missing aircraft. By the time the witching hour had arrived, she had dug into the missing / discovered / still missing remnants of Flight 19 and the Bermuda Triangle, lubricated by a fat glass of boxed white wine. She had never heard of the Great Lakes Triangle or the Mount Rainier encounter in 1947. As she sifted through Amelia Earhart's bones, she remembered a visit to the Manitoba Museum in the early eighties. *Wasn't there a UFO sighting at Falcon Lake?* She remembered the darkness of the planetarium and the projector that looked like an alien creature, as a booming recorded voice told the popular tales of UFOs, from the Barney and Betty Hill abduction to the Falcon Lake incident of 1967.

A quick Google search of the Falcon Lake UFO uncovered a new book about the sighting. The Royal Canadian Mint had just issued a commemorative coin that depicted the encounter in full force, with a startled Stefan Michalak shielding himself from the craft. Sam thought that the full-colour coin looked just as ridiculous as its price: $129.95. She changed her mind when she saw that the initial run of four thousand coins had sold out. *That's a lot of UFO geeks.*

The wine was starting to do what wine did to those sipping it in the wee hours. Sam decided to check her email before she turned in for the night. Her inbox had a bit of spam, an invoice from the food service for her mother and something from the accountant's association. She clicked on the message.

From: jbachynski@cpamb.ca
To: shutchings1970@gmail.com
Subject: Archives related to Gerald (Gerry) Hutchings

Greetings Samantha,
As per your request, I have checked our archives with regards to your father's name. Unfortunately, I have been unable to find any information within the timeline that you had specified in your initial inquiry. Please let me know if there are any other spellings or family names that would apply to your father. I suggest that you contact the associations in other provinces where your father may have worked.

Sam rubbed her eyes. She read the email again. *Unable to find any information?* A third and a fourth scan didn't change the text to her liking. *Was he certified in another province?* Sam knew that wasn't the case. Gerry Hutchings was as Manitoba homegrown as bison burgers and fresh goldeye. She went to the bookshelf to prove it. A musty legal-sized portfolio had plenty of pictures from her father's youth, still awaiting their placement in a proper album. There was a class picture on the steps of Polson School, dated 1946. Then high school, at St. John's in the North End, dated 1957. A smaller snap showed him next to his first car, a '46 Hudson Commodore that he bought for seventy-five dollars in '58. It was a story he would retell every two years when he rolled into the driveway with another new Buick. "Do you know how much I paid for my first car?" he'd say, as he unfurled the window sticker in front of his children.

There was a selection of candid shots from her parents' wedding in '65, a few embarrassing ones of her and Chris in the naked baby stages. The snaps from the seventies changed from bordered black-and-white to rounded Kodachrome, with the odd Polaroid stuffed in for good measure. These were the years at Bird Lake that held fast in Sam's memories. The living-colour years.

The portfolio had a few non-photo items that bore her father's name. A diploma of sorts from Polson School. His high school diploma from St. John's. Sam sifted through the pile to the bottom. *Where's his degree?* Sam looked through the pile of books and framed pictures on the shelf, the pictures that were still waiting to return to the wall after the new woodgrain panelling was installed in the summer of '89. A framed diploma was nowhere to be found. *Maybe it's in Mom's storage locker.* Sam made a mental note to check for it during her next visit to the Whispering Pines. Her next trip was now boarding, an eight-ish hour flight to dreamland.

She did remember to bring her slippers with her.

Norman Peale checked his Jazzmaster. The witching hour had been history for about fifteen minutes, along with his scotch. The cigar butts of the Whiskey Jack guests were barely visible in the ashes of the firepit. It had been a fat minute since the attendance around the fire had shrunk from three to two. Peale looked through the remaining flames at a face he knew all too well. Jake Kinsey's gaze had been silently concentrated on the lower flames of the dying fire. There was still enough scotch left in his glass to draw a dirty look if anyone tried to take it. It took another minute until he broke the silence. He lubricated his throat first, then placed the empty crystal on the ground next to his lacquered stump stool.

"There's purple in there."

Peale leaned closer. Kinsey was right. The hue could be clearly seen in the lower levels of the log remnants.

Kinsey continued his analysis. "Maybe a little bit of pink too."

"Must be the wood," said Peale.

Kinsey looked over at the stone half-wall that held the seasoned pile. "What kind of wood is it?"

Peale looked at the pile, then Kinsey. He smiled. "Dead."

Kinsey blinked, then let out a hearty laugh. "You are correct, Norman. You are correct."

Peale scanned the area. They were alone. He reached over to an ancient poker and pushed the remaining logs together in the centre of the firepit. "That is the one good thing about dead trees."

"How's that, Norman?"

"They stay dead."

Kinsey looked around the firepit. "A true statement, Norman. Mind you, I don't reckon that a Scotch pine has a ghost underneath all that bark and needles." Kinsey took another scan of the immediate area. "But we both know there are ghosts here. Catch my drift?"

"I do," said Peale. "Because we put them here."

"We did that, Norman. Directly or indirectly, we did. Most of them nowhere near here."

Most of them. Peale looked up at the night sky. A shooting star cut through the rising smoke.

"Did you see that, Jake?"

"I did, Norman. I did."

"I wonder whose ghost that was."

Kinsey rose from his stump. He gave the night sky a broad scan. He looked at Peale. "It's best not to wonder, Norman. I've got too many ghosts that the brass at the Pentagon know about, let alone the ones they don't. I prefer sleeping at night instead of lying awake." He gave the sky a final look. He tossed something resembling a sloppy salute at Peale. He was about ten feet from the firepit when Peale spoke.

"Jake?"

"Yep?"

"Do *you* sleep at night?"

Kinsey stopped. He turned back to the firepit and looked at Peale, grinning. "Sometimes, Norman. Sometimes I do."

CHAPTER
NINETEEN

Perhaps it was the conspiracy sites. Perhaps it was her brother's plastic model planes that Sam could see from her bed as she drifted in and out of sleep. Perhaps it was the vegan ground beef substitute in the tacos, flipping her unaccustomed constitution more than the pancakes at a church picnic. The wine? *No, never the wine.* Whatever it was, Sam knew that proper sleep wouldn't come again. She looked at the clock on her phone: 6:30 a.m. *Really? On a Saturday?* She was so groggy, she didn't even feel the chill of the dawn floor on her slipperless feet. She grabbed a bottle of water from the counter, a towel for the surely damp Muskoka, and her father's thin down curling jacket. She headed for the dock.

The water was dead calm, a morning mist hugging the surface with all its might. The Hutchings' family canoe had finally made its way to the water's edge, tipped on its side. Sam stared at the canoe. *I never was awesome at solo.* After a few minutes of trying to talk herself out of it, she was pushing the canoe off the sand. She used the life jacket that she should have been wearing as the kneepad for the centre position. She pushed off from the shore.

Sam's paddling technique was about as good as her typing skills on the ancient typewriter: capable but clumsy, with a hint of epic fail just waiting to happen. She moved along the shore, past the Janzen cabin, where Lisa's cooler bag stood open and empty of usable beer. Past the old Reynolds place, a plot of waterfront recently cleared of its original cabin for something involving three shipping containers, a steel girder framework, and probably half of God's money. Another old shack, another new money monster. Sam knew that Bird Lake was changing, and probably not for the better.

She thought about her father as she paddled the canoe he built, how she knew as much as any child of the seventies and the eighties would know of their father before the end of their teens: Dad goes to work in the morning, makes the money to buy the food, the clothes, and the cars, and comes home in the evening. That's what dads did. Few sons and daughters would question it, especially during their formative years. She knew of one family that had to move due to financial issues in the eighties. Even then, it was from a bungalow to a well-kept duplex. Families didn't collapse as easily back then. Or maybe the walls were just built thicker to absorb all the yelling.

Sam's parents had their arguments. Most of them dealt with her dad's work schedule. Through all the summers that she could remember, Sam knew that she wouldn't see her father at the cabin during the week. This meant that her mother would take the brunt of the childhood injuries, which Bird Lake provided regularly, especially when the dirt bikes showed up. After her brother broke his arm during one such event, Lena threatened to roll the Hondas into the lake, a lake which, like most lakes, heard the whole thing. Chris was riding that Honda two weeks later, a little more cautiously, his cast signed by most of the cottagers on Block Fifteen.

What did Dad do for a living? Sam thought back to the Buicks. He would take one of the kids along to pick it up from the old McNaught dealership on Portage Avenue. She remembered the process, wandering through the showroom as papers were signed, hands shaken, and licence plates moved from one Buick to the next. *The salesman always said something about the car that Dad traded in.* Sam dug into her memory. Nothing.

Sam dipped her paddle in the water, raising it to an angle that was supposed to run a trickle of water to her lips, another Dad trick. The water soaked her sleeve instead. She was rubbing the sleeve dry on her pant leg when she heard the faint opening riff of "Bobcaygeon" by The Tragically Hip. The wispy mist parted, revealing a well-worn T-shaped steel dock. Two Muskoka chairs bobbed ever so slightly on the floating section, which appeared to have a flotation barrel beneath that was taking on water. One of the chairs was empty. The other was occupied by a lone figure wearing a red pullover hoodie. White headphone strands emerged from the front pocket, heading into the ears of the unseen head. Sam knew the head beneath the hood. She couldn't resist. She turned the canoe to allow for a right-handed flick of her paddle, a splash that quickly brought the chair's occupant to their feet. The hood came off, revealing a mess of salt and pepper curls. The surprised look quickly changed to a smile. "Hey, Sammers."

Sam returned the grin. "Hey, Zack-Attack." Zachary Peeters got down on his knees at the edge of the dock. He reached for the canoe, pulling it to the side. Like most of the lake buddies from Sam's youth, Zach wore the usual scars of time, from wrinkles to paunch. His mischievous grin was still as timeless as ever. If he'd chosen the musty Mary Maxim sweater that hung on the hooks at his cabin door, he could have passed for a Halloween-grade Jeff Lebowski, sans goatee. He was born in 1970, a perfect fit as childhood playmate for Sam and her brother. Zach was riding the other Honda when Chris Hutchings broke his arm. That event almost resulted in a lifelong ban from the Hutchings' cabin. Zach promised to stay off the tough trails, volunteering for grass-cutting detail when Gerry was working during the week. There was a tiny bit of history between the two: a first kiss that Sam had planted on Zach in the Hutchings' treehouse, a kiss he had quickly recoiled from in disgust. He was there when the Canuck went screaming down the lake. He was there when the fire prompted the evacuation of all the cottage blocks. He was also there at Gerry Hutchings's funeral.

"Need some weekend coffee?" said Zach. He pointed towards the vintage Thermos next to his Muskoka.

Sam smiled. She knew what weekend coffee meant. "Baileys?"

"Carolans," said Zach. "It's the same shit, and it was on sale."

"Well, no, it isn't," said Sam. "But as long as it was a bargain." Zach steadied the canoe as Sam exited. He secured it to the cleats while Sam gave the other Muskoka a quick wipe. She leaned forward in time for Zach to place the Thermos cup in her hands. The smell of the liqueur was potent. So was the coffee-to-liqueur ratio. "Holy shit," said Sam, downing the first sip. "So, you're just heating the booze and nixing the coffee now?"

"I know! Genius, isn't it?" Zach unscrewed the Thermos for a quick swig. "I mean, let's face it. When you've decided to add a depressant to a stimulant, you start to ask yourself how much stimulation you actually want."

Sam nodded between sips. "Well, a noble experiment."

"So, how's the day job?"

Sam realized it had been a while since they talked. "Great, especially when you don't have to go to one and still get paid for it."

"Oh shit," said Zach. "You were part of that last round at the *Sentinel*?"

"Yeah. But no biggie. Nothing left to do but write 'The Great Canadian Novel.'"

Zach nodded towards the Hutchings' cabin. "Going to keep the place?"

Sam followed the nod. "I hope so. Chris is on me to sell it. Needs money for his latest failure."

"You'd be nuts to sell it." Zach pointed at his cabin. "I can't imagine life without the lake."

"Yeah, it's hard to beat. But—"

"But what?"

"Well, it's a lot of work."

"Which you've got time for."

"And then, there's the Dad stuff."

"Yeah," said Zach. "I know about that."

"How long has it been?"

Zach leaned forward in his chair. It had been almost twenty-eight years since the accident, the head-on collision on PR 315 that had taken his father, mother, and kid brother, Phil. "You know, my dad always said those Volvos were stupid safe."

Sam leaned forward in her chair. "I don't think any car is safe against a logging truck."

"Yeah, probably not." Zach reached back to the Thermos. He unscrewed the cap. "Probably not."

Sam remembered the weekend it happened. It was the second one after July Long, a weekend with a lot of rain. The crash happened at the top of a blind hill, about three miles from where the two friends now sat. Zach came upon the scene about an hour after it happened. He didn't even recognize the car. He drove around the RCMP, the useless ambulance, and the road flares. Two hours later, there was a knock at the door. By his own admission, Zach had not handled things well. The trucking company he inherited from his father continued to prosper, though he had little to do with the day-to-day. He didn't party as hard as he used to, lake parties that Sam vaguely remembered from her days of self-medicating to ease the loss of her own father. At her last count, Zach was winding down on his fourth marriage, a May-September pairing that had lasted about a year and a half. There was a kid each from the first three—kids who didn't come around, call, or write. The family cabin was an ongoing mess of half-finished renovations, thanks to hefty amounts of child support and alimony to pay out each month. The boathouse held his father's Glastron runabout, its Mercury outboard in a state of disassemble, easily seen through the garage door that had jammed midway in its tracks. Zach picked away at things when he felt the need, until the next distraction popped up on Plenty of Fish.

Sam deflected from the heavy remembrance. "Hey, do you remember when the Canuck went flying down the lake?"

Zach misheard the question. "The duck? I see ducks all the time. Mallard? Wood?"

"No, dipshit. The Canuck. The jet fighter?"

"Oh yeah, I remember that. That was wicked. Park Pontiac Brother Jake–wicked. What about it?"

"Oh, nothing, I guess. Megan found a picture that Dad painted of it."

"I'd like to see that. How's she doing?"

"She's good. Got her a summer gig at the lodge. She thinks there's more to that whole plane thing."

Zach frowned. "More? How do you mean?"

Sam explained the recent events: the discovery of the Canuck painting, the lack of markings on it, the remnants of paper at the Osis Lake radar station that apparently didn't exist. Zach listened attentively. He tried to remember what he could. It came to him.

"It was '82. Summer of '82."

Sam leaned in. "Are you sure?"

Zach smiled. "How could I forget the summer that Sam Hutchings put the moves on me in her treehouse?"

Sam felt her cheeks fill with colour. "*Moves?* I was eleven!"

Zach's grin grew. "Eleven going on twelve."

Sam slapped Zach's arm. "Eww. Gross. And as memory serves, you ran like a scared little bitch."

Zach leaned in, still smiling. "Strong women still scare me, Sammers. And strong divorce lawyers."

Sam rolled her eyes. "Well, you of all people oughta know. But the plane. The plane!"

Zach smirked. "Who are you, Tattoo? Am I wearing a white suit?"

"Zach, c'mon."

"Tell me your *fan-tah-see*." Zach poured on his best Ricardo Montalban.

Sam's patience collapsed. "For you to grow the fuck up and tell me what you remember, that's what."

Zach dropped the goof. "Hey, sorry. OK. The plane."

Sam nodded. "Yes, the plane." She watched as Zach rubbed his moustache. He looked up, his eyes seeming to follow the flight path of the phantom Canuck. His eyes went wide. He looked at Sam.

"Gimme a minute."

Before Sam could answer, Zach was on the move, still holding the top of the Thermos, splashing out its boozy contents as he headed up the path. She decided to follow him, grabbing the lower part of the Thermos. The wooden screen door still produced its signature slam as Zach flew inside. Sam made a point of letting it close slowly as she entered. The interior of the Peeters' cabin looked as she remembered, with plenty of pine, lacquered driftwood, and the Master Angler pike caught by the late Donald Peeters hanging over the wood stove. It was flanked by the first fish caught by his sons. Zach was pulling out photo albums from a built-in shelf. He was saying something as he went. Sam heard it clearer as she approached.

"Nineteen seventy-seven, '78, '79 . . ."

Sam saw the albums. Judging by the expert cursive, the labels that denoted the years of the albums were penned by

Zach's mother, Bertha. *Just like Mom's cursive.* He found the 1982 album. He smiled at it, then at Sam.

"Eighty-two. Duran Du-freaking-ran."

The two childhood friends moved to the kitchen table. The clear protective sheets that covered the photographs were dried out of their adhesive, with many of the pictures loose and jumbled. There was more cursive beneath the photos, describing the people and the events of the summer. The captions noted the arrival of two new photographers, Zachary, and Philip. *That's right*, Sam thought. *Mrs. Peeters never shortened their names.* There was a snapshot that showed the brothers holding their new-for-'82 Kodak Disc cameras. The next few pages showed the grainy offerings of the budding photographers. The cursive notes included the name of the shooter, along with their blurs. Some pictures were joined by three question marks, a mother's attempt to encourage the creativity in her sons while having no idea what the picture was about.

Zach turned to the next page. "Holy shit!" he blurted. "I knew we had a picture of it!"

Sam looked at the snapshot. Calling the image a picture was generous, though it was proof of the event. The pictures leading up to it appeared to be a child's study in clouds. Philip was the shooter.

Sam looked at Zach. "Wasn't Phil with us on the inner tubes?"

Zach rubbed his moustache. "I think so, until . . ."

"Until what?"

Zach sat up. He smacked his forehead with the return of the memory. "Kehoe!"

Sam looked puzzled. "Kehoe? Who the hell is Kehoe?"

"The black lab, the one that the McKenzies had."

Sam remembered. "Oh, you mean Stupid Dog." Kehoe, a.k.a. Stupid Dog, loved the water. He loved it so much that he wanted to be in it all the time, especially when kids were playing in it. He also loved to claw his way into inner tubes that children were using. A few shrieks, a little crying, and a shout of "KEHOE! COME!" and it was all over.

"Phil was bawling, that much I remember," said Zach. "Kehoe scratched him pretty good too. So Dad grabs the inner tube, calls old man McKenzie something colourful, then gets the bicycle patches to fix the holes. I think Mom grabbed Phil a Freezie and his camera to calm him down."

Sam looked at the pictures. *Phil was lying on his back.* Clouds, clouds, clouds, and then, the belly of the Canuck. Grainy, out of focus, though still clear of one thing: identifying markings of any kind. Sam looked at the date: July 14, 1982. In addition to the photo credit to Philip, there were three cursive characters. It was the only explanation Bertha Peeters could muster.

???.

CHAPTER
TWENTY

Sam paddled lazily back to the Hutchings' family cabin. Megan's shift didn't start until the afternoon, which would hopefully give Sam some time to determine if she was ready to ride solo to work. Sam's Honda rejuvenation had gone surprisingly well, with both dirt bikes running just as she remembered. The bikes were semi-automatics, with no clutch levers to teach for engagement. There was also the trail, which could ferry her daughter to the Whiskey Jack Lodge in such a way that the wheels would barely touch the provincial road.

The Chevy was a non-starter, as Megan, like most teens of her generation, had yet to obtain her learner's permit.

The sun felt nine-ish as Sam rounded the corner to the Hutchings' cabin. She was surprised to see Megan in a Muskoka, with something warm rising from her travel cup. "I hope that's what I think it is," said Sam, as she glided past the dock to the shore.

"Fresh brewed," said Megan. "I watched a video on how to brew it, but I think I made it a little strong."

Just what the doctor ordered, Sam thought. As she approached, Megan reached down next to her chair. She brought up the second travel cup. There was no way that she could have known whose cup it was. Sam tried to look past it, but the look on her face had nowhere to hide, short of diving off the dock. Megan caught it. "Mom, is this cup OK?"

Sam smiled, dulling the awkwardness of her recent expression. "It's more than OK, Megs." She took the cup from her daughter, cradling it with both hands. One observer may have thought it was to collect its warmth. Another would have seen the embrace of the vessel as much more. Megan chose the latter.

"That's Grampa's cup, isn't it?"

Sam smiled as she nodded. It wasn't fancy by any means. It was an old Mac's Convenience Store cup from the seventies, when the orange hue was truly a thing. "This cup was practically bolted to your Grampa's hand. Driving, fishing. I think he even gave me and your uncle Chris a few solid tongue-lashings while shaking it at us."

"He must have been careful with it when he did," said Megan. "The top is a little loose."

Sam checked the fit. It explained a lot of things, such as the minimalist sips that Gerry Hutchings would take from it and the reason he always kept the top clamped with his index finger. Sam took a sip, testing the finger-clamp system for herself. *Not bad engineering for an accountant.* "So, how's the job so far?"

"Pretty good," said Megan. "Rhee's pretty cool."

Sam leaned in. "Who's Rhee again?"

Megan gave Sam the basics on Rhiannon Koshelanyk. "She's going to Red River College in the fall. And she's got her own trailer at the campground!"

"Really? Her *own* trailer?"

"Yeah! Can I sleep over?"

Sam knew that a friend was a valuable commodity to have at Bird Lake. While their reunion had progressed well, mother-daughter time didn't have to be the only time spent. Somewhere in that realization, Sam felt the need to add a pinch of parent. "Do I get to meet her first?"

Megan rolled her eyes in the family way. "Yes, *mother . . .*"

Sam smiled. The two sipped their coffees, taking in the growing ripples on the lake surface.

Norman Peale sipped from his travel cup as he walked along the water's edge of the Whiskey Jack Lodge. The Yeti cups wore a new corporate logo, a tilted float plane much like the Norseman flying over the peak of the resort. The new cup kept things hot—*too* hot for Peale's liking. He popped off the cap to let the heat dissipate.

The path he walked was anything but even. It was bad for feet and even worse for wheels. A casual guest probably wouldn't have noticed the old damage to the trunk of the tree by the water's edge. Peale reached forward, touching the spot where his former employer's three-wheeler had hit on the night he died. For the tree, the wound had healed.

Peale looked down the path, towards the conference centre. The hands of his Jazzmaster were dangerously close to ten in the morning. He picked up the pace. The guests were emerging from the paths that led to their respective cabins. They carried no briefcases, no laptops. There wasn't even a yellow legal pad in sight.

Peale climbed the steps to the conference centre. He exchanged pleasantries with the attendees as they filed into the space. Apart from the timber theme, the room was unremarkable. The tables were folding, the chairs stackable. There was no grand fireplace, just a ceiling-mounted projector pointing at a lowered screen. Peale walked over to the only laptop in the room, and the attendees hushed. He reached down for the wireless remote before looking up at his eager audience. He smiled broadly.

"Gentlemen, this meeting of the Pinetree line will now come to order."

CHAPTER TWENTY-ONE

Sam was busy fishing, and not the kind that would upset the new Mrs. Goodman. The fishing expedition was among the shelves of the Hutchings' garage. Megan sat patiently on the dirt bike, pleased that she would soon be doing something that few of her friends had ever attempted. It might even be YouTube-worthy, depending on the safety equipment that was part of the deal. She started to laugh when she saw the helmet, hoisted high by her mother. "See?" said Sam, blowing off as much dust as her breath would allow. "And it's sparkly too!"

Megan reached for the helmet. The metalflake green dazzled with every contact of light. Apart from a few scrapes and nicks, the helmet was in good condition. She pushed it onto her head. She was looking at the straps, trying to figure out how they worked, when she noticed her mother's look of concern. "What?"

Sam held a clean rag in her hand. "I didn't get a chance to check yet."

Megan leaned closer. "For what?"

"*Spiders*, Megs. *Spiders!*"

Megan shrieked. She struggled with the helmet, convinced that it had shrunk two sizes since putting it on her head. She was still struggling when she realized that her mother was enjoying a hearty and sustained laugh at her daughter's reaction. Her panic subsided enough to remove the helmet. The interior had zero squatters. She looked at her mother, still laughing. "That's not funny," said Megan, feeling the laughter starting in herself.

"I know," said Sam, as she took the helmet from her. "Your uncle Chris would always try to get me with that. Every year." She wiped away the dust on the helmet's exterior. Megan leaned forward on the handlebars to watch. "So, what's he like?"

Sam felt the question hit her. *I guess that's my fault.* The siblings began to drift apart in high school. Their father's death didn't help matters, with the exception of Chris using academia to ease the pain. The scholarship to Simon Fraser University clinched it. Chris had met Megan, once, at the airport in Calgary. *She couldn't have been more than two.* Sam kept polishing as she answered. "Chris? Oh, he's OK, I guess. A little annoying, like most younger brothers."

"Do you see him much?"

"No. Not as much as I should. Not since he's been on the West Coast."

Megan pointed to the Chevy in the driveway. "We could take a road trip!"

Sam looked at the car. She could see the oil puddle glistening beneath the engine. "I think Pinawa is about as far as I want to chance it right now." She handed Megan the helmet. "Right now, let's see how much Evel Knievel you've got in you."

"Who's Evel Knievel?"

It took less than a half hour to go through the basics of the dirt bike operation. Sam was watching her daughter practise when she heard the telltale flip-flops of her childhood partner in crime. Lisa Janzen was still wearing her sleep pants, her travel mug smelling much like that of Zach Peeters. "Not bad," she said, taking a healthy swig. "All she needs now is her first scar."

"Don't jinx her," said Sam. She reached for the cup. "If she keeps it at jogging speed, that's good enough for me."

Lisa nodded. She held her hand open. Sam put the cup back in her hand without looking away from Megan's progress. She took another pull, wiping the drink from her lips with her sleeve. "As long as she's fast enough."

Sam continued to watch her daughter. "Fast enough? For what?"

"Bears. Especially mommas."

Sam reached for the cup. "I'm more worried about wolves."

"Wolves? There are no wolves around here."

"The two-legged kind, Leese. The two-legged kind."

"Want me to teach her how to use a knife?"

Sam shifted her gaze from her daughter to her friend. "You don't know how to use a knife!"

"Sure I do," said Lisa. "Ya stick 'em with the pointy end."

Sam rolled her eyes in the family way as Megan rolled up to the pair. She killed the engine, then fiddled with the helmet strap to remove it. "It sure gets hot in there."

"Better get used to it," said Sam. "Safety first."

"Yeah," said Lisa. "Especially after I teach you how to do a wheelie!" She grabbed the handlebars, motioning Megan off the seat. A few seconds later, Lisa Janzen was spitting as much gravel as her frame would allow. Sam shook her head as her friend did everything on the dirt bike she had told Megan not to.

The weekend was feeling quiet. *Too quiet*, Sam thought, as she topped up the gas on the lawnmower. Lisa had left for Winnipeg to see her husband, something about a proper thrashing. The rest of the cabins on Block Fifteen couldn't have been more than a third full, and with anything but revellers. The days of a family spending most of their summers at Bird Lake were gone. Both parents worked in this millennium, and right hard.

Sam had escorted Megan to the Whiskey Jack on the dirt bike previously used by her brother, helmetless, though with a solid dose of "do what I say, not what I do" over the din of the air-cooled engines. The trail had little bumps of concern, with plenty of solar panel–fed LED lighting in place, the kind that looked expensive and government funded. Sam dangled a final motherly safety carrot, the offer to pick Megan up in case she wasn't up for the solo return trip when her shift was done or if the old Honda gave her any grief.

The gaze into the fridge in the late afternoon did little to inspire. *Vegan tacos? Not bloody likely.* Sam pulled a store-bought tub of bruschetta out of the fridge. It made her Triscuit dinner feel decidedly uptown. She was finishing off the dessert portion of the cracker-fest when her phone rang. The caller ID said Whispering Pines. *Oh shit.* It was either nothing or everything. She swiped right on the screen. "Yes, hello?"

"Yes, greetings? Hello? Miss Hoo, Miss Hoo-chins?"

Sam tried to remember the name of the attendant, the one still newish to Canada. She remembered. "Yes, Milad?"

The attendant sounded grateful for the remembrance. "Yes! Yes, it is Milad. Your moth—, I mean, Lena, she wants to speak to you."

Sam heard shuffling. *Good,* she thought. *He called from the hallway.* There were a few murmurs, something that sounded like "a little privacy" that must have been her mother requesting it. A little more shuffling. Then, a voice.

"Hello, Samantha? Are you there?"

Sam bit the inside of her lip to achieve composure. *Are you there?* Sam had been waiting years for her mother to be there, a there that seemed as much a possibility as her dead father making a similar phone call. Now was not the time to argue it. Now was the time to grab it with all her might.

"Yes, Mom. Yes, I'm here."

"Samantha, did you want to come for supper?"

"Yes, Mom, yes, I do. I can leave right now." Sam wasn't waiting for any additional go-aheads. She had already put on her sandals, grabbing a sweater on her way out the door. She was heading up the path to the garage when her mother spoke.

"And Sam?"

"Yes, Mom?"

"Can you bring some blueberry pie."

Traffic did little to interfere with Sam's push to Pinawa. She still made a point of sounding her horn at the hill, the one that had taken the bulk of Zach Peeters's family. With all the improvements to PR 315, the hill, *that* hill, continued to be an issue. Sam had no idea if there had been additional fatalities through the years, though she did know of a few accidents that inflicted injuries that steel pins and massive casts were required to fix. There was no one at the crest of the hill upon the third blast of the horn. She pushed the needle up to sixty-five. She made it to the Solo store just ten minutes before closing. The blueberry pie didn't look fresh or wild. It would have to do.

There was a slight reduction in the scent that Sam had become accustomed to at the Whispering Pines, thanks to an extra-strength bucket of mop water. Milad looked up from his cleaning duties as Sam approached. He smiled. He leaned the mop handle against a door frame to keep it from falling. "You are a fast woman, yes?"

Sam smiled, partly because of how easily the phrase could have been misconstrued by Western ears. "Traffic was pretty light." She looked towards the open doorway to her mother's room. It sounded as though an older movie was in progress. She turned to Milad, cutting her volume to mid-whisper. "How is she?"

"Much more, what is the word?" Milad spoke the word slowly, as though the air it was travelling through had the consistency of syrup. "Pleasant."

Sam nodded her understanding. Her thank-you to Milad was barely audible, though she still made the effort to mouth the words slowly. She stepped into the room.

Lena Hutchings wasn't arguing with game-show contestants. She watched the flickering screen with awe, as though she was seeing the movie for the first time. Sam looked at the screen. Cary Grant was doing his best to explain that he wasn't George Kaplan. James Mason and a very young Martin Landau seemed anything but convinced. Then James Mason said something in the way that James Mason would say just about anything, with cadence and class. The phrase got Cary Grant's attention, as well as Lena's. She leaned forward in her chair. She looked up at Sam. She smiled.

"The opportunity of surviving the evening. That's a classy way to say you're going to kill someone, isn't it?"

Sam thought about what she had just heard in the movie dialogue and from her mother. She returned the smile to Lena. "That *is* a clever way to say it. It almost makes it sound more . . ."

"Sinister?"

Sam nodded. "Yes, sinister." She wondered if Lena knew who she was at that moment. Lena pointed at the pie.

"Thank you for bringing the pie, Samantha."

Sam looked at the pie. She smiled. "You're welcome. Store-bought, hope it's OK."

"I'll bet it tastes even better when the cellophane comes off."

Sam blinked. She gave a quick laugh, then pulled the Cool Whip from the grocery bag. They ate and watched as the hired goons secured Cary Grant, a full bottle of bourbon ready to be poured into him to ensure his compliance. Lena pointed at the screen with her fork. "That's going to give him quite the hangover in the morning."

"If he makes it to the morning," said Sam. "This is, uh, Hitchcock, right?"

"*North by Northwest*," said Lena. "Your father loves Hitchcock."

Loves Hitchcock? Sam remembered her Dementia 101: don't correct. She took a bite of her pie. She pointed at the screen with her fork. "So, they think he's a spy or something, right?"

"Yes," said Lena. "He just picked the wrong place and the wrong time to send a telegram."

Sam thought for a moment about that forgotten form of communication. She quickly returned to the communication occurring in front of her. It was so easy, so effortless. The years of vacant stares evaporated. She wanted to tell her mother so much. She knew she had to take it slow.

"I love the music in this movie," said Lena. "Real edge-of-your-seat music."

Sam nodded, finishing her bite before she spoke. "It's very intense."

"Are you still working for the *Sentinel*?"

Sam didn't know how to answer that one. She also knew that tonight's conversation could disappear as easily as the pie on her plate. "I took some time off, decided to write the Great Canadian Novel."

"Really? What's it about?"

Yeah, what's it about? Sam knew she had to tell her mother something. "Mom, do you remember when the plane flew down the lake? The Canuck?"

The look on Lena's face changed. Sam wondered if it was the effect commonly referred to as sundowning. She had seen it before: confusion first, then agitation, culminating in full-blown anger that had put her mother into Whispering Pines. This look wasn't a lost one. It looked like good old-fashioned remembrance. Lena looked up at her daughter. She smiled.

"Fast," she said. "Faster than a speeding bullet."

CHAPTER
TWENTY-TWO

Megan Goodman tried to think of something else as she watched her new boss explain the operation of the cordless vacuum. She had no idea what a HEPA filter was, but she did like listening to him as he explained the monthly cleaning procedure. *He could read the rest of the instructions in the manual out loud if he wanted.* Even the geek glasses that Vance McMasters wore had a certain sex appeal, a tortoiseshell keyhole frame that looked like they fell off of a famous Ryan. *Gosling*, Megan thought. *Definitely Gosling.*

"Dinner will be closer to eight tonight," said McMasters, as he handed the newfangled vacuum to his latest hire. "Most of the wives are spending the afternoon on the pontoon boat, but just make sure you knock a few times before going into the rooms, OK?"

"Yes Mr., uh, I mean sir, I mean Sir Vance." Megan felt the colour rise in her face.

"Just Vance," said McMasters. "Just Vance will do."

Megan's face was still red as the afternoon passed into the early evening, mostly from the bending and moving of furniture to ensure that the dust bunnies in the rooms were all accounted for. She straightened the Pendleton blankets. She folded the ends of the new rolls of toilet paper into a sharp point for an easy pull. She stacked the washcloths. Most of the rooms were decorated as expected for lake life. As she moved through the halls, she noticed a unique theme to the artwork on the walls. Loons and sunsets were replaced by pictures of military men in their prime. Some of the pictures seemed to be at military bases. Others appeared to be in active theatres of conflict. All of them were black and white.

The main hallway wound its way to a secluded room, a climb of three steps to reach a pair of double pine doors. The previous doors had the expected numbers, presented in cursive metal. This door had no number. It did have a name: The Pinetree. The letters were presented on a heavy brass plaque. Megan gave the plaque a proper wipe with a polishing cloth, as though the letters had requested her to do so. *Must be the honeymoon suite*, Megan thought. She tapped her keycard against the sensor. The lock clicked open. She pushed through the door with her cleaning gear.

The room was impressive. *Classy, not trashy.* Built-in shelves of lacquered pine held the perfect proportion of leather-bound books. The pine continued throughout, in the form of tongue-and-groove panelling, furnishings, and a desk with carved wilderness scenes, sitting near the bay window. The sun shone through the half-open Venetian slats, illuminating the dust particles that needed removal. Megan started vacuuming. The light in the space was in a losing battle with the afternoon sun and the trees outside. Megan went over to the bank of switches near the door. She flicked them on, but the resulting light came from the floor and table lamps. *Not much of an improvement*, she thought, as she continued with the vacuum swipes beneath the bed. A glint from the bookcase caught her attention. At first, it seemed to be a simple reflection from the fading sun. When she rose up from the floor, she realized that the sun had nothing to do with it. The light was coming from one of the shelves. She left the vacuum running and stepped closer to see what it was.

The glowing shelf was about seven feet from the floor. Megan couldn't see the object that caught her eye, though it appeared that one of the light switches had tripped an accent light. Standing back from the shelf didn't help. She looked around the room. The chair at the desk looked sturdy enough. She moved it over to the shelf and climbed up.

The backlighting was artificial, as she had guessed. The object on display was a glass orb, baseball-sized, an art piece that contained plenty of air bubbles, captured for eternity. Megan had seen them on display at various shops in Edmonton. A friend had attempted to create such a form at a shop that held glass-blowing glasses, with anything but spherical results. The shape of this sphere looked textbook-perfect. Something inside it was partly responsible for the backlit glow, a light that shone up from the bottom of a lacquered drift-wood base. She looked closer.

Gold?

The yellow particles that caused the glint were mixed throughout the sphere, seemingly random at first glance, but planned with expert precision in the second. The more she looked at it, the more the sphere seemed to resemble some far-off galaxy. The drone of the vacuum had become white noise. She picked up the sphere, cradling it like a stunned sparrow.

"Stunning, isn't it?"

Megan spun around on the chair, a motion that she instantly regretted. She didn't have time to register a face or a figure, but she did have time to lose her balance. The floor was coming closer, faster. She landed hard. She looked at her hands. *The sphere! Where is it?* She looked out from her vantage point. There were no broken shards, just a pair of brown Top-Siders. She looked up at the wearer. She took a guess, factoring in the location of the room and the vintage of the eyes looking down at her. She also remembered her mother's advice.

"I am so sorry, Mr. Peale. I was just . . ."

"Admiring what must be admired," said Peale. He smiled as he reached down with his right hand to help her up. "It's quite robust, actually."

Megan watched as her employer dropped the sphere from his left hand, the hand he must have caught it with when she lost her balance. She hadn't held it long enough to register its weight. The sphere returned little bounce as it landed on the rug in front of the bed. Peale reached down to retrieve it. He removed a chamois from a drawer below the first of the bookshelves before handing the sphere to Megan. "Would you mind?" He nodded upwards to its original position. "My knees aren't the model of articulation that they once were."

Megan obliged, quickly repositioning the chair, and depositing the sphere, trying to remember if it was in the exact position that she had retrieved it. Peale caught the pause.

"It could use a 'this side up' arrow, wouldn't you agree?" He reached his hand up to steady her as she made her descent.

"Uhm, yes," said Megan. "That could come in handy. But I'll never—"

"Your name is Megan, correct?"

Megan nodded, almost throwing in a curtsy. "Uhm, yes, Mr. Peale. Megan Goodman."

Peale kept smiling. "I understand you're a legacy."

"Yes, Mr. Peale. My mother is Sam—I mean, Samantha. Samantha Hutchings."

"I can see the resemblance," said Peale. "Are you enjoying the summer?"

"Uhm, yes. Yes, Mr. Peale. Bird Lake is very beautiful."

"It most certainly is." Peale walked over to the bay window. He cranked open one of the windows. "I know most of our guests prefer their air-conditioned environs. I just can't imagine keeping a scent like this on the other side of a pane of glass."

Megan caught the zephyr. She smiled. "Is that cedar?"

Peale smiled. "Very good, Ms. Goodman. What else?"

Megan took another whiff. "Pine?"

"Very good. Anything else?"

Megan lifted her nose. "Uhm, gasoline?"

Peale chuckled. "Well, aviation fuel, to be exact. Our Norseman goes through plenty of it." Peale pointed outside. Megan saw a pair of workers transferring fuel to a barrel from a large storage tank on stilts. It looked like smelly, greasy work, judging by the condition of the pair's coveralls. She wondered if that's where she might be heading next. She turned to Peale, her head cast down. "Mr. Peale? I'm truly sorry about the—"

"It's all right, Ms. Goodman. No harm done. Are you all done with my room?"

Megan shook her head. "No sir, I still need to do the washroom."

"Then I'll leave you to it." Peale extended his hand. Megan shook it. She watched as her employer exited the room, smiling to her as he closed the door behind him.

Megan waited for what seemed like a solid minute until she finally exhaled.

TWENTY-THREE

The light was starting to diminish through Lena Hutchings's window. Sam glanced over at the clock radio: 8:37 p.m. The pie had been a hit, with a respectable leftover slice. There had been more interest in the origin of the pie's blueberries than a list of the aircraft that had used Bird Lake for speed trials.

"Too many to count," said Lena, as she watched Cary Grant waiting patiently at the side of a dusty rural Indiana road in a grey flannel suit. Sam stretched what was left of the bunched-up plastic wrap over the treat before storing it in the compact fridge. She turned to look at her mother before she stood up. Lena was smiling, the kind of smile that any mother bestows on her child, regardless of their age. Sam smiled back. Lena followed up the smile with a yawn. Sam welcomed it. She hoped to have enough daylight left to assist the dim headlights on the Chevy for the ride home.

Sam adjusted the faded afghan on her mother. "Did you want to move to the bed?"

"I'll be all right here," said Lena. "Just resting my eyes."

"All right, Mom." Sam leaned over to kiss Lena on the cheek. Lena smiled, and her hand lightly trembled as she touched Sam's cheek ever so slightly. "Will I see you soon, Samantha?"

"Yes, Mom. I'll be back real soon. I promise."

"With more blueberry pie?"

Sam smiled at Lena. "Whatever you want, Mom. Whatever you want."

"Strawberry and rhubarb is good too."

"Yes, it is, Mom. Goodnight."

"Goodnight."

Sam moved into the hallway. She watched her mother from the doorway for a moment. If Lena could see her, she wasn't letting on. If Sam had left a few minutes earlier, she might not have seen what happened next. Lena rubbed her eyes. She leaned back in her chair, her left hand stroking her right in her lap. She started to sing, softly. There were no words, just a combination of la-la and hum that seemed very important to her. Sam couldn't make it out.

"It is pretty song."

Sam startled. Milad had moved to the doorway so quietly that she hadn't sensed him at all. She quickly composed herself, convinced that the flinch she gave was mostly internal.

"Yes," she whispered. "I wish I knew what it was. It's very . . . familiar."

"I ask one time. She say a bird."

"A bird? Did she say what kind?"

"Maybe outside. Many birds. They like to sing."

"A bird."

"Yes. Very happy bird."

Sam listened a little bit longer, hoping for a series of notes that would be an obvious tell. It wasn't a songbird, or at least not one that she had ever heard. There was something strange about the whole thing. It would have been easier to file the thought into the dementia file. Perhaps it was a song from her mother's childhood, when rope was skipped, and cans kicked. Whatever it was, Sam was sure of one thing.

She hadn't heard her mother sing since she was a child.

Sam pushed the Chevy down 315. The rearview mirror was empty. She decided to let the speedometer bob around fifty, not a bad idea with the arrival of the nocturnal residents that called the Nopiming home. She did see a deer at the side of the road, but it decided to leap back into the trees instead of across her windshield. She received a couple of text notifications after she hit the gravel but decided to wait until Block Fifteen to read them.

The cabin was cold. Sam debated a solid minute before opting for the electric heater instead of the fireplace. She changed into her sleep pants, a battered green Henley, and her fuzzy slippers. She debated another minute on the drink, instant coffee for writing, boxed Merlot for procrastinating. She sipped her wine as she checked her emails. Nothing new on Gerry Hutchings. She checked her phone. Megan had used her new friend's phone to ask if she could spend the night at their place. Sam hadn't met Rhiannon yet, something she had been led to believe that mothers were supposed to do before allowing their children to have sleepovers. She gave in, sending a simple thumbs up. A sunglasses-wearing emoji answered. Cool.

The second notification was from Chris. It wasn't about the cabin. Sam squinted at the screen.

> Hey Sam. Any chance you can
> take a few pix of the planes?
> I might want a couple of them, LOL

Ugh, LOL. Sam's brother put it on everything he texted. She sent the same thumbs up that she had just sent to Megan and went over to the bank of light switches near the door. There wasn't much in the way of light for the model aircraft. Sam played with the settings on her phone for a moment, finally getting the flash to fire for each picture. She sent them to Chris as she took them.

The Creativity Bug had little to offer, the sips of Merlot intent on silencing it entirely. Sam busied herself with dusty Facebook posts, cheesy entertainment news, and clickbait to things like the most amazing things you didn't know about just about everything. She closed the laptop. She fumbled with the electric typewriter. The keys felt satisfying as they struck the paper with purpose, even if it was just the practice exercise of a quick fox and a lazy dog, times ten. On the eleventh pass, a new text message hit her phone. It was Chris.

> Hey Sam. Did you build one of
> those planes? Maybe Dad, LOL

Sam knew that she hadn't. The smell of the glue always made her nauseous, so much so that she would volunteer to sleep in the screen house when construction was underway. She would always have to settle for an open window in her bedroom and an old fan that buzzed her awake for the duration of the night. She tapped in her message.

Maybe one of your friends?

Sam was able to tap out two more quick fox–lazy dogs on the typewriter before the next message.

The black one. The SR-71. LOL

The SR what? Sam looked up at the planes flying overhead. The black one was easy to spot. She tapped in her message.

Looks like a dildo with wings, LOL

An eggplant emoji popped up about fifteen seconds later. Sam came close to snorting her wine through her nose. She composed herself before she tapped out the message.

Which ones do you want?

Chris responded, without emojis or rude script.

The Canuck for sure, and the dildo, LOL

Sam looked up at the Hutchings' squadron. She sent a thumbs up to her brother.

TWENTY-FOUR

Megan watched through the flames of the camp-fire as Rhiannon entertained her with smoke rings from her two-thirds-gone blunt. Most of her friends in Edmonton were vaping their THC, with the rest indulging in the growing selection of edibles. She felt embarrassed about her coughing fit from her recent toke, until Rhiannon did the same note for note. "I think this is Lee River Kush," said Rhiannon, as she handed the remainder of the blunt to her new friend. "The Lucky Lager of Kush-related products."

Megan laughed, inhaled, then coughed. "It's a little harsh," she said. She wondered if any class of weed would have elicited a similar reaction. She handed the remainder back. She leaned back in the ancient lawn chair. The green webbing took on a new and strange sensation in her fingertips. Rhiannon stated the obvious.

"I think someone's getting high!"

Megan kept checking the texture. "This stuff feels like, like a, like a . . ."

Rhiannon leaned over. She looked down at the orange webbing on her chair. She touched it. She felt it. She said the first thing that popped in her head.

"A dragon . . ."

Megan stopped. She looked at Rhiannon through the flames. She burst into laughter, her motions almost folding the chair onto herself. The sensation made her laugh even more. She was starting to catch her breath. She looked at Rhiannon's trailer. She squinted. She looked at Rhiannon.

"So, we're, like, sleeping in an egg?"

Rhiannon looked at the vintage Boler. She saw it. She said as much. "It does look like an egg, doesn't it?"

"Totally," said Megan. "A big egg."

"Yeah," said Rhiannon. "Now I want eggs."

"Do you have any eggs?"

"No, just pancakes."

Megan paused, waiting for the Pot Genius Fairy to pay a visit. She looked at Rhiannon as though their heads pivoted on an unseen pulley. She revealed her revelation.

"Pancakes are the breakfast sister of eggs."

Rhiannon blinked. "So, if we don't have eggs . . ."

Megan finished the thought. "We MUST eat pancakes!"

The Late Show breakfast was underway. The pancake mix called for eggs. "Let's just add more milk," said Rhiannon, as she gave the carton a cautious sniff before dumping it in the bowl. Megan dripped out sizable blobs of imitation vanilla extract into the mix. She grabbed the bottle of syrup from the Boler's cabinet. Rhiannon stopped her as she attempted to pour the syrup into the bowl.

"Isn't that supposed to go on after they're cooked?"

Megan flipped the cap. "That's what the syrup Nazis want you to think."

Rhiannon nodded. "I hate syrup Nazis."

The ancient griddle took forever to heat up. Even with way too much butter to soften the blow, the sugar in the syrup made for a blackened pancake. They rolled the pancakes around some leftover hot dogs that Rhiannon had blackened the previous day. The rest of the syrup went into coffee cups for dipping the twisted piggies in their pancake blankets. The verdict was unanimous.

"These are freaking awesome," said Megan.

"The hot dog is like a kind of bacon," said Rhiannon.

The two gobbled their concoctions. Megan stopped. She pointed her hot dog pancake at Rhiannon, poking the air with drops of syrup. "I almost forgot!"

"Forgot what?'

"I was cleaning today, in Mr. Peale's office. I saw this, uhm. It was a—"

"Please not his dick."

Megan's face scrunched together. "Ewwwww! Gross! Number Two maybe, but Mr. Peale? Ick!"

Rhiannon perked up. "Number Two, as in Vanceypants?"

Megan blinked. "Who's the what's-it-pants?"

Rhiannon dipped her dinner in the last of her syrup. "Never that into gingers. The freckles can go sideways in a hurry." She gobbled the last bite. The sugar rush brought her back to her previous train of thought. "Was it all wrinkly?"

"It wasn't his dick! It was his ball!"

"Peale only has *one* ball? I knew it!"

"Nooooo! It was a golden ball!"

Rhiannon's glazed eyes grew wider. "What kind of guy has a fake gold nut?"

Megan tried to explain the size with her hands. Rhiannon's eyes grew wide.

"He should get that looked at."

Megan was feeling less stoned and more annoyed. She looked straight at Rhiannon. "Rhee, listen to me. It's not his dick, or his ball, or gold balls on his dick, which would be really weird. It's on his shelf. And it's glass."

"I thought you said it was gold."

"It *is* gold. And it's in a glass ball. Like, you know, stuck inside it. On purpose."

Megan told the tale of the sphere, and the surprisingly cordial encounter with Norman Peale. Rhiannon nodded along in stoned syncopation. "So, like, he wasn't mad or nothing?"

Megan answered through her chews. "Naw, he wasn't mad at all. Said something about me being a legacy or something."

"Legacy? What's a legacy?"

"I think it's 'cause my mom worked there in school, just a fancy way to say it."

Rhiannon nodded. "Yeah, a lot of people worked out here. My dad did, before he got creamed."

Megan stopped stirring her piggy pancake in the syrup. "Creamed?"

"More like sliced," said Rhiannon. "Fell out of his boat near Tulabi. Boat bonked him, and then the propeller messed him up. I think I was two. I never knew him, just got his last name. Mom had kicked him out for his drinking, something to do with some accident he had while driving a logging truck."

"What kind of accident?"

Rhiannon dabbed at the syrup pooling on her plate with her finger. "On 315. There's that bad hill where you can't see shit. Wiped out some family or something."

"Whoa," said Megan. "What was his name?"

Rhiannon looked up from her plate. She smiled at Megan as she slowly stated the painfully obvious. "Dad?"

The laughter erupted. Someone down the lake requested that they shut the hell up and go to bed already.

CHAPTER
TWENTY-FIVE

Norman Peale sipped his scotch as he perused the Whiskey Jack spreadsheets at his desk. Kinsey wasn't completely out of line for his complaints about the price increases, colourful as they may have been. *Maybe I should just jack up the mini-bar prices.* The thought was enough for the slightest of grins.

A flat-screen television had made its way down from a hidden ceiling perch. The volume was muted, probably a good thing, with the frantic gestures that were coming from the two financial analysts locked in a heated debate. The bottom of the screen scrolled with the usual commodity updates. Peale kept his gaze fixed on the paper printouts.

Peale heard the lightest of audible taps at the door. "Come in," said Peale. The door opened to reveal Vance McMasters. He pushed a small trolley cart into the room, its top adorned with the expected vessels that spoke of room service. McMasters began to remove the plastic wraps. "Not just yet," said Peale, his eyes still fixed on the spreadsheets. "I'll take care of it."

McMasters nodded. He swapped the empty coffee carafe on the windowsill for a full one. "Will there be anything else, Mr. Peale?"

"No, that's it. Thank you."

"You're welcome, sir." McMasters went to leave. He stalled at the door. Peale noticed. "Is something wrong, McMasters?"

McMasters spoke, still looking at the door. "I'm not sure if it's my place to say anything, Mr. Peale."

Peale had yet to look up from the desk. "The only way to know that is to speak up."

McMasters turned to face his employer. Peale was still deep in spreadsheets. "Have you considered all the risks, Mr. Peale?"

Peale seemed as though he might look up to meet the eyes of his subordinate, but his gaze landed on an upper column of a spreadsheet instead. "Since before you were born, McMasters. Since before you were born."

"But the exposure."

"Will be contained, McMasters."

McMasters almost bit through his lower lip. "Mr. Peale, and I say this to you with the utmost respect."

Now Peale looked up. He locked eyes with McMasters.

McMasters tasted blood from his lip. "I just want—"

"What, McMasters? For Christ's sake, spit it out!"

"YOU'LL NEVER GET AWAY WITH IT!"

Peale blinked. He started to chuckle, which grew to polite laughter. The laughter went higher, less refined, much more along the lines of his drunk ex-servicemen guests after too much scotch.

McMasters tensed. He had never heard this type of laughter from his employer before. It scared him.

Peale wiped his eyes of the laughter's tears before he spoke. "Let me allay your fears, McMasters," said Peale, his voice still cracked with laughter. "No endeavor of the Pinetree line has ever come into question. From its inception to this very day. Not now, not ever. Getting away with it is what we do, and quite successfully at that."

"But the current climate Mr. Peale. The concerns already being raised. It couldn't possibly—"

"There's a saying about the Canadian climate, McMasters. Ever heard it?"

"Sir?"

Peale grabbed as many spreadsheets as he could in his right hand. He threw them into the air over his employee. The sheets fell on McMasters like a soft snowstorm of gargantuan flakes. He looked at Peale.

"If you don't like the weather, McMasters, wait five minutes, maybe even less than that these days. The 24-hour news cycle isn't looking to the Whiskey Jack for their next fifteen-second sound bite. They're looking for the train wrecks, and there's a new derailment every fifteen seconds. We are insulated. We are hidden. We are *safe*. By the time they figure it out—"

"I want to believe that Mr. Peale," said McMasters. "It, it's just that—"

"What, McMasters?"

"It, the plan. It, it's just so—"

Peale smiled. "Genius?"

McMasters blinked. "I suppose that's one way to put it."

Peale continued to grin like the Cheshire Cat. "Help me pick up these spreadsheets, McMasters."

Sam knew better: the wine took *better* out of the equation. She knew there was a stepladder somewhere on the property, probably underneath the cabin. *Smothered in spiders for sure.* She looked into her memory, searching for a Gerry Hutchings method for attaching the plastic squadron to the open beams. Judging from the height, little thought had been given to ever getting them down again.

The kitchen table felt hefty enough as Sam dragged it into position. A quick ascent to the tabletop surface presented a wobble worth noting. *Don't stand on the sides. Stay right in the middle.* Sam wondered if she had thought that thought, or if it was the otherworldly advice of her dad wafting in the rafters. She descended with the help of a kitchen chair. She went to the clothes rack near the main door. A quick rummage found the help, an avocado green–handled squeeze mop, its sponge petrified beyond use. Sam tossed the sponge. She examined the rusted chrome carrier. The edges looked sharp enough to cut through the fishing line.

The plan was simple: lift mop, snag line, tug till it broke, then simply catch the plastic model as it glided to the ground. The procedure was without flaws until the catch. Perhaps it was the lack of propulsion, no headwinds, or the number of Chris-applied decals. Whatever it was, the planes plummeted faster than the career of a #MeToo offender. The first plane to shatter was the Sopwith Camel. *OK, that one was practice.* The Spitfire drilled its nose into the coffee table like it was the English Channel. The Zero slipped through Sam's outstretched hand, a hand that deflected the fuselage into a collision course with the bamboo blinds before snapping in half on the floor. Sam looked at the wreckage in disgust. She spoke to her brother who wasn't there. "Dad let you stay up late to finish this half-glued bullshit?" The squadron was taking heavy losses. She came very close to catching the F4U Corsair and the Messerschmitt Bf 109. She was ready. She steadied herself on the table surface. She raised the mop with steady conviction towards the strange black plane.

"Come here, you stupid dildo."

The mop head sliced through the line. The SR-71 made a beeline for the tabletop. Sam caught it with her free arm, hugging it close. She gave the mop head a victory thrust skyward, high enough that she caught the Canuck. It came loose. The table teetered. Sam lost her balance. She saw the Canuck explode against the wall as she fell. The coffee table broke her fall as its final act. Sam waited a moment before she checked her extremities. *Nothing broken.* There were no gashes, no cuts. The bruises in their various hues would arrive at some point tomorrow. Sam looked up at the remnants of fishing line. She looked for the dildo plane. It was gone. She went to raise herself, immediately realizing that the bruises were indeed deep. She didn't see the plane, but she did smell it: it had landed on the top of the wood stove. She flicked the plane off the fireplace with the poker. The brittleness of the decades-old model glue offered little protection as the fuselage hit the tiles. Sam watched as the plane split apart. It was the sound that caught her. She had heard enough plastic impact in the last few minutes to know that this sound was different. She rose carefully. She leaned down to inspect the wreckage.

That's when she saw the key.

CHAPTER
TWENTY-SIX

Jarrod Mulaney felt every one of the cop hairs on the back of his neck standing at attention. He gripped the wheel on his weathered Laurentian in front of McNaught Motors on Portage Avenue. He hadn't felt the hairs in a while. To be fair, he didn't have to. The nerve damage he had received from the glass shards that flew into his leg in '73 had fastened him securely to desk duty. He could keep up with his son, Steven, if the space wasn't much bigger than the backyard. Steven was fast for a soon-to-be two-year-old. Mulaney knew he'd be getting faster.

The bum leg had little effect on the family jewels. Peggy's due date for their second child was only a month away, a pregnancy nowhere near as difficult as her first. He had dropped the family off at Polo Park Shopping Centre to keep them occupied during his interview. *Why did he want to interview me at a car dealership?* Mulaney unzipped the leather folio on the seat. He retrieved the newspaper clipping from the *Winnipeg Sentinel*. He checked his Timex. He still had about fifteen minutes until the interview start at two. He read the clipping.

CORPORATE SECURITY POSITION
Law enforcement experience
required. Salary to be discussed.
Reply to Box 237
Winnipeg Sentinel

Mulaney had sent in his résumé two weeks prior. The phone call a week later had little in the way of cloak and dagger attached, until the meeting place was pitched. The interviewer had said something about renovating his home office, and that his new car was ready for delivery. No apologies for the location or its irregularity. Mulaney was intrigued. The date was set.

The folio was three-quarters zipped when Mulaney heard the tapping on the passenger-side glass. It was polite, not aggressive enough to startle. He reached over to the door lock knob with a modified wooden paint stick, a U-shape carved out of the end to fit under the crown of the knob. The door creaked open, the kind of creak that a Foley artist longed for. The man smiled. "I think some three-in-one oil would quiet that down."

Mulaney went to speak. A much smaller voice beat him to it.

"That door sounds like one in a scary movie, Daddy."

Mulaney looked to the man's right. A young girl no more than four was doing her best to hide from the stranger in front of her. She peeked around the houndstooth trousers of the man who must have been her father. Mulaney smiled and waved. The girl disappeared behind the slacks. The man did his best to allay her fears.

"Sam, this is Mr. Mulaney. You remember me mentioning him, don't you?"

The little girl peeked out again. Mulaney smiled. She retreated.

The man spoke with a firmer tone. "Samantha, please say hello to Mr. Mulaney."

Samantha slowly emerged from the safety of her father's polyester weave. There had been some rehearsing on the greeting, Mulaney was sure of that. The delivery was classic four-year-old, in timbre and grammar.

"I'm very please to meet you."

"I'm very please to meet you too, Samantha," said Mulaney, mimicking the error in her delivery. "Are you having a good day?"

"Daddy's getting a new car today! It's blue!"

"Wow, a *blue* one! Did you pick out the colour?"

"And we're going for ice cream at Dutch Maid, but only if I'm really good."

Mulaney thought of Steven and the pending arrival in his household. He wondered if it would be a girl or boy. "Well, Samantha, I think you're doing just fine."

The girl smiled then.

Her father reached inside. "Gerry Hutchings," he said, as

they shook hands. "And thanks again for meeting me, I mean *us* here." Hutchings smiled at his daughter. She smiled back ten-fold.

Mulaney slid across the bench seat, exiting on the passenger side. He followed the father and daughter into the dealership. The girl was at the age where skipping overtook classic left-and-right steps three to one. She continued her skipping around the cars in the showroom. Gerry Hutchings took the lead.

"So, you've been with the OPP since?"

"Sixty-seven, sir."

"Call me Gerry. You're OK with Jarrod, right? Jerry with a J would be pretty confusing."

Mulaney nodded. "Jarrod's fine sir, I mean Gerry."

Hutchings pointed to Mulaney's left side. "The leg won't be an issue. There is some legwork with the job, but nothing like chasing down a perp on angel dust through Osborne Village."

Mulaney nodded. Gerry Hutchings knew how to talk cop, but he didn't *seem* cop. *Government? Military?* Mulaney was just about ready to ask as Samantha skipped by them.

Gerry put the brakes on Mulaney's thought process with his next question: "So, what can you tell me about May Long of '67?"

Mulaney knew at that moment that this was no run-of-the-mill security gig. There had obviously been some type of background check on him, maybe a sift through his reports. He decided to play it as cool as he could.

"It was pretty warm that day. A few speeders, nothing much."

Hutchings smiled. He unzipped his folio. As his daughter pranced past singing of Rosie and posies, he removed a glossy colour eight by ten. It was a picture that Mulaney had never seen. It was a picture that he did not know was being taken. The vantage point was from above. It showed a wide-eyed OPP rookie standing next to the detachment shitbox. The remains of a shattered Pepsi bottle could be seen at his feet. The mic from his radio was inches from the rookie's lips.

Like his younger self, Mulaney wondered what to say next. *It's some form of test.* He looked straight at Hutchings. He was about to answer when the little girl completed the verse, falling squarely on his foot. He winced. He looked down at Samantha Hutchings. She smiled back as wide as the wheel cover on the Buick behind her. She leapt to her feet for an encore lap.

Gerry Hutchings watched as his daughter disappeared behind the fender. He went to speak. Mulaney beat him to it.

"I stand by my report."

Hutchings grinned. "I know. That's why you're here."

"Excuse me?"

Hutchings stuffed the photo back into the folio. "My employer has plenty of unique tools to help in selecting potential candidates. What you saw in '67, or, more importantly, what you didn't see, is extremely valuable in this field."

"And what field would that be, exactly?"

"Your T4 would list you as a Security Supervisor for Consolidated Industries. The non-disclosure agreement is as thick as the *Winnipeg White Pages*."

"So, what kind of *security* would I be supervising?" The second that he said it, Mulaney realized that Hutchings didn't care for the tone. He moved in close.

"Mr. Mulaney, the goings-on of this company are instrumental in providing the daily protections that keep the free world as we know it on an even keel, the kind of steady sailing that gives us nylon slacks, whitewall tires, and all the Harvest Gold appliances your kitchen can swallow."

Mulaney thought of the old Norge fridge back in Kenora, its compressor song sounding more and more like a Gregorian chant. He glanced at the only whitewall tire on his rusty Pontiac. The time had come for better. Hutchings leaned in to let him know how much better.

"I can double your salary to start, with annual bonuses based on performance. Oh, and a company car. You'll be based out of Winnipeg, moving expenses covered, of course."

Mulaney felt like he was going into shock. "Yes, of, of course. Yes."

Hutchings had one more question. "Are you a wagon or a hardtop man?"

"Am I a what?"

Hutchings pointed at the dark blue 1976 Buick Electra 225 hardtop at the front corner of the showroom, the glass doors being opened to allow its escape. "I like rolling down all four windows when the weather is just right. It's like driving a convertible without the sunburn."

"Gerry Hutchings, you miled out another one, you no-good son of a bitch!"

Gerry turned. He smiled at his insulter, a red-headed version of a civilian Santa Claus. "How are you doing, Patch?"

"Three sheets to the wind. How you think I'm doing?" Patrick "Patch" Kaniuga introduced himself to Mulaney as the chief, cook, and bottle washer of everything car for Gerry Hutchings. "Been putting this son of a bitch in a new Electra every two years since '63. Made me come in on the Saturday after JFK got shot. Brand new '64, blue on blue, loaded to the nuts. Beautiful car."

"Patch, did the mobile get installed?"

Patch winced. *"Of course* it got installed! This isn't Carter Motors Chubby Old Slow-Wheels. Why didn't you just use the phone from the '74?"

The '74? Mulaney felt the need to confirm what he was thinking. "Why are you trading in a '74?"

"I know," said Patch. He pointed out the open showroom doors. The plates from Gerry Hutchings's '74 Electra were being removed. "I could back that in right now and no one would be the wiser, until they saw the round headlights. Almost everything in the lineup is square for '76."

Mulaney walked through the open showroom doors to the trade-in. He opened the driver's door. The odometer read like a new car, with four zeros, a seven, and four-tenths on the white dial. The odometer had turned over. One hundred thousand miles on a car that was barely two years old. *That's a lot of driving,* he thought.

Mulaney felt a tap on his shoulder. It was Hutchings. He pointed at Mulaney's rusty Laurentian.

"So, what's it gonna be? Hardtop or wagon?"

Mulaney looked in the showroom. Samantha Hutchings was dancing around a red Pontiac Grand LeMans Safari, with just enough woodgrain. He turned to Hutchings.

"This year, it's the wagon."

TWENTY-SEVEN

Gerry Hutchings stood in the centre of a cluster of birch trees at the shore of Eastland Lake. He watched as each one of the trees began to smoulder at the forest floor. The flames were small at first, growing as they wrapped their way around the trunks of natural parchment. He looked down at his jacket. The flames had leapt onto his sleeves. The cuffs of his pants had ignited. He reached for his Black Label cap, flinging it as high as it would go. An updraft that must have known the wings of unseen angels carried the cap to the top of the highest spruce.

This is how they will know it's me. He waited until he was completely engulfed in flames. That's when he screamed. That's when Samantha would always wake up.

The nightmare had first presented itself during a cram session in the fall of '89. Sam had been told to expect them from a counsellor at the university. They seemed to diminish through the years, with work and a family of her own. Maybe it was the recent discoveries, the confusion as to her father's true occupation, but it had reappeared. On this night, the startled reaction occurred on the lumpy couch. She squinted through the initial haze at the flattened coffee table. The key that she had found in the shattered model looked back at her.

Sam sat up. She leaned forward to retrieve the key. It was unremarkable, the type of key that might have opened a neighbourhood mailbox, perhaps a small padlock. There were no numbers on it, just a logo from the manufacturer. *Yale.* Sam flipped the key around a few times to confirm that no other markings were present.

The key was well used. The cuts of the shaft were rounded, with a touch of sheen. Sam pressed her mind for a memory of the key, her father using it somewhere, anywhere. Nothing. She shuffled over to the kitchen cabinets. The junk drawer truly lived up to its name, in contents and operation. The insides were stuffed with all manner of nails, thumbtacks, tools, and sleeves of playing cards, some that were anything but PC. *Another time,* Sam thought. She pulled the drawer free, placing it on the counter. She knew that other keys lived here. She found their home in an old Player's tobacco tin, the logo obscured by a piece of masking tape. The script was her father's hand. *SPARE KEYS.* She jimmied the top from the tin.

Sam knew some of these keys. Some were spares to door locks, a few for the Master padlocks that protected such valuable lake things like propane tanks and the old Lund fishing boat at the water's edge. There was a spare set for the Chevy, and locksmith cuts for the dirt bikes. Some keys appeared to be for other cabins, in case a neighbour might ask to have their place checked over, or for their sheds, if a special tool was needed. The Sykes' key was where the cement mixer lived. The Parthenays' shed had the levelling jacks for the posts that held up most of the cabins. Most of the other names were faint on their swatches of masking tape. Some were probably for sheds that the money monster places had leveled. None of the other keys said Yale.

There was no need for a clock face to confirm the hour. The slightest rays of dawn were starting to remove the darkness from the lake's glassy surface. The birds hadn't heard the alarm yet. It was quiet. It was also right chilly. Sam clicked on the space heater. A tap of her phone confirmed that it was pre-5 a.m. It also confirmed that there was a missed call from the Whispering Pines at 11:34 p.m. the previous night. *Mom!*

Calls from the nursing home were rare, even rarer if her mother was the one on the phone. Megan's suggestion of vegan food might be the reason. When clarity would come was always a guess with Lena. 11:34 p.m. didn't sound like a Lena; it sounded like bad news. To make matters worse, no voice message had been left. Still, there had been the recent call through the orderly Milad, a call that occurred much earlier in the day. Sam decided on a callback for seven-ish. She picked up the plane wreckage as the early birds serenaded her.

The first call went straight to voicemail. *Shit, too early.* Sam waited five minutes, blaming the no-answer on the skeleton crew that had yet to pass the baton to the day shift. She dialed. The call was answered on the third ring by a disinterested female voice. "Whispering Pines, can I help you?"

"Yes, good morning. I was just checking in on Lena Hutchings. I received a call late last night, around eleven thirty."

There was the shuffling of papers. Sam heard the woman softly reciting Hutchings over and over. A pause. Then the question.

"Are you a friend or immediate family?"

That can't be good. Sam mustered up the courage, trying not to waver. "I'm, I mean, she. She's my mother."

"Name, please."

"Lena, Lena Hutchings."

"No, ma'am, *your* name."

Sam gave her forehead a slight slap. "Sorry. Yes, I'm Samantha Hutchings, her daughter."

A little more shuffling. "I have a Samantha Goodman."

"Yes, that's me. I mean, that was me."

"We do need to be updated when name changes occur, ma'am."

Sam felt like updating her name to this staff member with a free throat punch. She kept her calm. "Yes, I'm sorry. I can bring in my ID to make the changes. Is, is my mother all right?"

A little more shuffling. "Well, we had a bit of an incident last night."

Sam felt her voice rise, feeling completely unable to control it. "Incident? What kind of incident? Is she all right?"

"She's all right, ma'am. However, we did have to sedate her."

"*Sedate* her? What for?"

"Your mother had become quite agitated. She, let's see here. She wouldn't stop singing."

Sam remembered the recent tune, the one that the orderly Milad had blamed on the birds. As she asked the next question, she felt the ridiculousness immediately follow it.

"What was the song?"

The exhale of the woman on the other end of the line had no words, though Sam could swear that she heard her eyes roll. "I don't know, ma'am. All I know is that she wouldn't stop singing."

"So, I can come there now?"

The woman's exhalation this time was very close to forming words. "Yes ma'am, you may visit your mother now."

Sam grabbed the keys to the Chevy. She was halfway out the door when her phone warbled an alert for an incoming text. It was the number that she hadn't recognized the night before, from the Rhiannon that she had yet to meet. Sam swiped her screen to read it.

> Mom, it's Megan. The Honda won't start. Can u pick
> me up?

The message had an adorable cartoon character emoji beneath it asking an animated please. Sam exhaled. She told Megan to be ready in five.

CHAPTER
TWENTY-EIGHT

Megan Goodman clutched the Chevy's minimal armrest as her mother drove. The speed was faster than she had remembered, the slowing for the hills apparently forgotten. The genius of pancakes and wieners and weed the night before hadn't mentioned anything about the aftermath. Sam kept her eyes on the road as she doled out the advice. "Roll down your window, get some fresh air. Do you have any water?"

"I don't think that's a good idea right now."

Sam grinned. "Smells like you got into the Lee River Kush last night."

Megan squinted at her mother. "I thought the smoke from the campfire would mask it."

"Nothing masks that skunkweed," said Sam, as the Chevy bounded over another hill. "Not now, and definitely not back in the day."

"Mom, can you slow down? I think I'm going to throw up."

Sam looked down at the bouncing needle, quivering just below seventy. *That's pretty fast for gravel.* She backed off the throttle, stabilizing around fifty. She looked at her daughter. "Better?"

Megan went to nod, then screamed. "Mom! Deer!"

Sam turned back in time to see the yearling. She swerved to the left to avoid it. The deer changed course, heading back to the safety of the ditch. That's when one of the tires that Stan Buckmaster had concerns about decided to rupture, the right rear. The bang brought a scream from both mother and daughter. Sam controlled the skid well, keeping the Chevy straight. She pulled the car into an empty load-check station.

The tire was done. Sam pulled the keys from the ignition. Megan asked where she was going.

"I'm going to change the tire."

Megan blinked. "You can *do* that?"

Sam smiled. "*We* can do that. I used to do it all the time on my Bobcat."

"Mom?"

"Yes?"

"What's a Bobcat?"

Sam felt Gerry Hutchings's presence as she explained the procedure to Megan, the procedure that her father had shown her. "Not many pay phones out here to call for help," said Sam, as she jacked up the rear bumper. She added a touch of contemporary to the life lesson. "Or cell towers for that matter."

Megan looked at the ancient spare. "What's the white stripe for?"

"It was kind of a thing in the seventies," said Sam. She showed her daughter how to loosen the lug nuts. The work was dirty, greasy, and actually fun. Sam showed Megan the length of steel pipe in the trunk. "Your Grandpa used that to make sure the lug nuts wouldn't fall off." She slipped the pipe over the tire iron for an extra smidge of tight for each nut. Megan was impressed. She said as much.

"Grandpa was a pretty smart guy."

Not smart enough to outrun a forest fire. Sam instantly regretted the thought. Megan read the change in her face. "Mom? Are you OK?"

Sam composed herself. She grabbed her right shoulder. "Rotator cuff," she said, giving it a quick massage. "Old writing injury." She threw the tools and the flat in the trunk.

The Whispering Pines felt busy for the early morning hour, until Sam remembered that most octogenarians rose before the birds. She had once thought that it was a clever ruse to beat the Grim Reaper out of a fresh soul. She stopped at the front desk, making sure to update her name with the appropriate ID. The attendant was someone other than the woman on her throat punch list. She explained the goings-on of the night before. "She wasn't singing any words, just a melody."

Sam leaned closer. "Does anyone have any idea what the melody was?"

The attendant shook her head. "It's not the first time it's happened with a resident. We've even had some start playing the piano in the middle of the night. But Lena's song, it was so . . ."

Megan leaned in, mimicking her mother. "It was so what?"

The attendant leaned closer. "Familiar. It was very familiar. It might only be missing a note, or maybe a different key. I just know that I know it."

Sam nodded. She headed towards her mother's room. The attendant added some more news, the kind that stops anyone in their steps.

"We did have to put her in restraints, and she might still be a little groggy. I hope you understand."

Sam bit her lip. Megan caught it. She chomped on hers as they headed down the hall. There wasn't any singing coming from Lena Hutchings's room, just an old Carpenters standard as the music bed for the Environment Canada weather channel. They got to the part where he was breaking her heart as they entered the room. Lena Hutchings had been moved to a hospital-style bed. There had been generous attempts at providing her comfort, judging by the extra pillows. She was asleep, though it seemed anything but restful. She was muttering something. Megan gripped Sam's hand. They headed to the bedside.

Sam reached in to brush the hair off her mother's forehead. Lena's muttering blended into a blissful sigh. The sigh stopped. Lena began to sing. It was soft, a volume that no one could complain about, especially if their hearing aids had yet to be inserted. There were no words, just like the attendant had pointed out. Sam and Megan leaned in.

"*Lah-la la-la-la-la-la-LAH-LAH . . .*"

Sam and Megan looked at each other. It did sound familiar. Lena repeated the melody.

"*Lah-la la-la-la-la-la-LAH-LAH . . .*"

Megan nudged Sam. Sam looked at her, a non-verbal "What?" on her face. Megan pointed at her mother's purse and mimed a phone. Sam pulled it out of her purse. Megan tried to mime the rest. She eventually had to go for a whisper.

"Mom, unlock your phone. We need Shazam."

Sha-what? Sam nodded and keyed in her passcode. It took about a minute for Megan to bring up a blue screen with some kind of stylized S. She hit the S icon. The phone captured Lena's melody, but the results made little sense. The lack of words returned a list of club mixes that were anything but familiar. Megan tried again. Nothing.

"If only we had some words," Megan whispered.

Sam didn't know if the melody was of any importance. She did feel the need to preserve it, for a time when her mother could shed more light on it. She asked Megan if the phone could do that. Judging from the eye-roll, it could.

Sam and Megan stayed with Lena for a little more than an hour. The effect of the sedative gave little indication that it would let up anytime soon. Sam decided to head back to the cabin. She knew that her daughter would need some rest before her evening shift. She also knew that Megan could use some proper food, warm 7-Up, and a generic pink antacid.

The Solo store was deserted. The shopping cart had the perfect noisy wheel to amplify Megan's pounding head. It reached a crescendo when Sam rounded the corner. The blind spot of a coffee special and a barbeque giveaway caused a head-on collision into the cart of another morning shopper. It was Milad. He immediately apologized in his fractured English. "Accident, so sorry. Hope broken nothing."

Sam smiled as she checked the eggs. "They survived. And I think the bread was already in an accident."

Milad nodded in agreement. "Bread here, many times must be fallen on. And expensive always." He noticed Megan rubbing her forehead. "Daughter, yes? Is she flu sick?"

"Self-induced," said Sam. "Probably the first of many life lessons."

"I hope her feeling is better. I use the ginger tea."

Sam made a note on her impulse list. "Good idea. Thank you, Milad."

"Is no trouble. Is Lena singing still?"

Sam realized that Milad must have just come off his evening shift. He was still wearing his scrubs, his nametag pinned above his pocket. *He must have seen most of what happened.* She decided to ask.

"Milad, do you remember what happened when my mother started singing?"

"Not exact. Was in the hallway with floor, cleaning. She sang, how you say. It was hard."

"Hard?"

"Yes, very hard. Everyone hear."

Hard means loud. "Milad, do you know what song it was?"

"I think was birds," said Milad. "Just like time last, and time before."

"Birds," said Sam.

"Pretty birds," said Milad. "Very pretty birds."

Sam nodded, though she had no idea what it meant.

CHAPTER
TWENTY-NINE

Megan slept for much of the drive home. Sam kept her speed around forty-five on the gravel, with no one in the rearview forcing the issue. As she crested the hill that had silenced most of the Peeters clan, she slowed. The morning yearling was lying at the side of the road, dead. Sam watched the carcass grow smaller in the mirror as she accelerated.

It didn't take much time for Megan to resume her car snoring in her room. Sam was able to coax a Tylenol and some water into her before she assumed the starfish position. She was so tired that she didn't notice the flattened coffee table. The light snoring went medium, then medium-high. When it hit eleven, Sam decided to check the Wi-Fi signal on the dock.

The emails were few, mostly Facebook notifications from groups she hadn't remembered joining. Lisa had sent a private message that she would be back at her cabin later in the afternoon, needing some rest after numerous eggplants. Sam remembered that she needed some gas for the lawn-mower. Lisa messaged that there was plenty in her shed. She sent a nuclear explosion GIF to drive the point home.

A quick tip-toe into the cabin retrieved the key from the Player's tin. The Janzen shed had the usual lake things: fishing rods, tackle boxes, and ancient life jackets that afforded anything but maneuverability. The gas cans were marked for the things they fed. Sam grabbed the one that said mower. She was just about to leave the shed when she saw the tackle box on the shelf. It was old, at least sixty years young, with the Janzen Magic Marker scrawl still visible on the side. Most of the green paint had been replaced with scratches, dents, and rust. The cobwebs around it were thick. The padlock on the tackle box wasn't out of place. Sam had seen such padlocks on tackle boxes throughout the years, standing guard over the luckiest spoons and rigs. The padlock was secured. *Probably rusted shut*, Sam thought. She brushed away the cobwebs. She stopped. She blinked.

The Yale logo looked back at her.

Norman Peale stood at the water's edge of the Whiskey Jack Lodge. There was enough protection from the waves during the morning to allow for a little practice. He reached into the old washtub—a rustic piece mounted on a newer wrought-iron frame—and removed one of his favourite things, a perfectly formed skipping stone, made even more perfect with a clear lacquer coating. He cocked his wrist. The flick was good for five healthy leaps across the water's surface, with six shorter skips before the stone slipped below the surface. He was searching for the second perfect stone when Jake Kinsey appeared. "I've never seen anyone take skipping a stone to such extremes, Norman."

Peale studied the second stone. "Extremes are the way of the Whiskey Jack, wouldn't you agree?"

Kinsey rummaged through the washtub. "Well, the missus did paint some old stones for a garden once, at the base in Grand Forks. Or maybe it was Nellis, I truly can't remember."

Peale launched his second. "Memory can be a most valuable commodity, Mr. Kinsey."

Kinsey cocked his wrist. The stone contacted the surface thrice before its death dive. "And you should be remembering to call me Jake, Norman. All my friends do."

"Friends are rare in my field, Jake. You of all people should appreciate that."

Kinsey rummaged for his third stone. "I do, Norman. With friends like us . . ."

"Who needs enemies?"

Kinsey smiled. He tossed his chosen stone in the air for an easy catch. "You really think you'll be able to pull this one off? It's a pretty big one."

Peale launched his third. The flight was flawless, a baker's dozen of skips, evenly spaced. "I do, Jake. I truly do."

"So, on Wednesday?"

"Yes, Wednesday."

"Why Wednesday?"

Peale smiled. He looked at Kinsey instead of the water as he launched his fourth stone.

"Because, Jake. It's a Wednesday. At the lake. In *July*."

Sam heard plenty of jangle inside the old tackle box as she took the path back to the Hutchings' cabin. She held it close, tucked under her arm like a running back at the twenty, the fifteen, the ten. It was the easiest way to carry it: the handle had broken off at some point in its rusty life. She burst into the cabin, her thoughts of her sleeping daughter a distant memory. She slammed the tackle box down on the counter. Sam went over to the flattened coffee table and retrieved the previously hidden key. She brought it back to the lock that bore its name and tried to insert the key into the lock.

It stopped at the halfway point. Sam jiggled. The lock refused to budge. *Shit. Seized.* Sam opened the cabinet doors beneath the sink. She rooted through the bottles of cleaners and chemicals until she found it at the back of the cupboard, an economy-size can of WD-40. She sprayed the penetrant into the lock. The sickly solvent smell filled the air. All it did was make the lock wet. She sprayed it again.

She jiggled. Nothing.

She removed the key, flipping it around to re-insert it. No dice. *What the hell is it for?* Sam had been quietly asking that question since the black dildo plane gave up its secret. *Secrets.* The cabin, her father, her very life as she had known it appeared to be full of them. She felt the anger in her rise, the anger of not getting to say goodbye to her father, the rage of not being able to slow her mother's decline. *Secrets.* The secrets were bringing her to the boiling point. It was one thing to find out about Cooper's side piece when her marriage was going down the toilet. Every divorce had them, and you didn't have to possess much of an imagination to figure out what they were. But this was different. *Who was he? Who was Gerry Hutchings? Who was my father? Why couldn't you tell me, Dad? Did Mom know?* The answers could be on the other side of a rusty padlock. She decided that she needed to know, and now.

Sam rooted through the junk drawer. The tools it offered were weak, a hammer with a loose head, a rounded screwdriver, a broken pair of vise-grips. She grabbed the tools and the key to the Hutchings' shed. There were plenty of woodworking tools within, but little in the way of tackle box safe-cracking. She looked at the lock. She looked at the shore's edge. *Fisherman's Rock!* It had bordered on monolith in her youth, a glacial erratic on the shore of the Hutchings' property that was just the right size and angle for all levels of childhood imagination. Today, it looked like the perfect medium to bust a rusted padlock loose.

The first whack of the box made more noise than headway. The metal construction, the tackle inside, and the water's edge amplified the sound. It was the only thing that Sam could hear. She was committed. She didn't hear or see Zach Peeters on his stand-up paddleboard as he watched her new workout regimen. She did feel the water when he flicked his paddle at her. She looked at her watery assailant with eyes of fire. "What the FUCK was that for?"

Zach didn't answer. He slowly crouched down and dismounted from the paddleboard in the knee-deep water. He placed the paddle on top of the board, slowly pushing it to the shore. He approached Sam with his hands out, palms down, seeming to dribble the invisible basketballs of Please

Calm Down, You're Scaring the Hell Out of Me. "It's OK, Sam. It's OK. Everything is going to be OK."

Sam answered with her language of the moment. She raised the tackle box over her head, landing it once more on the surface of the great rock with a soul-clearing grunt. The lock refused to yield. She pitched the tackle box to the side of the rock. She dropped to her knees in the wet sand. Sam was still panting from the exertion as Zach placed his right hand carefully on her back. He tried to defuse the situation with a joke. "So, you're going fishing today?"

Sam let out a pant laced with a laugh. "Not without my lucky spoon."

Zach looked towards the tackle box's landing spot. It was hidden from view, on the other side of Fisherman's Rock. "That must be some spoon. Like Elwood's microphone."

Sam smiled at the *Blues Brothers* reference. "You traded the Cadillac for a microphone?"

Zach smiled back. "Yeah, I can see that."

Sam let out a clearing exhale. "We must have watched that movie a hundred times."

Zach nodded. "Yep. Every time we'd get the big rain."

"I liked the big rain."

Zach looked out at the water. "It would get so thick that you couldn't see the other side of the lake."

Sam mirrored Zach's gaze. "There are a lot of things I'm seeing for the first time at the lake."

"What do you mean?"

She pointed to the other side. "I think it's about two miles east of that beach."

"Your dad."

"Yeah, my dad." She leaned in closer. Zach rubbed her back. She accepted the only comfort he could offer.

"At least it's hidden."

Sam realized what she had said, and who she had said it to. *He drives past his dad all the time. And his mom. And his brother.* "Zach, I'm sorry, I didn't—"

Zach shook his head. He added a little more dialogue from *The Blues Brothers* to soften things. "It's 106 miles to Chicago . . ."

Sam smiled. "We've got a full tank of gas . . ."

"Half a pack of cigarettes . . ."

"It's dark . . ."

"And we're wearing sunglasses."

Sam picked up a stone. She threw it into the water. "Hit it."

"Mom, what was all that noise? And who's the *dude*?"

Sam turned to see her daughter, sporting an impressive bedhead. "It's nothing, Megan."

Zach looked annoyed. "Oh, so now I'm nothing to you, *again*. Just like when you were eleven."

Megan rolled her eyes. "Eww, gross."

Sam rose to her feet. "Megs, this is Zach Peeters, one of my lake buddies, like Lisa."

"Well, I've got prettier legs."

Megan's eyes did a 360. "I'm surrounded by weird, old people."

Sam nodded. "No argument here."

Megan rubbed her eyes. "So, what was that noise?"

"That was me," said Sam. "I was trying to get the lock off an old tackle box."

Megan pointed next to Fisherman's Rock. "You mean that green one?"

"Yeah," said Sam. "But the lock wouldn't budge."

Megan looked over at the battered box. "Well, it's open now."

CHAPTER

THIRTY

Gerry Hutchings looked up at the starburst clock. The buzz was in fierce competition with the fridge at the cabin. Throw in the old space heater and the resulting trio could probably have a hit record. *Record. Now that's dating myself.* There was an old record player at the cabin, with a worn-out needle that he kept forgetting to replace. He retrieved a briefcase from the shelf, one that held cassette tapes instead of important documents. He pulled out *Gunfighter Ballads and Trail Songs.* The B-side was already cued up, just the way he liked it. He listened to Marty Robbins as he sang the tale of the Mexican girl.

The plastic model offerings at MacLeod's in Lac du Bonnet would be slim. That meant Gooch's in Winnipeg. The aisles were thick with model kits of cars, planes, and ships. He worried that anyone who knew the goings-on of the organization would put two and two together with his selection. In some way, he was hoping that it would finally happen. To see the whole thing come crashing down, consequences be damned. What had started out as a clandestine arm of the Canadian and American governments under the guise of national security had morphed into the overseer of the most shrouded of operations, operations that just kept getting dirtier. He didn't feel like much of a Boy Scout anymore. He was simply an enabler.

The rapping at the screen door was expected, though it still gave him a start. "Come in, Jarrod, it's open," said Gerry. "And grab some beers out of the fridge." Jarrod Mulaney entered, his limp as common to his gait as his rumpled Tilley hat was to his head. Gerry shook his head. "Why do you always wear that thing like you're AWOL from an Australian regiment?"

"Crikey," said Mulaney, a swing and a miss for his Crocodile Dundee impression. "Must be all those Foster's and shrimps on the barbie!" He placed the cans of Black Label on the table.

Gerry shook his head as he opened his beer. He pointed at Mulaney's right ear, where the Tilley's flap had been snapped up. "You'll probably get melanoma on that ear. Look at the freckles on that pork rind."

Mulaney pointed at the Black Label trucker hat on the table. "Your ears will probably fall off if you keep wearing that thing."

"Probably," said Gerry. "Did you bring the key?"

Mulaney fished the key out of his pocket. "Are you sure we can talk about this here?"

Gerry pulled the model kit out of the Gooch's bag. "I swept an hour ago. Does he know about the other keys?"

"Nope," said Mulaney. "One padlock, one key. That's what he asked for, plus the ammo box. And that's all he gets."

"That prick," said Gerry. "The old man is starting to slip, and he's closing in for the kill. He's an arrogant opportunist."

Mulaney pulled his beer tab back. "'Arrogant opportunist.' I remember when we used to call those guys assholes."

Gerry chuckled. He found the weak spot in the seam of the cellophane wrap on the model. He opened the box. "Aw shit."

Mulaney leaned forward. "What's wrong?"

Gerry tipped the contents of the box forward. "Why the hell would they sell a model plane that's never been anything but black molded in white?"

Mulaney smiled at the box. "Well, looks like we get to inhale glue *and* paint fumes. In Kenora, we used to call that Saturday night."

The glue and paint sniffing wrapped up just before four. The double beeps of Gerry's pager intruded. He checked the number. "Speak of the asshole."

Mulaney finished his sip. "Did he put a 911 on the end of the number?"

"Yeah, that seems to be his new thing. Well, duty calls."

"Do you need me there?"

"Naw, it's probably about the next ill-gotten shipment. Crossing the T's, dotting the I's."

Jarrod tipped his Tilley on the way out. Gerry opened a few extra screens to air out the cabin. He locked up the cabin doors before leaving, something he seldom did. He walked up the timber steps to the garage, adjusting his Black Label hat. Samantha's Bobcat had decided to eat its water pump, a good-sized coolant stain beneath it in the driveway. Lena had been staying in the city for the last two weeks, convalescing from the removal of an ovarian cyst that had proved to be benign. Sam had taken the Chevy to work at the lodge. Gerry wasn't thrilled with his latest Buick for the conditions of the gravel road. He was going through touch-up paint like gas through his first Electra. He did like the power, when he got a chance to use it on the pavement. Patch Kaniuga swung a sweetheart deal on the leftover '87 coupe, Gerry's first ever. With both Sam and Chris driving, the need for a massive family truckster seemed like a waste.

He wondered when the lake would become less of a concern for his children. Their young lives were getting plenty busy, with Sam at school and the summer job at the lodge. Chris was working at the Loblaws warehouse in Winnipeg part-time, making enough to buy a four-year-old Chevette. *Why blow it all up?* He thought back to the truths, the ones he had protected for what he had believed was the greater good. Nothing was black and white anymore, just a dull, soul-sucking grey. *Even the smallest truth demands accuracy.* Gerry wondered when the last truth had occurred that he truly believed in.

Gerry opened the garage door. The Grand National looked ridiculous with the padded nose bra, but it did keep some of the stone chips at bay. He checked the odometer. It sat at 58,367 kilometres and four-tenths. The second roll of the odometer happened sooner with the kilometres cluster on the Canadian cars. It meant that the Grand National was closing in on a hundred thousand miles. The car was almost done. So was Gerry.

He headed for the Manitoba-Ontario border.

CHAPTER THIRTY-ONE

The starburst clock on the wall said barely two, but it was five o'clock somewhere. The dose of Merlot was more than Sam's usual pour, though she wasn't used to using red Solo cups to dispense her medicine. She was removing the items from the mangled tackle box on the kitchen table. Megan and Zach watched, the steam rising from their coffee. It was probably too late for that drink, though both had had late nights.

The items within the tackle box didn't seem out of place: spoons, barbed jigs that were now very illegal, fishing line, and a few rubber bait grubs in Day-Glo colours. The fish bonker looked like something out of a Sam Spade novel. *Maybe I'll use that in my Great Canadian Novel.* Everything in the tackle box was fishing-related. *No secrets.*

Megan and Zach had kept quiet through the cataloguing. Neither was expecting the brutal murder of a tackle box that afternoon. There were no straws to be drawn, just a desire to find out what had sent Sam over the edge. Megan got the ball rolling.

"Mom, is everyth—"

Zach decided to parrot. "Yeah, Sam, are you all righ—"

Sam slammed the top of the tackle box shut. Megan and Zach's mouths did the same for a solid minute. Megan tried again, a page from The Concerned Child.

"Mom, you're scaring me. What's going—"

"Yeah, Sam," said Zach, with less filter. "I mean seriously, what the fuck?"

Sam pushed back from the table. She brought her Solo cup along for the ride. She walked towards the kitchen sink. She looked down. She saw her father's Mac's coffee cup staring back at her. "I'm sorry, guys," she said to the cup. "I'm just trying to figure some stuff out."

"Is it about Grandma?"

Sam exhaled. "No Megs, well, maybe a little bit. It's more about Grandpa."

"Gerry?" said Zach. "Sorry, I mean Mr. Hutchings." Zach hadn't forgotten about the tongue-lashing he had received from Gerry Hutchings when Chris broke his arm on the dirt bike. *You address me as Mr. Hutchings, understand? I'm not one of your little schoolyard friends.*

Sam smiled. "I think it's OK to call him Gerry, Zach. I don't think he'll mind."

Zach looked around Gerry's former domain. "Yeah, I'm not taking any chances."

Sam returned to the table. She explained what she knew from the information that she had: the lack of records, the discovery that the only accounting that Gerry Hutchings was involved with was the family chequebook. "All I know for sure was that he had a job. And that he drove a lot."

Megan raised her hand slightly as if to ask permission to proceed. "How do you know he drove a lot?"

Sam tilted her head back. She blinked. "You miled out another one, you no-good son of a bitch!"

Megan looked at Zach. Zach looked at Sam. "What did you say?"

"The guy," said Sam. "At the dealership. That's what he always said about Dad's cars. 'You miled out another one.'"

Megan didn't understand. "Miled out? What does that even mean?"

"The cars didn't last as long back then," said Zach. "I don't think my dad kept anything past a hundred thousand, until he switched to Volvos. Those things go forever."

Sam thought of Cooper's new Volvo wagon, and his new wife. She thought about saying something snide about Volvos, then remembered what Zach's family died in. "Anyway, Dad worked out of the house. He had an office in the basement. We could go in there when he was working, but he kept it locked when he wasn't there."

"That doesn't sound too weird," said Zach. "My dad's office in the house was the same way. I think he just didn't want us dicking around with his hole punch or the fax machine."

"I remember Dad's fax machine," said Sam. "It was noisy, spitting out paper at all hours."

"Mom?" Megan had her hand raised again.

"Yes, Megs?"

"What's a fax machine?"

The seriousness subsided for a moment, as Sam enjoyed her first good-hearted laugh of the day. Zach nudged Megan in the shoulder. "Old-people tech."

A thumping on the steps outside heralded the arrival of Lisa and Rusty. The dog was already jumping up on the respective legs of the Hutchings' cabin as the screen door slammed shut. "Which one of you fucktards left my shed open?"

"Sorry, Leese," said Sam. "My bad. And I'm sorry about the tackle box."

Lisa looked at the mangled metal. "Looks like I *had* a tackle box. What were you doing with it, using it as a vibrator?"

Megan snorted. Zach added a proper chuckle groan. Sam gave the Hutchings eye-roll.

Lisa inspected the gouges. "Yeah, most of these will buff right out. Why didn't you try the key? It was hanging in the shed, on the C-minus key rack they forced me to make in wood shop."

Sam's fixation on the lock had missed that, though now she wanted to see what a C-minus key rack looked like, especially knowing Lisa's predilection for exaggeration. "All I saw was the lock. It said Yale, just like the one on the key I found in the model airplane that looked like a black dildo."

Megan blinked. Zach blinked. Lisa blinked. Even Rusty the Fifth cocked her head.

Lena Hutchings watched the goings-on of the current contestant on *Let's Make a Deal*. A wandering Pinawa yearling had stopped at her window for a moment to investigate her commentary. It had no idea what a zonk was or which door the trip to Switzerland was behind. It was more interested in the sensation of the window screen on its nose. The birds were unseen but very vocal. So was Lena. "Why would you take the door? The last one found a Monte Carlo behind the door! What, you think there's *two* Monte Carlos behind the doors this week? And look! You've won a sheep! What are you going to do with a sheep? Shear it for sweaters?"

A light tapping had started at the door. It became louder on the second round. Lena finally heard it on the third attempt. "Yes? Hello."

Milad entered the room with her lunch tray. "Hello, Lena. Lunch is late today, I am sorry for this."

"That's fine," said Lena. "What kind of mush are we having today?"

"Is soup," said Milad, as he removed the tray cover. "Good soup. Squashed butternuts."

"I hope it doesn't give me gas," said Lena. She stirred the soup slowly. "This new food can do that."

"Is good for brain," said Milad. "Thinking more better."

Lena pointed at the TV screen with her spoon, ignoring the drips of soup. "A lot better than these ten-watt light-bulbs."

Milad looked towards the window. "The pretty birds are singing at you today, yes?"

Lena responded with a healthy slurp. "That's all they ever do. Not much of an existence if you ask me."

Milad leaned forward. "What is song they like to sing for you?"

"Song? It all sounds like gibberish to me." She took another spoonful before finishing her thought. "Like jazz."

Milad clarified. "The song they sang to you, the one you sing."

Lena chuckled. "I can't sing. The birds would go quiet if they heard me sing."

"You have pretty voice. It went like, sounding . . ." Milad did his best rendition of the song that had caused the need for sedatives and restraints for Lena. She listened. She smiled as he repeated it.

"You have a very pretty singing voice," said Lena. "You should do that, what's it called. Kar-a-jokie?"

"Yes," said Milad, not realizing the mispronunciation. "Kar-a-jokie. Singing words on screen. You try."

"Oh, I don't think I—"

"Is very pretty. Please?"

Lena cast her eyes to the ceiling. She gave the tune a run-through. Milad smiled. "Pretty, yes?"

"It is," said Lena. "Very pretty."

"Can do again?"

Lena smiled. "I might have to start selling tickets. We can have a buffet in the hall."

Milad nodded. He smiled. Lena took it as her cue. She sang the tune stronger, but not strong enough to send the other attendants running for the restraints. Milad kept smiling. He looked at her tray. "Do you want more soup for now?"

"I'm not too hungry," said Lena. "You can leave the roll."

Milad put the tray together. He left the roll and the butter pats within easy reach. "I come later if you need."

"It was good soup."

"Yes, soup good. I tell them."

Milad carried the tray out to the cart in the hallway and pushed it away from Lena's door. He then reached into the front pocket on his scrubs, removed his phone and pressed the red button on the screen to end the voice recording.

CHAPTER THIRTY-TWO

The Yale key was making its way around the Hutchings' kitchen table. Sam had retrieved the remnants of the shattered plastic models from the trash. There weren't any more keys inside the wreckage. No notes, no inner scrawling to point anyone in a direction of discovery. There were only two more planes left in the rafters. Zach retrieved the wooden stepladder from beneath the cabin, a ladder that had little in the way of the spider worries Sam had originally feared. He carefully brought down the remaining planes, an Avro Lancaster that was missing two of its four propellers and a de Havilland DHC-2 Beaver float plane. Like the rest of the squadron, the two remaining planes cracked open like dropped eggs. There were no keys to be found.

Sam threw the rest of the planes into the trash bag. She looked at Megan. "Well, I guess your Uncle Chris is going to have to build his own models."

Megan looked up at the strands of fishing line that remained in the rafters. "I don't think they would have shipped well."

Lisa flipped the Yale key back and forth between her fingers. "It looks well-used, doesn't it? It's like, all rounded on the edges."

Zach folded the ladder, lowering it to the ground. "Is there anything else around here that has a padlock on it?"

"A Yale padlock," said Sam. "And no, nothing that I've seen." A buzzing noise started to fill the room. Sam looked at the counter. She had left her phone on vibrate. The call was from Stan Buckmaster. She swiped right to answer. "Hey Stan, did you find a spare tire?"

"Well, it's almost the right size," said Stan. "A little wider, but it should fit no problem. Used to be on my old Blazer, so it's a little aggressive. Twenty bucks and it's yours."

"Deal," said Sam. "See you in ten." She ended the call. She addressed the crew at large as she grabbed her keys. "I'll be back in twenty. First one that finds something locked up with a Yale padlock gets a Coke."

Sam hit the switch for the power trunk as she pulled up to the Oiseau Garage. Stan was waiting with the better tire. She pulled the old tire out. "It blew up pretty good on us."

Stan looked at the ruptured tire. "Just old and dry."

Sam smiled. "Just like you?"

Stan laughed out loud. "You wait till you get to my age! I wish I were dry. I piss seven times a night. Too bad I only get up for four of them."

Sam laughed. She went to square up. Her wallet was empty. "Shit. Stan, do you have debit?"

"Of course," said Stan. He closed the trunk. "It's a little slow. None of that tap dancing payment stuff. You wouldn't believe what they want for that box." He motioned for her to follow him to the convenience store. "I'll make it total out to twenty with the taxes."

Sam looked around the store space as the debit machine booted up. Salty snacks, doodoo coils, and the new Muskol that didn't work anywhere near as good as the old took up dusty residence on the shelves. A very dusty blister pack caught her eye. She pulled down the package. It had a decent heft to it. She brushed away the dust. "Hey, Stan?"

"Stupid machine," said Stan as he checked the data cable. "It's got a mind of its own."

Sam showed the package to Stan. "How do these work?"

Stan looked at the package. "Oh, those old things. I've had those for years. Do you need some? They're all keyed alike. Kinda handy that way, unless you lose the key. Then somebody could get into all three of them."

"Good to know," said Sam. She put the triple pack of Yale padlocks back on the shelf.

Gerry Hutchings chafed at the collar of his
new Arrow short-sleeved shirt. His mother
had insisted that he "dress for success" for
the job fair at the Winnipeg Auditorium. The
thin black tie felt like a noose. His high school
graduation was a month away. Most of the
old Polson Avenue gang had sewn up their
next steps. Larry Smith had just received a job
offer from the Manitoba Telephone System.
His brother Ron was in line for a promotion
to assistant produce manager at the Shop-Easy.
Donny Park had been accepted as a recruit

with the St. James Police Department. Gerry's part-time delivery job at A-B Hardware on McPhillips put gas in the Hudson, and a quart of oil a week. It needed a ring job if he planned to spend any time at Winnipeg Beach this summer. The fix would be slightly more than he paid for the car.

Most of the fair's attendees had visited during the week. There were the usual careers on tap: Hydro, the city, Great-West Life. He was scanning the room when he felt a tap on his shoulder. He turned to see a man about his father's age, trim, clean-cut. He wore the same style of Arrow shirt. His thin black tie didn't seem to bother him one bit. "A little overwhelming, isn't it?"

Gerry nodded nervously. "There's, there's an awful lot to choose from, I guess."

"Very true," said the man. "Very true indeed. The only question is—"

Gerry completed the thought. "Which one to choose."

"Which one to choose," the man repeated. "That is a very good question, son. It's a question I asked myself when I was your age. Unfortunately, the answer I got was as a tail gunner in a Dam Buster."

Gerry nodded. "At least there isn't a war going on now to worry about."

The man smiled, then went deadpan. "Son, there's always a war going on." He started to walk away from Gerry. Gerry followed as though he had been tethered. The career table that the man occupied had zero to offer in the way of glossy brochures or oversized posters. The banner above looked as though it had been a generic one placed by the organizers. The name gave away very little. It sounded downright boring. Gerry said it out loud to see if that would change. "Consolidated Industries." *Nope. Still boring.*

The man felt Gerry's tone. He addressed it directly. "I know, sounds pretty boring, right? Unfortunately, trying to fit everything into what we do at Consolidated would require about twenty of those banners."

Gerry crossed his arms. "So, what exactly does Consolidated do?"

"Depends on the day," said the man. "We have interests in everything from mining to aerospace to hospitality. If everything goes smoothly with government down the street, we'll be part of a new atomic energy project. We also maintain automated sites for National Defence."

"Automated?" said Gerry. "You mean, robots?"

The man let out a hearty laugh. "Sounds like you've been watching too many of those little green men double features down at the Lyceum. No, we don't have any robots or death rays or slime monsters, just generators and battery packs. Most of it is secondary sites for older radar systems. The DEW line has pretty much taken over that job."

Gerry looked puzzled. "DEW line?"

"Distant Early Warning," said the man. "Detects an incoming Russian missile faster than the earlier radar lines. Pretty much killed the Arrow."

Gerry remembered the excitement around the Avro Arrow in the fall of '57, the Canadian all-weather delta wing interceptor developed in response to the Soviet bomber threat. He also remembered the annoying beeping noise from the Sputnik satellite on the news reports that same week. The Soviet bomber threat quickly became the Soviet space threat, then something called a missile gap. The pride of the RCAF had become the victim of bad timing, just like the Ford Motor Company had with that ridiculous Edsel. By February, Prime Minister Diefenbaker had put the brakes on the Canadian supersonic dream for good. The whole mess had thrown thousands out of work. Gerry had no way of knowing that the remaining Arrows were being sliced into pieces in Malton as he spoke about his future.

The man continued. "What we're looking for is a few select candidates to learn the ropes, expand into other operations as needs change. Have you graduated yet?"

Gerry stammered. "Uh, next month, sir."

The man smiled. He extended his hand. "Edgar Van Cleef," he said, giving Gerry's hand a firm clasp. "But you can call me Ed."

Gerry released from the clasp when it felt right to do so. "So, how do I apply?"

Edgar smiled. "You just did. I'll be in touch."

June and graduation came and went. Tony Bachynski at A-B Hardware had a few side jobs that helped pay for the repairs on the Hudson. Gerry met a sophomore named Lena Dumka on the boardwalk at Winnipeg Beach. She was Donny Park's second cousin. After a little cajoling, he convinced her that a ride on the roller coaster was in order. These were early days, but it was progressing well.

Something else was new. Gerry would catch glimpses of it in the rearview mirror of the hardware store's Sedan Delivery. He would see it parked near his family's house on Polson. He swore that it had even been at Winnipeg Beach. It was a black Plymouth sedan, plain Jane, no trim, looked like a '57. He didn't get a clear look at the driver, though he did see what looked like a police-style radio antenna on the roof.

That wasn't all. At first, Gerry thought it was a door-to-door salesman. Half the street had fallen prey to them, from storm windows to aluminum siding. He had the typical folio that salesmen would carry. Seemed to be asking questions, writing things down. Went to every house on the block but the Hutchings. Didn't leave any brochures. *Weird.*

The man he knew as Edgar Van Cleef from Consolidated Industries had yet to reach out. No mail, no phone calls, no telegrams. Gerry was starting to wonder if he hadn't made the cut. He tried to look up Consolidated Industries in the Henderson Directory. The name didn't exist.

By the beginning of July, the black Plymouth was gone. Gerry was delivering paint to a decorating company on Corydon. It was hot, almost ninety. He needed something to cool off. He parked in the back lane to drop off the delivery, then crossed the street to the Shop-Easy. He kept the lid on the Coca-Cola cooler open as long as he could to turn down his thermostat, until he caught a dirty look from the store manager. He paid for his Coke and left.

When he rounded the corner to the back lane Gerry found a pink Nash on the driver's side of the Sedan Delivery with maybe six inches to spare. *The nerve of some people.* Gerry walked over to the passenger side door. When he opened it, a manila envelope fell into the gravel. He picked it up. It was addressed to him. There was a single type-written sheet inside. The letterhead was from Consolidated Industries. When he read the weekly salary, he gasped, and the Coke bottle slipped from his grasp. It shattered.

He drove back to A-B Hardware to quit.

CHAPTER THIRTY-FOUR

Sam drove back to the Hutchings' cabin. She was starting to feel the pain in her arms from her tackle box–cracking workout. It was getting close to Megan's shift at the Whiskey Jack. The Honda was still at the campground. Sam thought about retrieving it. Then she thought about her arms and lifting it into the trunk. Ouch.

The padlock key. Sam kept doing as many mental searches of the Hutchings' property as she could. As she pulled in the driveway, it was immediately evident that great minds thought alike. The garage door was open. Megan, Zach,

Lisa, even Rusty the Fifth were searching the shelves. She turned the Chevy off in Drive. "Any luck?" she said, as the driver's door creaked open.

"Just a bumper crop of spider webs," said Lisa. She removed her hat to wipe her brow. "Checked the shed too. Nothing else is locked up."

"Hey, I think this is mine," said Zach. He had found another metal-flake helmet, a dark blue one. Sam smiled. "If you can squeeze it on your melon, it's yours. I might want to take a video of you trying, though."

"I think it'll look cool on a shelf," said Zach. He brushed off some of the dust. "They always tried to get me to wear one, but I never did."

Megan looked at Sam, hoping that she would get a similar OK. Sam nixed it. "My dirt bikes, my rules."

"But it pinches my head," said Megan.

"A rock will pinch it worse," said Sam. "Besides, I've got to give you a ride today. You better get changed."

Megan trudged out the back door, exhaling hard as she went. Lisa smiled. "If she knew half the crazy shit we did without helmets and life jackets."

"And she never will," said Sam. She surveyed the garage. "Well, whatever that key fits, it doesn't look like it's here."

"You're sure it's not for a safety deposit box?" said Zach.

"Different shape," said Lisa. "I remember going through my parents'."

"Me too," said Zach.

"Me too," said Sam. An awkward silence ensued. *The children become the parents.* It still felt too young, but Sam knew it wasn't. Dad was dead. Her mother was three-quarters gone, in the home stretch. One day, it would be Megan's turn to use such a key. Sam hoped it wouldn't be any time soon.

It took about twenty minutes for Megan to get ready for work. Sam dropped her off at the main gate. Her new friend Rhiannon was arriving at the same time. Megan introduced her. "Mom, this is Rhee."

Sam waved from the driver's seat. "Hi, Rhee. Thanks for keeping her out of the weather the other night."

"Wow, this car is bitchin'," said Rhee. Sam wondered if the admiration had a stoner tint. She watched as Megan's new friend scanned the inside of the car like it was a hotel ballroom. "I bet you could fit a dozen people in here," said Rhee.

"In clown suits," said Sam.

Rhee looked at Sam. The extra glazing was obvious. "I don't like clowns. They're always trying too hard."

"They sure are," said Sam. She looked at Megan. "Around eleven?"

Megan pointed to Rhee. "But Mom, I was thinking—"

Sam said it again. "Around *eleven*?"

Megan exhaled. "OK . . ."

Sam watched as the girls ran up the steps. She thought she heard a whispered comment about how lame she was. Sam knew that her seventeen-year-old self would probably agree.

Norman Peale studied the spreadsheets on his desk. *McMasters has a point.* The current plan was ambitious, to say the least. It had also been in play for the last eighteen months. He looked at the stories he had printed off from the *Sentinel*'s website. It was good news for Pinawa, a reprieve from the expected closing of the Whiteshell Laboratories, which had been slated for lights out by 2024. More than three hundred jobs were on the table, three hundred people who were smack dab in the middle of not being old enough to retire, with too much mortgage and not enough money. *Secrets* thought Peale. The employees at the lab were used to keeping them. It was a firing offence to divulge any of the legitimate goings-on. There was banter, of course, the kind that stayed in the rec rooms of friendly Pinawa gatherings, the kind where listening devices had long been installed. The people were worried. They didn't have anywhere else to go, unless you counted Winnipeg, where they'd make half the money they were earning. *Desperation.* His contacts within the lab assured him that everyone was on board, the way it had always been.

The cover story seemed plausible: an American company interested in the development and testing of small modular nuclear reactors at the lab, to power such things as remote work sites, like the Trans-Mountain Pipeline. A growing number of Indigenous communities with infrastructure challenges had expressed serious interest in the mini reactors. All of a sudden, nukes had become green. The Whiteshell Laboratories checked all the right boxes for the venture. *Optimism.* Peale looked at the spreadsheet of the towns-people's financials. New trucks were being bought. Trips were being planned. Credit lines were expanding. *Opportunity.* The reactor research would occur, with plenty of checks and balances in easily accessible files. Maybe two or three of the reactors would eventually get built and sold, after years of testing, a small price to pay for the millions in profit gleaned from the clandestine ventures. *Location.* It was the location that greenlit the lab and the town in '59, not too close to Winnipeg, but not too far for the employees of Consolidated Industries to keep an eye on initiatives that were anything but nuclear. *Greenlit.* Green lights were never questioned, like the one that flashed go to drill a thousand feet down into the Canadian Shield in '74 to retrieve the secret gold deposits for

Consolidated, all under the guise of building a research laboratory for the long-term storage of nuclear waste. No one batted an eye when it was announced that the Underground Research Laboratory would be closing, or that it would be flooded to the brim to ensure that no access could ever occur. No one questioned *anything*.

Peale knew that they wouldn't start now.

CHAPTER
THIRTY-FIVE

Gerry Hutchings pulled into the parking lot of Osis Building Supplies in Lac du Bonnet. He needed to pick up a few things: nails for the loose boards on the dock, new spring hinges for the screen door, and a gallon of stain for the front steps. It would only take about five minutes out of the trip to Pinawa, then a little farther down the road to the Underground Research Laboratory access. There weren't enough items to warrant the shopping cart. *Maybe there's something else I need on sale.* The bad wheel on the right-hand side spun with happy abandon.

The aisles were thin, the shelves tall. Head-on collisions with other carts were a regular occurrence. Aisle Three was the scene of the accident, a glancing impact with a much younger store patron. He went to curse, then realized who it was. "Sorry about that, Mr. Hutchings. It was all my fault. I was going too—"

"It's all right, Brendan," said Gerry. "I might not have to get the stain mixed in the paint shaker now."

Brendan paused, then laughed nervously. "Yeah, well, I didn't think I hit it that hard."

Gerry looked at the contents in the other cart. "Doing a little electrical?"

Brendan nodded. "Finally running power to the bunkhouse, for the family reunion."

Gerry smiled. "That's going to be a lot of Koshelanyks."

Brendan nodded. "And a lot of vodka."

Gerry laughed. "Sounds like a typical family reunion then." A mutual laugh was shared. "I passed my Class One last week, with air brakes," Brendan said.

"Congratulations," said Gerry. "Going to start driving the logging trucks?"

"Hope so," said Brendan. "Mr. Peeters has me doing the delivery routes now, plus the fuel truck run to the Whiskey Jack."

"I'll put in a good word," said Gerry. "You've done plenty of gravel, haven't you?"

"With the three-ton," said Brendan. "Just have to be careful of the shoulders."

Gerry nodded. "True. They can suck a truck right off the road. Cars too."

"Like quicksand," said Gerry. "Almost have to drive in the middle in some places."

"I'll bet you use your horn a lot on the hills."

"Have to," said Brendan. "That's how I stay in one piece."

Gerry smiled. "Well, I think they need to put horns on these carts. See you around, Brendan."

"See you, Mr. Hutchings."

Gerry didn't have to offer up his security pass at the gate to the Whiteshell Laboratories. The Grand National was a regular visitor. He waved as he passed the guard shack. He parked next to a dusty Rolls-Royce. He heard the honk behind him before he saw the car. He turned to see a red Volvo station wagon approaching. It took the empty spot two cars down. Gerry walked up to the back of the car. He pointed to the tailgate as Donald Peeters exited. "Since when does Volvo make a turbo?"

"Been making them for years," said Donald. "Remember my GLT?"

Gerry blinked. "You mean the silver one?"

"That's right," Donald pointed at the dusty Buick. "How's your turbo?"

"Plenty of poke, and plenty hard on gas."

"Yeah, that's what happens when you keep your right foot on it all the time."

"But that's where all the fun is."

The two men laughed. They headed towards the side door of the administration building. A small foyer greeted the two, with another door and an intercom switch. A closed-circuit camera pointed down from the ceiling. A voice crackled overhead from an unseen speaker. "Please identify, last and first."

The man stepped forward. "Peeters, Donald."

There was a pause. The speaker spoke again. "Please identify, last and first, subject two."

Gerry stepped forward. "Hutchings, Gerald."

The door gave an audible click and buzz. Donald opened the door. "After you, Mr. Hutchings."

Gerry smiled. "Why, thank you, Mr. Peeters."

The two men proceeded down the corridor. Greetings were a mix of nodded and verbal as they passed other workers. The destination was about halfway down the hall. The conference room had floor-to-ceiling glass windows facing the hallway. The windows were sealed as to the goings-on within, the venetian blinds closed tight. *Another presentation*, Gerry thought. *Another bad idea.*

Donald pushed the door open. Gerry followed. Half the lights had already been dimmed. A man of standard build stood at the front of the room, adjusting the angle of the overhead projector on the screen behind. Even in the dim light, it was obvious that the man was in a losing battle for his thinning brown hair. He wore a dark green button-down shirt, a logo on the pocket that looked like a plane of some sort. He had a briefcase open on the table. In front of it was a portable tape recorder. The man nodded at the pair as they sat at the table. He reached over to the recorder. He pressed Play and Record at the same time. He waited about ten seconds for the tape to reach the magnetic medium. Then he spoke. "Meeting of Consolidated Industries administration team, July 22, 1989. Principals Gerald Hutchings, Donald Peeters . . ." The man stopped. He hit the Pause button. He looked at Gerry. "Where's Jarrod?"

The door to the conference room swung open. "Sorry I'm late," said Jarrod. He slapped his zippered folio on the table, his gait fast, his limp pronounced. The man in the button-down shirt released the Pause button. "And Jarrod Mulaney. Meeting called by Secretary Norman Peale. Not present, Edgar Van Cleef, Chairman."

CHAPTER THIRTY-SIX

Sam was finally alone. The search for the missing padlock was starting to sound like the title for a Scooby-Doo mystery. Zach and Lisa were anything but a Fred and Daphne in their mystery-sensing skills, nor a Shaggy and Velma for that matter. She snickered to herself when she thought of what Fred and Daphne were *really* up to in those spooky old castles. She had another thought. *Shaggy and Velma?* No, Scooby would have said something.

The garage door had been left open. Zach and Lisa had returned to their respective cabins.

She took one last run through the dusty shelves and dustier corners. Nothing. She returned to the inner confines of the cabin, with two plastic milk crates that were still the property of the long-defunct Silverwood Dairies. Five minutes later, the coffee table was fixed.

The remnants of fishing line in the rafters were still swaying in the breeze fed by the open screens. Sam watched them dance, enjoying them at first, then remembering the encounter with the jellyfish she had had in Mexico on her honeymoon. It never got around to stinging her, but the reaction made the locals think that it had. For her sake, Cooper had put the camcorder down on the boat when she started screaming. *He wasn't always a complete asshole.*

Sam scanned the living area from her vantage point. There were still bits and pieces from the obliterated plastic squadron underneath the chairs. She moved back the chairs to retrieve them. She didn't know what the names of the parts were in the aeronautic sense, though she did realize that they probably took plenty of time to glue into place. Most of the pieces were small, easily concealed in a closed hand. She went to move the magazine rack, then stopped. One of the floats from the float plane had landed on top of the ancient *Chatelaine*s. When she retrieved it, she noticed the wing. It must have sheared off the top of the float plane on impact. The top of the wing was plenty dusty from all those years in the rafters, its yellow paint almost turning grey. There was some form of marking beneath, possibly a decal. Sam wiped away the dust to see it. She blinked. She flipped the wing over. She flipped it back. She dug through the bag of wreckage to find what was left of the float plane. She placed the rest of the pieces on the table. She was remembering something that she had seen on the planes, or something she *hadn't* seen.

The flat surfaces of the coffee table, kitchen table, and the kitchen counters were starting to look like miniature Transport Canada crash investigations. She had no idea what the planes were called, though quick test fitments helped determine which parts belonged to which plane. The different colours were also helpful. Sam had never made a plastic model in her life. She knew someone who did.

The first rings to Chris Hutchings's phone went to voicemail. Sam was about to leave a message when her brother's number came up as an incoming call. She hit the speaker. "Hey, Chris,"

"Hey, Sam," said Chris. "How's the Styrofoam peanut-packing going on those planes?"

Sam gave herself an unseen pat on the back for not using the video call feature, a feature that she had only instigated once, and by accident. "Yeah, I'll have that heading your way shortly. I was just remembering that thing that Dad had said to you, about the Canuck."

"What, the little truth, accuracy-schmaccuracy thing?"

Sam remembered. *Even the smallest truth demands accuracy.* "Yeah, something like that. But you said it was when you were putting the stickers—"

"Decals, Sam. They're called decals."

"Right, decals. Sorry, not stickers. And it was because the Canuck didn't have any on it, right?"

"I think so. But that was almost forty years—"

Sam pressed her brother. "Try to remember, Chris. It's important."

"Important? Why is it so—"

"CHRIS!"

There was an awkward pause. Sam broke it with her best condensed version of what she knew and what she didn't know about their father. She came clean about how the models had shattered like peanut brittle when she tried to retrieve them and the discovery inside the black dildo plane. Chris listened. Something clicked. "Wait a minute."

Sam held the phone closer. "What? What is it? What do you remem—"

"It was before the Canuck. When I first started making the models. Might have been the Spitfire, maybe the Zero."

"What about them?"

"He said I didn't have to, that no one would ever see them, so why bother."

"See what?"

"The decals," said Chris. "I didn't put them on the top of the wings, because you'd never see them anyway. I don't know if that helps you any."

Sam looked at the shattered squadron. None of the planes had any decals where the cabin dust would have obscured them from view. None of the planes except for one. "Chris, did you ever build a float plane?"

"Float plane? Naw, nothing like that. I just liked the fighters and the bombers. Too bad it's all garbage now. Can I get that Canuck pic—"

"The key, Chris. Any idea about the key?"

"Sorry, Sam. I never hid anything in them. Come to think of it, I could've stowed my weed in the bottom of the Lanc. I think the bomb bay doors flipped open."

Sam thanked Chris for his recollections. She apologized for the downing of the squadron and promised to send him the rendering of the Canuck when she had time. Sam returned to her examination of the float plane wreckage. *The decal.* Sam knew the logo. It was identical to the one that was on her button-down shirt when she worked at the Whiskey Jack

Lodge. *A promotional thing?* The logo was different now, probably because the plane was different. It wasn't anything that she'd ever seen in a storeroom or something that she was asked to retrieve for a guest. If it was a gift, it was for a select few. *Was Dad the accountant for the lodge?* Sam stopped herself. *Dad wasn't an accountant.* There had to be someone that knew. There had to be a padlock somewhere that the key from the shattered plane opened.

Sam wondered if the answers were at the Whiskey Jack Lodge.

Most of the seasonal campers at the Pinawa Campground preferred the sites that were closest to the Channel. Block Seven was more of an overflow block, for campers who had forgotten to make a reservation, or maybe an overnight for folks who were headed further into the wilderness. It wasn't a great spot for families. The ticks had been particularly aggressive, more so in the sheltered areas. Anyone staying in one of the campsites on Block Seven was either impervious to blood-sucking parasites or a garden-variety loner.

The tenant in the eighth stall of Block Seven was quiet, kept to himself. There didn't appear to be anyone else staying at the site. There wasn't any loud music around the campfire at night. Actually, there wasn't *any* music, ever. The same was true of the firepit, its remnants of ash long since removed. The trailer, an old 1970s Prowler that still had the cartoon cat decal looking down on the site from above, would have lights on at odd hours, and the tow vehicle, a rusty silver Dodge Ram, would come and go sporadically.

No one was quite sure of the name of the man who stayed in the eighth stall of Block Seven. Someone in Block

Three had seen him at the bear-resistant trash containers. He did wave as he hopped back in his truck, not overly friendly, not overly unfriendly. One of the older campers who rented a seasonal site had said that he looked "ethnic," which was probably about as politically correct as the septuagenarian would get for the new millennium. The man respected the posted rules. He drove below the ridiculously low campground speed of ten kilometres per hour. Whoever he was, he wasn't a problem.

Someone said that he thought he worked at the Whispering Pines in town.

CHAPTER
THIRTY-SEVEN

Gerry Hutchings looked over at the plastic model kit of the Beaver float plane on the passenger seat as he drove towards the Underground Research Laboratory site. It was a promotional gimmick, the latest from the mind of Norman Peale. He had big plans for expanding the Whiskey Jack Lodge, the hospitality arm of Consolidated Industries. He also had other plans. Gerry didn't care too much for those.

The red Volvo wagon in his rearview mirror followed at a safe distance. Gerry couldn't see Jarrod Mulaney's white Parisienne Safari, but he knew it would be bringing up the rear. The Underground Research Laboratory was about fifty klicks northeast of the Whiteshell Laboratories. Officially, the site had been built to study the feasibility of using the Lac du Bonnet batholith for the storage of nuclear waste. Sounded downright heroic on paper. It also wasn't bullshit. Teams had come in from around the world to do experiments to address their own nuclear waste concerns, in a footprint that took up less than a third of the underground labyrinth. As far as the public was concerned, it was a major project with considerable inspection and oversight. There had never been anything approaching *The China Syndrome* fiction or a Three Mile Island reality. *Nothing to see here*, Gerry thought, as he keyed in his access code at the automated gate. *Nothing to see here.*

Gerry idled the Grand National along the freshly graded gravel. He went past the access to the main shaft. The gravel road took a slight left into the canopy of the trees. There was another automated fence to pass, then a third, and a fourth. A curve to the right lasted for almost half a klick. It opened to reveal a large gravel parking area with a hangar-sized steel Quonset. A faded windsock flapped in the breeze. There was no runway in sight.

Gerry parked near the main door. About thirty seconds later, Donald's Volvo pulled up on the left, followed by Jarrod's Safari on the right. All three drivers killed their engines at the same time. They reached the main door together. Gerry flipped up the all-weather cover that protected the keypad from the elements. He inserted his key and turned it to the right. He heard a beep and keyed in a series of digits. A buzzer sounded, along with the release of the main door. The three men entered the Quonset.

The air inside the cylindrical hut felt stale. Jarrod flicked on the bank of light switches on the wall nearest the door. The large fixtures overhead flickered on one by one, followed by the overhead fans. The lights revealed three drive-on chassis dynamometers. Donald opened the oversized front doors to the Quonset. Within fifteen minutes, all of the cars were inside, strapped down, hooked up to exhaust hoses and adding the miles expected to be on the odometers of very busy men. Jarrod looked inside at the odometer of his Safari. "I don't know why we don't just crack them open and spin 'em ahead like a crooked car dealer." He had to raise his voice to be heard above the cruising speed engines.

"They can tell if they've been cracked," said Gerry. "There's no way anyone can argue with it."

"Who would argue with it anyway?" said Donald.

Gerry smiled. "They."

"I thought *we* were They," said Jarrod.

"There's always another They," said Donald. "All kinds of them actually."

The three men moved further into the Quonset. Gerry found the next bank of lights on the wall. Their illumination revealed what was left of the heavily modified Avrocar, the one that had snapped the picture of Jarrod Mulaney in his rookie OPP gear on May Long 1967, plus those of a curious and accidentally burned Stefan Michalak at nearby Falcon Lake. Gerry had watched the whole thing from the dusty remote-control console pushed up against the wall. *How could the poor sap have known that he was standing in front of the exhaust vents for the turbine?* He remembered the recording of the man's voice, asking in a few languages whether or not the experimental pilots within were having the aeronautic equivalent of car trouble. The curious Michalak didn't venture far enough inside to see that the craft was empty. If he had, he would have seen that it didn't have any seats. The story that followed, that Michalak had come face to face with a flying saucer, was all that was needed to place the story in the Nutbar Section of the *Winnipeg Sentinel*.

The next set of lights revealed the sectioned remains of RL-207. It was the lost Mark II Avro Arrow, squirrelled away in early 1959, just before the cancellation of the Arrow program. Wilfred Curtis, the former head of all things Royal Canadian Air Force, had almost let its existence be known in a 1968 interview. Luckily, Curtis had been cagey enough to deflect an all-out inquiry. Gerry had been involved with the movement of the airframe components as one of his first assignments with Consolidated Industries, coordinating shipments from various warehouses across the country through Peeters's trucking company until it all ended up in Manitoba by the fall of '63. The poking and prodding by various military aircraft designers from around the world had left their scars over the years. Norman Peale had suggested that it be scrapped when he arrived at Consolidated in 1973. Edgar Van Cleef had scolded the young Peale for his insolence. "That plane has far greater worth than numbers can imagine," said Van Cleef. "I suggest you leave well enough alone."

Gerry knew that Peale was going to be trouble, he just didn't know exactly when. The arrangement with the principals at the Whiteshell Laboratories at its inception was all about the secure site, a place for government secrets and experiments both small and winged to be tested, evaluated, and hidden away from prying eyes. The remnants of the Pinetree line had been used for the type of Cold War–justified surveillance that would raise the hackles of anyone defending present-day civil liberties, surveillance that had been pointed directly at citizens with radical ideas on both sides of the border. As for 1989, it didn't feel a thing like 1959. Former global enemies were getting downright friendly, so much so that the hidden runway that had landed and launched things both winged and hovering was being reclaimed by the forest, the manufactured foliage intertwined with the real. The last time it had been actively used was for the testing of surplus RCAF fighters, like the Sabre and the Canuck. They were sold for scrap value by the federal government, supposedly for their repurposing as static displays for communities that asked. An exposé by CBC's *The Fifth Estate* had grounded that venture, after it was discovered that better than half of the planes labelled as scrap were completely operational. A few private pilots who never got the joke of being nicknamed Crash ruined it for everybody.

Gerry knew that there would always be an enemy to fight. He also knew that the best way to fight was to pay someone else to do it for you. For that, you needed money, and lots of it. Those worries ended in '74, when the holes were drilled about forty feet away from where he stood, and the vein of gold was found. *The best money is never green.* Where the gold went and for what purpose was not his concern. It was the new gold that worried him.

"The world is forever in the precarious state of losing its balance," said Edgar Van Cleef, shortly after hiring Gerry in 1959. "Like the scales of justice, certain things, certain *events* need to occur as required to keep the balance within the agreed specification."

Gerry had nodded as though he understood. It was obvious to Van Cleef that he hadn't. He dumbed it down. "This girl you're sweet on. Lena, right?"

"Right," said Gerry. He felt the colour in his cheeks beginning to appear.

Van Cleef looked straight in Gerry's eyes. "How do you think she'd feel if you had relations with her sister?"

Gerry's eyes went wide. "What? Why would I—"

"And what if you murdered her family outright? Like that Starkweather fellow."

Gerry couldn't find the words. Van Cleef continued. "And what if I told you that the failure to do so would result in famine, genocide, the end of days?"

Gerry remained dumbstruck. Van Cleef clasped his shoulder. "Son, I will never ask you to do those things. But I will ask you to do things that no one has ever asked you to do before. I will provide you with as much truth as possible. These will not be half-truths. These will be facts, backed up by research, backed up by intelligence, backed up by even more intelligence. Some of these facts may seem as dry as a saltine, while some may be hotter than a cat on a hot tin roof. But I promise you this, Gerald Hutchings, they will be accurate, for even the smallest truth demands accuracy."

Gerry thought for a moment about his aging mentor as he looked around the dusty warehouse of secrets. *Where is he?* Peale had been handling more of the weekly meetings for Consolidated. He was even driving Van Cleef's car. It all still *sounded* Van Cleef, with the briefings, the spreadsheets, the graphs. But something was missing.

Gerry decided it was time to find out what.

THIRTY-EIGHT

Megan knew that she could never tell her mother, her father, even her whacked-out stepmother who wanted to be her best friend what she had discovered that summer. *I actually like vacuuming!* She knew it was probably the new lightweight unit that she had been handed at the Whiskey Jack Lodge. For whatever reason, it didn't seem to be work worthy of payment. She decided that it would be wise to keep that revelation to herself.

The rest of the rooms within her housekeeping footprint at the lodge were hardly a step down from Mr. Peale's Pinetree room, though there was definitely a different feel to them. It was almost as though the rooms were specifically designed for their patrons, who were few in number but plenty important. The rooms in the main lodge had name plaques on the doors that honoured the types of trees that swayed nearby. The outdoor cabins were a new assignment. McMasters had given her a quick primer on how to use the electric service cart. She hoped that he hadn't seen her blush during the training.

The naming of the cabins followed a sporting fish theme, then the local animals. The engraved door plaques of the main lodge had been replaced by expertly carved hanging wooden signs for the cabins, depicting the creatures in poses that seemed ripped from the pages of *Manly Outdoors Monthly*. Megan smiled to herself at the made-up magazine name. The names switched to birds for the remaining three cabins, clustered in a cul-de-sac at the rear of the property. Like the rooms of the lodge, each of the cabins had plenty of black-and-white photos of the region, as well as the military themes she had first seen in the hallways of the main lodge. Megan got to work inside the Chickadee cabin, lugging in the vacuum and the cleaning caddies in one trip. The first thing that she noticed was the dated tech accessories. Instead of a flat-screen TV, there was a massive silver beast that was as wide as it was long. The clock radio had no iPod dock, not even an auxiliary plug. It did have plenty of woodgrain on it. *This must be what Mom means by roughing it.*

The Chickadee cabin didn't have any guests staying in it. Neither did the Blue Jay next door. The final cabin of the three had the hooks for the chains but no sign. Megan didn't see it anywhere inside the cabin. She spritzed her sprays, dusted the things that needed dusting, and ran the vacuum on the floors and carpets. One of the black and white pictures above the bed seemed a little off-kilter. She climbed up on the bed, inching towards the picture on her knees. She moved the picture into a level position. She looked at it for a moment to make sure it was better than before. She stopped. She looked again. She blinked. The group of crew-cut men standing in front of a steel Quonset were looking back at her. A dark-coloured car's rear fender was intruding from the right. It had some cursive script on the side that she couldn't quite make out. *Electra?* There was a man leaning up against the fender. His haircut wasn't as tight as the other men. The shot was candid. Some of the men were laughing. The man against the fender seemed to be in the middle of rolling his eyes, just like her mother did and just like she did when the joke was lame.

The man was her grandfather.

Sam couldn't let the padlock thing go. She checked and rechecked all the cupboards in the Hutchings' cabin. She looked under all the beds. She opened every drawer. There was no Yale padlock, though there was a yell, when she found the bones of a long-dead mouse beneath some dusty wool blankets.

The Moleskine seemed as good a place as any to map out what she knew. *Dad wasn't an accountant. Dad drove a lot. Dad hid a key in a model plane. Dad knew somebody at the Whiskey Jack.* Sam thought back to her time there. She tried to remember her interview. *Did I even have an interview?* She sifted through her memories, back to 1989, back to July. *God, it was hot.* She remembered her mother staying in town, due to her recent surgery. She remembered Chris making money hand-over-fist in Winnipeg. *Dad*. She didn't remember seeing him too much, but she knew he was around. He had been dropping some pretty large hints to her about heading into Winnipeg to keep an eye on her mother over the weekend. She remembered that she had received little to no friction for asking for the weekend off from the Whiskey Jack. *That weekend*. Dad was at the cabin by himself, said he had to do something to the septic system. *Dealing with shit*. She remembered hearing about the fire. She remembered calling the lake. She remembered the phone ringing from all her dial attempts. She remembered getting the call. *That call*. She wondered if they remembered anything, anything at all. She decided to go and ask. She grabbed her Moleskine for the short trip.

Sam's destination was only three doors down. It was one of the cabins that the Player's tin had a key for, three keys actually: the shed, the cabin, and the boathouse. The cabin didn't have a garage, but it did have a gravel driveway built up over the metal culvert. A dusty but newish Ford pickup was parked next to an old man's car, a Grand Marquis with all the chrome trimmings. An old red station wagon was parked off to the side, slowly being devoured by rust and sap. It had the cheesy wood panelling that all station wagons used to wear. *An old lake car*, Sam thought. She headed down the path to the cabin. She knocked on the old aluminum storm door with the initial M. She could see movement within, slow but determined. Sam waited patiently. The man opened the door wide. "Samantha Hutchings! Why, you haven't changed a bit."

Sam smiled. "Then you should get your eyes looked at, Mr. Mulaney."

"You can call me Jarrod, you know. Maybe even Uncle Jarrod." Jarrod Mulaney had said the words as he moved back into the cabin, his gait assisted by a cane with a quadpod base for stability. Sam wondered if a walker was more in order. The pictures in the hallway started off with Mulaney in his younger days as an OPP constable in Kenora. The rest of the walls were lined with family pictures, clustered in collage-style frames. There were the anniversary-style frames, the department store–grade ones for the milestone markers. The last big number had been the Mulaneys' fortieth. Peggy Mulaney had dressed up for the occasion, but hadn't been doing well. In the photo, she was hunched over in her wheel-chair, her right leg removed due to complications from diabetes two years previous. She was blind by then, so she couldn't have seen how badly her wig needed an adjustment. The colon cancer that was found shortly after the party was Stage 4, the same stage as the pancreatic cancer that had taken her daughter Candace in 2005. Peggy had made it to Thanksgiving. There were no pictures of that.

Jarrod Mulaney had made his way to his powered recliner, still in the raised position from his recent exit. He slowly lowered himself into a more comfortable position. Sam looked around the cabin. It was as time warped as hers, with plenty of chrome, Naugahyde, and bric-a-brac on permanent display. The short trip had winded her host. "Do you need something to drink?" Sam asked.

"You know, I could really go for a beer," said Jarrod. His grin and eyes were full of mischief when he said it. Judging from the number of pills on the TV table next to him, Sam knew that he probably wasn't supposed to have any. "Let me check the fridge." She was looking through the fridge when she heard the sliding door open behind her. "What," said the voice. "You don't have food at your house?"

Sam turned to see a smiling Steve Mulaney. Sam smiled back, in expression and in memory. There was a smidge of a paunch showing, but he was still an imposing shadow, all six feet, four inches of it. His threadbare T-shirt spoke of Mercury Outboards. Judging from the grease on his hands, that's exactly what he had been tending to in the boathouse. He had a hat to match, with salt and pepper hair peeking out. Sam couldn't remember which eye was the glass one, the one that he had earned from a shotgun pellet during the serving of a warrant in Dauphin in 2012. He had opted for desk duty over disability, working with the RCMP's D division in Winnipeg until his retirement in 2015.

Sam smiled back. "Looks about as full as my fridge." Sam rummaged a little further. "I was looking for a beer for your old man."

Steve looked over at his father. "Dad, what did the doctor say?"

Jarrod Mulaney held up his hands in defeat. "You got me, copper."

Steve reached down into a small bar fridge that Sam hadn't seen. "You can have a Budweiser Prohibition." He brought up three cans, handing one to Sam. "That's the rules with the new meds."

Jarrod continued to protest. "I thought they repealed Prohibition."

"Well, it's back in full force in Mulaneyville." Steve opened the can before handing it to his father. "I'm on the wagon with you, remember?"

Jarrod changed the subject. "Is the boat fixed yet?"

"I think it's a bad coil," said Steven. "Picking one up tomorrow."

Jarrod turned to the window. "You hear that, fish? You've got till tomorrow to put your affairs in order."

Sam took a sip of the beer substitute. It was surprisingly good. She raised the can at Steve. "I almost can't tell the difference."

Steve motioned her over. "I got Crown Royal in the boat-house," he whispered.

"What was that?" said Jarrod.

Steve didn't miss a beat. "I said I need Sam's help in the boathouse."

"Okey-dokey," said Jarrod. "I'm going to watch a movie." Sam watched as Jarrod fast-forwarded to the beginning of a Clint Eastwood spaghetti western. It was something with dollars—maybe *Fistful*, maybe a *Few Dollars More*. She followed Steve to the boathouse.

When she entered, Sam noticed that the motor on the boat wasn't disassembled. There weren't any tools at the ready or on the bench. There was an open tub of grease on the workbench. Steve grabbed a rag to wipe off the grease he had placed on his hands. He pointed at the late-model outboard. "Those Yamahas never break," he said, as he lifted the bottle up from the bottom shelf. "He probably thinks I'm working on his old Gale." Steve emptied about half of his can of near-beer into the water. He filled the rest with Crown. He reached for Sam's can. "Think of it as a diet boilermaker."

Sam handed over the can. "Well, as long as it's diet." The drink was potent, but without the sting of the straight whisky. Sam grabbed a folding chair from the wall. She was just about to get comfortable when she stopped. She looked at Steve. "Are you sure he's OK up there by himself?"

"He won't get far," said Steve. "Doc says it's mild dementia, had these little micro-strokes. Vascular dementia, I think that's what he called it. And his B-12 is down. And he can't drink anymore."

Sam sipped before she asked. "Is he still driving?"

"I've been able to convince him not to," said Steve. "But I had to hide his keys. He keeps forgetting about his leg."

Sam nodded. "From that bomber in Kenora."

"More of an exploder than a bomber."

"I don't know how you'd forget something like that."

Steve looked at Sam. He closed his eyelid over his good eye as he waved his hands around in front of him. "I'm sorry, who said that?"

Sam laughed. "You're a sick bastard, Steve Mulaney."

Steve nodded. "Guilty as charged." He got back on topic. "Anyways, we're going to try this stuff, see if it helps. How's your mom doing?"

"Actually, a little better," said Sam. "We got her on this vegan food service thing at the home. Seems to be opening up a few pathways a crack. But she still goes a little off the rails. She's singing."

"Singing?" said Steve. "What song?"

"Here," said Sam. "Let me play it for you."

Sam played the la-la recording that Lena had sung in her sleep at the Whispering Pines. Steve listened. "Not exactly a dance number, whatever it is."

"Does it sound familiar?"

"I think music is a lot like fashion," said Steve. "Been there, done that, and go back, Jack, do it again. They even say that Zeppelin ripped off 'Stairway to Heaven.' That song was a bitch to slow-dance to."

Sam thought back to the school dances and socials of her youth. "Yeah, when it speeds up, what the hell do you do?"

Steve finished his sip. "Grab the ass tighter, I guess."

234

Sam laughed along with her lake bud. *Lake bud. Now that's not entirely accurate.* There had been a time. Well, a couple of times, anyway. The first comfort involved a two-six of Southern Comfort, an ugly crying fit, and an angry session of young love in the screen house at the Hutchings' cabin a few weeks after Gerry's funeral. The Peeters' three-casket send-off had brought it all rushing back. At least it was in a hotel room that time, Sam making the trek from school in Alberta, Steve in from RCMP training in Regina. *Still angry.* She waited for the laughter to subside. The pause was almost uncomfortable until she broke it. "So, I'm dealing with a little weirdness on the dad front myself."

"Shit," said Steve. "Is he haunting you?"

"In a way," said Sam. She detailed the Coles Notes of the recent events.

Steve listened attentively. He rubbed his chin, looking for the answer. "Maybe we can ask Dad if he remembers anything. I always remembered them as being pretty tight."

"Do you think he's up for it?" Sam asked.

"Today's a good day," said Steve. "Tomorrow could be major depression—why me, woe is me, forgetful kinda shit. I wouldn't wait on it."

The two lake buds finished their drinks. They headed up to the cabin.

CHAPTER
THIRTY-NINE

The volume was up on the TV. Sam was getting ready to open the cabin door. Steve stopped her. "This is his favourite part," he said quietly. "The getting-the-three-coffins-ready part."

"I have no idea what you're talking about," Sam whispered.

"How do you not know *Fistful of Dollars*?" Steve whispered back.

Sam peeked through the screen. "I remember some of the Dirty Harry movies. Dad liked those."

The pair waited on the steps until The Man with No Name updated the number of coffins to four. Sam opened the door as Jarrod Mulaney added his commentary to the screen. "That's why you don't shoot at another man's mule!"

Sam and Steve had each taken chairs near Jarrod. Sam knew that she might be interrupting but decided that it was a chance worth taking. *Besides*, Sam thought. *That's what the Pause button is for.*

"Mr. Mulaney, I wanted to ask you—"

"Uncle Jarrod sounds a lot better than Mr. Mulaney, don't you think?"

Sam smiled. "Yes, Uncle Jarrod. I think you're right about that."

Jarrod paused the movie. "What is it that you want to ask me?"

"It's nothing really," said Sam.

"Then why ask it?" said Jarrod.

"I'm just trying to fill in some blanks about my dad."

Jarrod looked at Sam. He looked at the TV. He pressed the Power button on the remote to turn off the screen. The image of a gritting Clint Eastwood disappeared from view. He pressed the Up button on his recliner. He started shuffling towards the front door, grabbing his faded Tilley hat from a hook on the wall. He was halfway there when he stopped. "Steve, can you grab the tin of keys in the junk drawer?"

"Sure, Dad," said Steve. He shot Sam a confused look as he went to the kitchen. Sam watched as he rummaged through the drawer. He removed a Player's tin similar to the one in the Hutchings' cabin. "I found it, Dad."

"Bring it. Meet me at the wagon," said Jarrod. The screen door slammed. Steve and Sam followed. Jarrod was moving as purposefully as he could, trying to fight the loss of balance that age and injury had bestowed upon him. He told Sam the tale as he huffed and puffed. "I met your dad in the fall of '75. He hired me as a security consultant for Consolidated Industries. In fact, you were there the day that your dad hired me, Samantha. You were skipping around this very car."

Sam looked at what was left of the Grand LeMans. The sap had obscured most of the windows, Mother Nature's tint job. Inside was a mess: a pile of fluff and upholstery that had been a winter nest to whatever could crawl through the holes in the floorboards. Jarrod reached for the Player's tin that Steve had retrieved. The elder Mulaney's hands were touched with age-related tremors, though he knew the secret to popping the tin open. He added to the tale as he looked through the keys. "This was my first company car for Consolidated," said Jarrod. "I kept it for us as a second car when I got the blue Suburban." He looked at Steve. "Your mother thought we'd won the lottery when I pulled up in this."

Jarrod continued. "We bought the cabin here in '76. When the engine started using oil, we parked it here as a back-up. Lost Reverse when I got it stuck getting water at the Tulabi well, so that's when I parked it." Jarrod found what he was looking for, a pair of keys held together by a produce bag twist tie. He stuck the door key into the driver's door. It took a few jiggles and twists, but the lock eventually clicked open. Jarrod pulled the driver's door open. He leaned in towards the centre console. He was about halfway there when he stopped. "Oh. Uh, Steve?"

Steve leaned in. "Yeah?"

Jarrod let out a grunt. "I don't think my body moves the way I need it to for this."

Steve helped his father exit the wagon. He pointed to the interior. "It's in the console."

"What's in the console?" Sam asked.

"The key," said Jarrod. "As long as the mice haven't learned how to digest metal."

Sam moved into the car without asking Steve. She flipped open the weathered console lid. It had been spared from becoming a mouse condo, but not for lack of trying. Something had been gnawing at the lid during the previous winters.

The inside of the console was stuffed with old registrations, road maps, and some ancient condiment packets that no one would ever risk squeezing. She saw it at the bottom of the console. *Yale.* "Hey, Uncle Jarrod?"

"Yes, Sam?"

"Who has the third key?"

CHAPTER
FORTY

Norman Peale rummaged through his desk drawer at the Whiskey Jack Lodge. He had grown partial to the fine-tipped refills for his Parker ballpoint, an ancient blue Jotter that he just couldn't part with. He had money pens throughout his office, many of them given as gifts by patrons and business partners alike. The Jotter just felt right, in heft, in motion, and in the satisfying click of its plunger.

The desk drawer was in serious need of a purge. He found one of the carded refills at the back of the drawer, a corner of the card wedged into a gap. As he pulled it out, a key revealed itself. Peale retrieved it. There was no ring, no identifying marks as to what the key opened, just the Yale logo on both sides.

It had been years since Peale had checked on the contents of the locked container, a weather-sealed surplus ammunition box that his former security consultant Jarrod Mulaney had picked up at Princess Auto in Winnipeg. *Out of sight, out of mind.* He knew that no one would come looking for it. Everything from those days had been digitized, hidden under multiple layers of encryption. Mulaney had retired from Consolidated Industries in 1995, a little early due to his wife's failing health. McMasters had been keeping tabs on Mulaney over the last few years during his summers at Bird Lake. "He's thinking about as fast as he's moving," McMasters had said. "He isn't a threat."

The third key had been in the possession of Gerry Hutchings, the main provider of friction between Peale and Van Cleef. Whenever Peale pitched taking three steps forward for Consolidated, Hutchings had reduced it to one, sometimes zero. *Missed opportunities.* Hutchings's untimely death in the summer of 1989 had removed the first set of roadblocks. The feeble Van Cleef had been easy to dispatch in the fall, a two-handed log that Peale delivered to the back of his head. The blow sent Van Cleef's forehead into the sharp flagstone that surrounded the mid-century fireplace in the main lodge. The rain was heavy that night, rain that would have made the rocks slick enough to send Van Cleef flying from his battered Honda trike. Peale had sent the trike into the tree three times for the desired crash effect as the rain fell on Van Cleef's corpse. There were no witnesses. The lodge had already been prepared for the winter shut-down by the summer staff. There were no interruptions as

Peale cleaned up the blood around the fireplace. He waited until the morning to call the RCMP.

The Koshelanyk kid. He wasn't the sharpest tool in the shed, but Peale had seen an opportunity to mould the youngster into a useful tool when Donald Peeters had introduced him as a driver for his trucking company. Brendan Koshelanyk had been doing the main run for Consolidated Industries from the Quonset at the Underground Research Laboratory site. He never asked a question about the cargo. The security tags on the truck doors were never a twist out of place. He didn't speed, kept his driving courteous. He enjoyed the money he was making, treating himself to a new truck, a boat, and a double-wide on the Winnipeg River. *Not bad for a Grade 11 dropout.* But Peale noticed a shift after he had sent Koshelanyk to dispatch the Peeters clan in 1990, a task he had carried out with a Peeters logging truck.

The drink that initially calmed him turned to recreational drugs, then the harder variety. He also liked to talk. When Hap Anderson had slurred his recollections of a conversation that he had had with Koshelanyk about the Peeters' crash, Peale arranged for the boating accident, assisted by his then-new protégé McMasters. That was fifteen years ago. He could still hear the motor of the fishing boat as it cut across Koshelanyk's strangled body in a sheltered cove near Tulabi Falls. The cuts from the propeller and a belly full of the lodge's finest scotch were all that was needed to rule the death as accidental.

Peale wasn't worried about the ammunition box. He was more concerned about what leaned against the wall next to his desk. It had just come back from a local artist. The flaking paint had been replaced with fresh. The red wing accents had more pop than before, the black in the eye glossier than the feathers. Peale wasn't sure how many coats of protective lacquer had been added to the relief carving. The thickness made it seem like it had been dipped as opposed to brushed or sprayed. Peale put the sign for the cabin that stood between the Chickadee and the Blue Jay under his arm. He was halfway out the door when he stopped. He returned to his desk to retrieve the Yale key. He looked at it. He looked at the sign. He smiled.

"Two birds, one stone."

FORTY-ONE

Sam had a problem, and his name was Jarrod Mulaney. He'd just told her where her father worked, and the new information felt like a nuclear explosion GIF going off in her head. Gerry Hutchings wasn't just tight with his three-doors-down neighbour: they worked together, for something called Consolidated Industries. *That name sounds like complete bullshit.* A quick Google on Steve Mulaney's phone returned little information, just variations of the Consolidated name. None of them used Industries in their description.

Jarrod pulled his hat back from his forehead to wipe his brow. "I know there were three keys," said Jarrod. "I had one, your dad had one, and . . ."

Sam and Steve watched as Jarrod tried to remember. Steve felt the need to explain. "I'm sorry, Sam. He gets like this—"

Jarrod slapped the sap-covered fender with his right hand. He pointed his left-hand index finger at his son, the way a parent would wag a finger at a ten-year-old. Sam knew what it was. *The Alz-Anger.* Her mother had reacted in a similar fashion in the early days of her dementia journey. Lena had almost upended the kitchen table on one occasion, banging down on it with both fists. It scared Sam then. Uncle Jarrod was scaring her now.

Steve did his best to calm his father. "Dad, I'm sorry. We're just trying to—"

"I know what you're trying to do! You're trying to put me in a goddamn home for the feeble farts and the pants-pissers, that's what you're trying to do!" He continued, "First, you say I can't drive. Then you say I can't drive the boat. Then you say I can't ride on the goddamn lawnmower. All you tell me is that I *can't.* Well, maybe you're right." The tears were welling up in Jarrod's eyes as he searched for the words. They were clear, concise, and perfect for the occasion. "But I've still got some *can* left!"

Sam watched as her Uncle Jarrod started to sob. She didn't know if he'd fight her off but figured it was a chance worth taking. She approached with her arms open. She held him close as he continued to weep. "I'm sorry," he said, his voice muffled against Sam's shoulder. "I'm sorry that I don't remember."

Steve had moved in. He wasn't much of a hugger, but he did offer a reassuring hand on his father's shoulder. Things started to level out after a minute. Jarrod patted his son's hand as he moved back. He patted Sam on her shoulder. He turned back towards the car.

"You know, Sam? You were there the day that I got this car. You were dancing around it without a care in the world."

They remember the old stuff better than the new. Sam had had similar moments of recollection with her mother. That's when it hit her. She turned to Steve. "My notebook. I think I left it inside."

"Notebook? Uh, OK. For what?"

Sam looked at Jarrod as he kept looking at the rusty wagon. "We're going to take a trip. Down memory lane."

Megan Goodman had made her way into the bathroom of the nameless cabin. She turned off the vacuum for the small floor space, opting for a spray cleaner and a microfibre cloth. She was missing her phone terribly, a phone that had her playlists. The clock radio was more a clock than a radio, with only static for any station that she tried to tune in. The television wasn't much better, offering up nothing but snow-storms for the channels she flipped. It appeared to be DVDs or videotapes for entertainment. Like the black and white pictures, the selections on a small shelf kept with the military theme. Silence felt like the best option. She returned to the bathroom spritz.

The dust bunnies were in full force around the back of the toilet. The other cabins weren't this bad. She wondered why no one had cleaned here recently. Megan swapped the micro-fibre cloth for paper towels, making sure to glove up before giving the area a wipe. The wet dust bunnies were resilient, doing their best to cling to the side of the vanity cabinet. As she wiped towards the front of the vanity base, the trim piece on the front decided to dislodge. *Shit.* Megan wiped around the void, glad that no mouse skeletons were grinning back at her. She grabbed the trim piece, taking care not to poke herself on what must have been loose nails. That's when Megan noticed something strange. The front of the board had what looked like nail heads, finished off with a wood filler before they were lacquered. The rear of the board had no nails protruding. She looked closer at the board and where the board would attach. Four shiny circular objects had been inset into the wood, two on each side, and two metal strips had been attached to the board. She brought the board close to the circular objects. The objects sucked the board in with an audible clunk. *Magnets.* It didn't seem too strange. Megan had plenty of them at home in Edmonton, holding all sorts of things on a metallic whiteboard in her room. *Plumbing access?* She leaned down to take a look. There weren't any pipes, but there was a box of some kind. She pulled it out slowly, hoping that a mouse army wouldn't be escaping from behind.

The box was metal, olive drab, and locked up tight. Megan flipped up the lock to get a better look. *Yale.* She dropped it back against the box. She heard someone on the steps outside. She pushed the box back in place, slapping the board back into place too. She threw her cleaning items into the caddy. She exited the bathroom. She stopped. The door was open. Norman Peale was looking at her, smiling like family. "Sorry to interrupt your duties, Miss Goodman."

Megan could feel herself becoming flustered. She stammered through it the best she could. "I, uhm, sorry, Mr. Norma—, I mean, sorry, Mr. Peale."

"No apologies necessary," said Peale. "Can you give me a hand with something outside? I think you're probably a little steadier than me."

Megan didn't feel steady. She felt like she was shaking like a leaf, that it would be obvious to everyone, especially Mr. Peale. She found the courage to calm. She followed Peale out to the porch. He picked up a wooden sign, the one that had been missing when she arrived to clean the cabin. It had two short chain links attached.

"No matter how hard I try, I always get it crooked," said Peale. "Do you mind? I can guide you."

Megan took the sign. She counted off the links of the chains, making sure they were an equal number per side. She hoisted the sign upwards to the hooks. "Is this good?"

"A little higher," said Peale.

Megan obliged. Peale gave a thumbs-up with the new position. She came down the steps to see the sign, a sign that had her employer smiling from ear to ear. He told her why. "It took me a while to find the right artist to restore the colours, one that really knew their birds. Especially the birds around here."

Megan looked at the carving. "That looks like a pretty hard thing to carve, Mr. Peale."

"It was," said Peale. "I've always had a steady hand with my chisels, not so much with a brush." Peale walked up to the carving. He held it to keep it from swaying. "These red markings are important. There are other blackbirds in North America, but these are the ones that call Bird Lake home."

"It's very pretty," said Megan. "What does it sound like?"

Just then, the blackbird in question uttered its song. Peale's eyes lit up. He pointed upwards to the trees. "Hear that? I believe our feathered friend approves of the corrections." Peale let go of the sign, and a slight sway was induced. "Because Miss Goodman, even the smallest truth demands accuracy." He smiled at Megan.

She smiled back, nervously.

"Well, I'll leave you to it."

Peale walked down the path. Megan looked back at the swinging sign with alarm.

CHAPTER
FORTY-TWO

Milad was annoyed. The primary power needs for the trailer he called home in the Pinawa Campground were for the computer, the one with the kind of encryption systems that would send an MIT professor in search of a strong drink. The web pages he was monitoring were in the moonless-night nether regions of the dark web, a clearing house reserved for automatic weapons, human trafficking, and the building blocks required to produce the kind of global breaking news that would make Wolf Blitzer trip on his words. The temperature for the liquid-cooled computer had yet to spike, in sweaty contrast to the interior of the trailer. Milad had stripped down to his underwear to beat the heat. The solar panel on the roof powered the miniature desk fan that blew at the sweat droplets on his forehead.

His back story had all the necessary elements required to ensure a quick and easy hire at the Whispering Pines. He had been a paramedic in Surrey before he was recruited by the Canadian Intelligence Security Service. He missed the Subaru WRX that was his daily back in Vancouver, though the rusty Ram parked outside wasn't a slouch. The CSIS office in the Prairies region had been operating a skunkworks garage since the mid-eighties, around the time that most cars had anything but performance. The Ram had a larger Hemi out of a wrecked Dodge Challenger, a special tune, and high-performance brakes. It made for quick commutes to the field office in Winnipeg.

Norman Peale had been difficult to track, much less observe. Putting a GPS tracker on his dusty Rolls-Royce was out of the question. The same was true of listening devices and phone taps at the Whiskey Jack. Even a drone fly-by could arouse suspicion. Whatever toys that CSIS had, Milad's superiors knew that Peale would have countermeasures in place.

It hadn't always been this way, as Milad had learned during the original briefing. The relationship with the Whiskey Jack Lodge and its original owner went back to the early days of the Cold War. The original Pinetree line had been touted as an early warning system for enemy bombers. While that duty was legitimate, the placement of the line's unmapped secondary locations made it useful for classified military experiments, such as the creation of phantom objects that would be viewed on radar, requiring an immediate intercept. After the tragedy and cover-up of the Kinross Incident in '53,

Van Cleef, the private-sector contractor who managed the secondary sites, decided to branch out into other areas. He had an interest in the tantalum mine at Bernic Lake, as well as the gold operations in Bissett. In '54, Van Cleef had placed all of his holdings under a larger umbrella, Consolidated Industries. There was mining, timber, hospitality, and numerous government contracts for the supply of vague services. There were also the Americans, the ones from the branches of the Armed Forces who visited the Whiskey Jack frequently while on leave from their duties at the Pinetree stations. There had been a lot of talk, everything from experimental aircraft testing to nuclear propulsion systems. Nothing had been confirmed.

Things started to pick up in 1974. Consolidated had been a major player in the construction of the nuclear reactor site in the Whiteshell and the building of the newest Pinawa. The next project that Consolidated was on the contractor list for was the creation of the Underground Research Laboratory. A lot of digging. A lot of removal for said diggings. A lot of drilling into solid Precambrian stone, the same kind of stone that had the potential for all sorts of mineral deposits within. At the same time, Consolidated had branched into acquiring surplus items from National Defence. It wasn't spent shell casings from Shilo or surplus Jeeps from Dundurn. Consolidated bought aircraft, retired jet fighters, and trainers, with names like Sabre, Canuck, and Voodoo—as many as they could get their hands on.

Milad studied the grainy scanned documents. Most of the aircraft purchases appeared legitimate. Small air forces in developing countries that Canada had friendly relationships with were customers. A good portion of the Sabres were sold to a company in California that worked with the American military, where they were converted into pilotless drones for target practice. The rest were deemed scrap value, the only problem being that no paper trail existed as to where the scrap metal ended up.

The plot thickened in the summer of 1989. A key member of the Consolidated team had made an initial contact with the fledgling intelligence agency. The details were few, but the gist of the communiqué was that the planes labelled as scrap were very airworthy, fitted with all manner of radar-cloaking technology, with additional cargo of interest that had yet to be confirmed. The contact was a Gerald Hutchings. The agent in charge, a Richard Middleton, had hoped to speak to Hutchings again. The notes that existed were thin, but there had been talk about an extraction plan to allow Hutchings to detail the goings-on at Consolidated without fear of reprisal by his current employer. That hope evaporated with Hutchings's death in a forest fire at Eastland Lake in late July. Middleton had made notes that hoped the fire was a ruse to allow Hutchings an easier escape. When Hutchings had failed to call in after a month, Middleton had concluded that the death had actually occurred, an unfortunate cottage country accident. In the fall, Edgar Van Cleef joined Hutchings in the passed-away department, the victim of an ATV accident. The day-to-day operations of Consolidated Industries were officially transferred to Van Cleef's personal secretary, a gentleman by the name of Norman Peale. Middleton died in '94, a massive heart attack while vacationing in Ixtapa.

Milad rewound to his latest briefing about Consolidated, at the CSIS Prairie Office in Winnipeg. "Things were pretty quiet after Van Cleef's unfortunate accident," said Gordon Sesko, Milad's CSIS handler. He pointed at another set of pictures on the whiteboard. "Then Donald Peeters, his wife, and one of his sons gets smoked by a truck from his own company in the summer of '90. The trucking firm had been used by

Consolidated since the sixties." Sesko pointed to the second-last picture on the whiteboard. "It seems that even working part-time for Consolidated can be hazardous to your health." Sesko explained the strange circumstances surrounding the death of Brendan Koshelanyk in 2003. "The body was pretty mangled up, but no water in the lungs. Drunk as a skunk, though. Might have been guilt."

"Guilt?" said Milad.

"Koshelanyk was the one driving the killer truck," said Sesko. "He was working part-time for Consolidated when that happened. Trucking companies tend to show you the door when you wipe out the owner and most of their family. Then, instead of two part-time jobs he's down to one, for Consolidated. Funny thing, though. Didn't seem to affect him in the pocketbook. Four new trucks from '90 to '02, all paid for with cash. Snowmobiles, quads, best of everything for his double-wide. No estate money, no inheritances. His tax returns didn't list anything else coming in."

Milad scratched his chin for a moment. He thinned it all down. "OK, Consolidated is a government contractor. They're doing some prospecting on the government dime and light smuggling to help finance American black ops. Heavy involvement with Whiteshell Labs since the first shovel hit the ground. Something goes down in the late eighties. People start dying." Milad pointed to another picture on the whiteboard. "Who's that again?"

"Jarrod Mulaney, security consultant," said Sesko. "How much he secured or consulted on is anyone's guess. He's also more scrambled these days than a four-dollar omelette."

"Dementia?" Milad asked.

"Probably," said Sesko. "Doubt he can be of much help. Anything come from Hutchings's wife?"

"She's not much better," said Milad. "Keeps saying her husband will be in on Friday, he's an accountant, blah-blah-blah. I've been through her stuff seven times now, including what's in storage. Sweet zip. Then there's that song she started singing."

Sesko crossed his arms. "And why does that matter again?"

"It was the timing," said Milad. "Her daughter shows up with the granddaughter. She starts getting better food. The fog starts clearing between her ears. Then she starts singing like there's no tomorrow."

Sesko's arms crossed tighter. "I don't see how that means anything."

"I *know* it means something," said Milad. "My great-grandmother had Alzheimer's really bad. She'd sing too, but it was almost like the music was getting in the way of what she really wanted to say, like the song actually meant something else entirely. Like it was the only language she had left."

Sesko turned back to the whiteboard. "Do you think Peale is going to go ahead with it?"

"The traffic I'm seeing supports it. It has to be nuclear."

"Dirty bomb building blocks. Christ. Do we know who he's selling it to?"

"Too many layers in the encryption. But it's definitely someone we're not inviting over for Thanksgiving."

Sesko pulled the cap off a red dry-erase marker. He circled the picture of Norman Peale in the middle of the whiteboard. He capped the marker. He looked at the picture. "So, Wednesday?"

"Yes," said Milad. "Wednesday."

"Wednesday," said Sesko. He wrote the day on the whiteboard. He underlined it. Milad got up from the table. He handed back his ID badge, the one that had his real name on it.

CHAPTER
FORTY-THREE

It felt like old times. Sam had set up her writing materials on the Mulaney kitchen table. Jarrod and Steve Mulaney sat across from her. Jarrod's Prohibition beer had been upgraded to an actual Budweiser. She looked at the man who had worked with her father. "Uncle Jarrod, can you tell me about the day you bought that old station wagon?"

Jarrod Mulaney obliged. The detail was thick, right down to the temperature outside, the colour of the leaves on the downtown trees. "You were pretty shy," said Jarrod, smiling at his niece of a different bloodline. He even remembered that she would be going out for ice cream, if she was really good. "Did you get your ice cream? I think we have some in the freezer. Steve?"

"Just ran out," said Steve, a lie to keep things on track. "I can pick some up when I go to the store."

"That sounds great," said Sam. She placed her hand on Jarrod's. She smiled at him. "Because Uncle Jarrod, you've been really good."

Jarrod smiled back. "Do I get to pick what kind?"

"Just name it," said Sam.

"Then I pick chocolate," said Jarrod.

"A man after my own heart," said Sam. She checked her notes. Jarrod had gotten into some good detail on the memories of his interview. She entertained the idea of being more pointed with her questions about the goings-on of Consolidated Industries. *Keep it light, get it right.* The chat about the station wagon hadn't resulted in any agitation. "Uncle Jarrod, tell me about your next station wagon."

"Well, I guess it was a station wagon," said Jarrod. "But it was a lot bigger. GMC Suburban, three-quarter ton. Your dad thought it would be good for moving the gold to the planes. Wasn't very good on gas, though." Sam scrawled frantically as Jarrod relayed the story about the surplus aircraft, the gold from the Underground Research Laboratory dig, the fattening of the mileage on the company cars, and the final destinations of the gold and the planes. "Toppled a few banana republics with what was in the belly of those old clunks."

"Clunks?" said Steve.

"That's what the pilots called the Canuck," said Jarrod. "Something to do with the sound the landing gear made when it retracted. Never felt brave enough to go for a ride." Jarrod went on to explain the location of the camouflaged airstrip. "They would check out the planes there before they left. Used to fly down Bird Lake for kicks. Had a lot of neat stuff in there too, like a Canadian area fifty-something."

The conversation progressed through the rest of the company cars. Sam and Steve's eyes grew wider with the stories surrounding every new model. They were getting closer to the year that Gerry Hutchings perished in the fire at Eastland Lake. "I had just got a new Safari wagon," said Jarrod. "But things weren't good at work." He looked at Sam. "Your dad was really upset."

"What was it?" Sam asked. She worried that she might start squeezing the ink out of the pen with her grip.

Jarrod leaned closer. He crossed his hands together, somewhere between contemplating and praying for some kind of forgiveness. It wasn't a search for the memory—it was a search for the right words. "Sam, I . . ."

Sam put down her pen. She leaned closer and gently held his forearms. "It's OK, Uncle Jarrod. You can tell me."

Jarrod's eyes were getting moist. "I remember that Safari. Had blue velour. Your dad had that Batmobile."

Sam smiled. "The Grand National?"

"That's the one. Anyways, the gold was starting to dry up. The government had been under pressure to scrap the planes instead of selling them. The company was doing good. That tantalum stuff, it was going in every electronics thing you could swing a stick at. The lab, the underground research thing. All that space. Peale got this idea to—"

Sam stopped writing. "Peale. You mean *Norman* Peale?"

"That's right," said Jarrod. "He started out as Van Cleef's assistant just before I came on. More of a glorified gopher at first, but an ambitious gopher. Your old man didn't trust him as far as he could throw him."

"So, the Whiskey Jack, it's part of Consolidated Industries?"

"Always has been. Didn't your dad get you a job there when you were in school?"

Sam remembered. *I never had an interview.* The weirdness of the lodge was getting a lot weirder for Sam. *Megan!* Was that why she'd been hired so easily? Was she in danger? Had Sam put her in harm's way? What was really going on there? Sam dug into her memory, looking for anything that stood out. The military pictures on the wall. The military haircuts on the men. The pricey scotch. The Cuban cigars. *Money, and lots of it.* Dad never mentioned any of it. *The model float plane. The key in the black dildo plane.* Clues had been left behind, clues that someone was meant to find. Sam didn't know if it was supposed to be her.

She was lost in her thoughts when Jarrod broke the silence. "How's your mom doing?"

Sam snapped out of it. "Mom? Oh, not too bad. She's at the Whispering Pines in Pinawa. Been singing a lot lately."

Jarrod smiled. He got up from the table. He shuffled over to an ancient hi-fi next to the television. He lifted the top. "I'll bet you five dollars I know what she's singing," said Jarrod. He flipped through the albums that were stored in an inner cubby and pulled out an album with a generic sleeve that didn't look like much. Jarrod pulled out one of the discs. Sam saw the green apple. "Is that The Beatles?"

"The White Album," said Jarrod. He set the disc on the spindle. The record changer made a few chunky noises as it started up. Jarrod guided the tone arm to the third track. "This was your mom's favourite song." He lowered the needle.

A few cracks, a couple of pops. Then, an acoustic guitar. Sam knew it instantly. The song played on a variety of mediums over the years in the Hutchings' household, as well as in the vehicles. Vinyl, eight-track, cassette, compact disc. Sam knew that she had it on a playlist somewhere. It felt like an old friend had come to call.

"I can't remember the last time I heard 'Blackbird,'" she said.

"So," said Jarrod. "Do you have cash or cheque?"

Sam listened. The melody was familiar. "It sure sounds close. Maybe not five dollars' worth, but close."

"Typical Hutchings," said Jarrod, as he steadied himself over the spinning disc. "Always looking for a deal." Jarrod kept looking at the revolutions. "Blackbird," he said. He said it three more times. Something clicked. It wasn't the hi-fi. He turned to Sam. His face was starting to droop on one side. "Blackbird, Sam. Blackbir—"

Before Sam or Steve could jump up to help him, Jarrod Mulaney fell to the floor with the rest of his revelation.

CHAPTER FORTY-FOUR

Megan did her best not to freak out. She kept seeing the olive drab metal box under the vanity, with the Yale padlock looking back at her. *Why did I have to find that?* She stowed her cleaning supplies in the rear of the service cart. She passed Norman Peale on the path. He was moving at the slowest stroll possible. He gave a polite wave, topped off with a courteous grin. She drove the cart back to the main lodge.

Megan entered. There didn't appear to be any mandatory meetings for the day if the lack of letters on the glass case bulletin board could be believed. She looked out at the cove. The warmth of July had beckoned a few of the guests into the water on floating chaises, though the only cardio that seemed to be occurring was the lifting of beer cans to lips. A couple of canoes were making lazy loops in the sheltered bay. The building by the water had no guests on the deck. No ladies getting facials, no men having cigars.

There was no need for a fire. McMasters had given Megan the primer on how to stack the wood in the massive fireplace, open the flue, and crumple the newspaper to start it. But McMasters was nowhere to be seen. The only person present was Rhiannon. She was using one of the new vacuums on the rugs around the fireplace. She wore wireless earbuds. Whatever the tune, it was a motivating one. Megan decided to move in front of her, instead of a back tap that could be frightening. Rhiannon didn't startle when she saw her. She paused the playlist on her phone. "You all done in the cabins?"

"Yeah," said Megan. She thought about relaying the weirdness of the cabins and the discovery of the lockbox. *Peale*. She decided to stay on task. "What's next on the list?"

"Master McMasters said to pull the fishing rods out of the garage," said Rhiannon. "Some of the guests are getting tired of having someone else catch their supper, I guess. Or the steaks have started to clog what's left of their arteries."

Megan looked confused. "Doesn't the garage have a security code?"

"Real tough one," said Rhiannon. "One, two, three, four."

Megan chuckled. "Must be some valuable stuff in there."

The overhead door rose with ease. Megan scanned the space as Rhiannon entered. The garage was well organized. None of the fishing rods were tangled together. The tackle boxes were stowed on a custom-made shelf that seemed fitted to the boxes' exact dimensions. Mr. Peale's Rolls-Royce was parked in the centre, its position aided by a red rubber ball that hung from a length of fishing line at the rear of the garage. The ball rested between the backswept wings of the hood ornament.

"Sir Vance-a-lot also wants some more life jackets," said Rhiannon.

Megan looked around the garage. "Where are they?"

"I think they're behind that old three-wheeler," said Rhiannon.

Megan shimmied past the battered Honda trike on the driver's side of the Rolls. She found the extra life jackets, all hanging from wooden coat hangers in an open closet. It looked as though it would be easier to bring the jackets around the front of the car than past the trike. The first two trips went well. On the third trip, she dropped one of the jackets on the ground by the driver's door. As she went to pick it up, she froze. The shelf held a stack of plastic model kits. She slid the top-most kit off its perch. She wiped off the dust. The box was a photograph of a float plane, a picture that must have been taken as it was gathering speed across the water for takeoff. The plane wore a familiar logo, slightly different from the ones on the shirts of the Whiskey Jack staff. "Hey, Rhee," said Megan. "Ever see one of these?"

Rhiannon nodded. "I think my dad had one. It was hanging in our trailer for the longest time. Knew that plane more than I ever knew him."

Megan flipped the box over. "How come we don't sell them with the shirts and stuff?"

"I think it was a promo gift thing once you'd worked here for a long time. Guess I'm still a newbie."

Megan slid the model kit back onto the shelf. She grabbed the life jacket from the ground. She dusted off the dirt as best she could. She glanced inside the vintage Rolls as she rose up with the jacket. A lot of leather and a lot of wood looked back at her. *I guess it was a thing.* The interior of the car was tidy, with one exception: a stack of papers that must have come off a laser-jet printer. She tried the driver's door. *Locked.* The vantage point from the driver's side wasn't the best. She went around to the passenger side. She tried the door handle but found no success. She looked through the glass.

The sheets on the passenger seat appeared to be printouts from a website. There was a Canadian flag in the upper left-hand corner. The grayscale images weren't very detailed. The punch came from what a red marker had circled a few items. "Hey, Rhee," said Megan. "Take a look at this."

Rhiannon peeked through the window. "Wow, that wood is crazy."

"Not the wood," said Megan. "The papers. On the seat. What's that from?"

Rhiannon looked closer. "Oh, that's GC Surplus."

Megan had never heard of it. "GC what-plus?"

"Government of Canada Surplus," said Rhiannon. "It's like an online auction for federal government stuff. My mom goes on it all the time. They got all sorts of weird shit for sale. My bike came from the nukes' place in Pinawa."

"Why would a nuclear power plant need a bike?"

"To get around, I guess. Nothing special, just a beach cruiser with a big-ass basket on the front. Doesn't even have hand brakes on it."

Megan looked back at the papers. "So how do you bid on stuff?"

Rhiannon had already called up the site on her phone. "All you do is look up the area that's closest to you. When you find something you want, you put in a bid. It's not like eBay, so you don't know what the other people are bidding." She clicked on a listing for a lot of tools at the Pinawa labs. "So it says the minimum bid is forty bucks. You put in a little more than that, or a lot more, if you really want it. If you bid the most, you get it. My mom's got a system. She'll do weird numbers."

"Weird? Weird how?"

"The small change. Let's say these tools are worth fifty bucks. That's what a lot of people will bid. All you need to do is bid more than everybody else. Mom throws in some change. Instead of fifty-three bucks, she'll bid fifty-three bucks and seventy-nine cents. That's how we got the bike."

Megan took another look at the papers. She couldn't see the images clearly. Then she got an idea. "Rhee, bring up the rest of the Manitoba stuff."

Rhiannon brought up the page. "OK, now what?"

"Start scrolling through," said Megan. "I want to try to match up the page."

"Why?" said Rhiannon. "You want to outbid old man Peale on some ball-peen hammers?"

"Just scroll," said Megan. "I'll tell you the rest later."

Norman Peale waited until Megan Goodman had finished with the Blackbird cabin. He smiled and gave a friendly wave as she drove the service cart back to the main lodge. Once she was out of sight, he doubled back. He tapped the door open with his master key. He headed for the bathroom. He steadied himself against the vanity to lower himself to the floor. He removed the trim piece with the magnetic catches and placed it on the top of the vanity. He retrieved the ammunition box. The trip upwards was a little slower than he would have liked. *Damned arthritis.* He brought the box to the small dinette table in the bedroom. The Yale key took a few jiggles to open the lock. He opened the lid and removed a blue three-ring binder.

The three rings were running out of room. The first set of pages dated back to the eighties. Pre-internet. The sheets were official documents from the Government of Canada's Assets Recovery Department. They were notifications of successful bids for various items that had started their life in the Whiteshell Laboratories. He flipped through the older entries to the newest, papers that now bore evidence of the dawn of online bidding. The items ran the gambit, from tool cabinets to machinery. Successful bid after successful bid. *Successful smuggling.* He retrieved his phone from his shirt pocket. The current items on offer from the labs were ending soon, at 9 a.m. EST on Wednesday. Tomorrow. Peale knew what would happen next. The emails would arrive shortly after the auctions closed, informing him of his successful bids. He would be instructed on how to pick up the items. The point person at the labs would already be moving the items into position—items with sizable voids that held things that hadn't made it into the official auction descriptions. The pickup, then the transfer of the items to the rooms of his American guests. Where they went after that was not his concern. The payments had been received in advance.

Peale slid the binder back into the ammunition box. He locked it with the padlock. He slid the box back into its hiding place. He reached up to the top of the vanity to retrieve the trim piece and brought it down to the magnetic catches.

Peale walked back to the main lodge.

CHAPTER
FORTY-FIVE

Gerry Hutchings headed west on 315. The road to Werner Lake was still passable as he crossed into Ontario, as long as you knew what you were doing. Anyone dumb enough to barrel down the stretch would lose an oil pan within ten minutes. Slow and steady.

The forest wasn't happy about the road. It appeared to be actively trying to reclaim it. Branches from neighbouring trees brushed into the glass and paintwork of the Grand National along the route. *It's almost time to retire it anyway.* Gerry checked his pager. He had lied to Jarrod

Mulaney. The caller wasn't Peale, though the subject matter for the meeting would be.

There weren't any other motorists around to warrant a turn signal for the right turn. Gerry did it out of habit. The tree branches were even closer. Gerry hoped that the scratches would buff out. The road opened into a clearing on the shore of Davidson Lake. It was an old campground, one that Ontario had seemed to have forgotten about. It had seen plenty of visitors over the years, judging by the scorched fire marks on the rocks and beer bottle remnants.

There was another car at the campground site, a gold Plymouth Gran Fury that screamed Undercover Cop. *And these guys are the Canadian CIA?* The car's sole occupant was leaning up against the fender. He wore a white short-sleeved shirt, a blue tie, and black slacks with blacker shoes. His hair was jet black, though the wrinkles on his face meant that the black was courtesy of Grecian Formula. He had a Pepsi can for an ashtray. The man took one last drag before putting the half-smoked cigarette in the can. He walked towards Gerry. Gerry killed the engine and exited the Grand National. "Middleton?"

"Call me Rick," said Middleton. He gave Gerry a textbook example of a firm handshake. He looked around the site. "Might have to come up here and do some camping with the kids, if I can pry them away from that goddamn Nintendo."

"Mine haven't got into it, thankfully," said Gerry. "School and work mostly."

"Lucky man," said Rick. "So, find anything else out since we spoke?"

Gerry went through the high points of the last meeting. Rick nodded as he produced a notebook, adding to it as Gerry explained what he knew. "All I know for sure is that August is supposed to be a busy month."

Rick finished scribbling his thoughts. He closed the notebook and looked at Gerry. "You do realize how crazy this whole thing sounds, don't you?"

"I do," said Gerry.

"And you have access to the records?"

Gerry thought about the freshly hidden key. "Accessible. Locked up tight."

Rick tapped the notebook against his chin. "Here's the thing, Gerry. We keep in close contact with anything involving nuclear energy. We have to. If any of this stuff gets into the wrong hands—"

"There's more to it than that," said Gerry. "A lot more."

"Jesus," said Rick. "Do I get a fucking hint?"

"Can you guarantee protection?"

"Well, we do the best we can, but we haven't even had an official statement on—"

"Not for me. My family."

"Does your family know anything?"

"Nothing. Not a thing."

"Then, what's the problem?"

Gerry went to say what the problem was. That's when he realized that there wasn't any. He had kept Lena and the kids well insulated from the goings-on at Consolidated. He could look himself in the mirror for most of what he had done for the firm. *Not anymore.* Peale's moral compass had started to spin faster, out of control. *Creative in all the wrong ways.* He had to be stopped.

Rick snapped him back. "So, what's the plan?"

Gerry looked at Rick. "Underground. Six months. I'll give you everything."

It was clear to Sam that Jarrod Mulaney had suffered a massive stroke. It took about twenty minutes for the ambulance to arrive. He was conscious, but non-verbal. Sam stayed close to him as they waited. Steve was frantically communicating with the 911 operator. Sam offered to secure the cabin for him. She thought about going with him to the hospital. Then she thought about Megan. "I need to pick her up later, and you'll probably be a while."

Steve looked at the paramedics as they secured his father to the gurney. "That's probably the understatement of the year."

Sam went to the table. She scrawled her number on one of the paper scraps. "Text me and let me know what's going on. Are you going in the ambulance?"

"I better," said Steve. "Can you come get me once I know?"

"Of course I can," said Sam. She gave him the quickest, biggest hug possible. She followed the group to the ambulance.

There weren't many cottage dwellers on Block Fifteen that week, but the ones who were there came out to see what was up. Lisa Janzen was one of them. She had just arrived in her flip-flops as the ambulance door was closed. "Was it the old man or the old-ish man?"

Sam rolled her eyes in disgust. "Jesus, Leese."

"What?" said Lisa. "Steve-Oh's gotta be getting up there."

"He's our age," said Sam. "And it was Mr. Mulaney." She knew that saying it as such would mean the elder to a child who grew up in the seventies.

"Oh shit," said Lisa. "How old is he?"

"Old enough to have a fucking stroke, that's how old!"

Lisa bristled. "Hey! What the fuck?"

Sam wasn't having any of it. She started walking back towards her cabin. Lisa trotted as best as she could in her poor footwear choice. "Hey, I'm sorry. I didn't mean like, that he's *supposed* to be having a stroke at that age or nothing. I'm just saying."

"He wouldn't shut up about 'Blackbird.'"

Lisa stopped. "Bees are on the what now?"

Sam kept moving. "'Blackbird.' You know, the Beatles song? Said it was Mom's favourite. Then he started saying it over and over and over. Then he hit the floor."

Lisa picked up the pace. "Do you think that's the one that your mom has been singing?"

"Maybe." The two lake buds had reached the Hutchings' cabin. Sam flung the door open, almost clipping Lisa. She swore under her breath at the near miss. Sam grabbed the laptop off her makeshift desk and brought it to the kitchen counter. The boot-up was quick. Sam Googled Blackbird. The first entry that came up was the 2009 remaster of the song. She started playing it. She looked at the lyrics that accompanied the search. "Is there anything here, Leese? Any big-ass clue jumping out at you?"

Lisa scanned the lyrics. "I dunno. *Moment to arise* sounds a little like code."

The pair listened to the song. Two minutes and eighteen seconds later, Sam brought up the images tab of the Google search. There were quite a few species of blackbirds throughout the world. Lisa stated the obvious. "Some of them got a lot of colour on them to be called a blackbird, don't you think?"

Sam scanned the pictures. She stopped. "What the fuck?"

"Where?" said Lisa. "What is it?"

Sam couldn't believe it. If she hadn't scrolled down a few rows, she may have never seen it. It was in the Related Searches field. She pointed at the picture. "The dildo."

Lisa squinted at the image. "That's not a dildo. That's a plane."

"Right," said Sam. "The black dildo plane! The Blackbird!"

Sam clicked on the image. It was the same plane that had recently hung in the rafters, the one her brother Chris hadn't built, the one with the Yale key that had been hidden in the fuselage. *The SR-71 Blackbird*. Sam did a quick scan of the Wiki information. The plane had been used for high-altitude reconnaissance missions, a task that it could accomplish at over three times the speed of sound. It didn't have to worry about surface-to-air missiles: it could simply outrun them.

"The Blackbird," said Sam. "It's a spy plane."

Lisa's voice spiked. "Your dad was a spy?"

"I have no idea. I guess leaving all these breadcrumbs lying around is a spy thing, isn't it?"

"But spying on what?"

"There was stuff going on, Leese. Hinky stuff." Sam explained the revelations from the recent chat with Jarrod Mulaney. She flipped through her notes. "Cold war, on the QT, very hush-hush."

"And it was still going on? Even after your dad died?"

"I was hoping to ask Mr. Mulaney that. Then he hit the floor."

Lisa lifted her Oiseau Garage cap for a quick head scratch. She slapped Sam with a revelatory backhand on her shoulder. "What about your mom?"

Sam winced at the point of contact. "What about her?"

"Maybe now that we know it's all about 'Blackbird.' It might flip a switch."

Sam thought about the switch that had just flipped inside Jarrod Mulaney's head. "I dunno, Leese. Might freak her out into a stroke too."

"We'll be delicate."

Sam blinked. "You? Delicate?"

"Let's take Mongo," said Lisa. "You drive like an old man."

FORTY-SIX

Sam wasn't sure who knew the road better: Lisa or the battered Jeep that was grabbing air over the hills of 315. Even the horn was as loud as the personality of the driver. "Put in some air horns out of an old Kenworth," said Lisa, over the din of the mechanicals. "Turns a white-tail into a brown-tail when they hear it!"

Sam was starting to think she might become similarly afflicted. "I don't think they have another ambulance in Pinawa to come and get us!"

Lisa hit the horn for the next hill. "Just because you have a pussy doesn't mean you have to be one!"

The Lisa Janzen Jeep Experience shaved a solid eleven minutes off the commute time to Whispering Pines. She hit the brakes hard in the gravel parking lot, sending a plume of dust into the front of the building. Sam made it to the front door first. She did get a dirty look from the staffer at the front desk as she trucked past, with Lisa in hot pursuit. If it had been high school, someone in authority would have told them to slow down. They had to deke around a couple of slow-moving walker pilots and Milad the orderly, who just about lost the finished food tray he was transferring to the cart. Sam turned and mouthed sorry to him. Lisa turned and shrugged for punctuation.

Sam peeked inside Lena's room. The TV was off, something that she thought wasn't possible. Lena had donned her reading glasses for the task at hand, a puzzle of the Manitoba Legislature. It was about sixty percent finished. Sam smiled. *The lines are now open.* She tapped on the wall to enter. "Hi, Mom?"

Lena looked up, removing her reading glasses for a clearer view. "Samantha? I didn't know you were coming. Did you bring a blueberry pie?"

"Have to pick up some more Tenderflake at the Solo," said Sam. "How about Thursday?"

Lena shook her head. "You must be doing something wrong if it takes you two days to make a pie."

Lisa snorted. Lena heard it. She knew the snort. "Lisa? Lisa *Janzen?*"

Lisa pulled off her ball cap, adding three full seconds of primp on her hair before answering. "Hi, Lena. How's the puzzle going?"

Lena looked down at her work. "I think it's going quite well. I wasn't planning on constructing The Manitoba House of the Lying Bastards, but that's what Milad brought me."

Sam was impressed. *Me, Lisa, even the right name for Milad.* She moved in closer to admire her progress. "Looks great, Mom."

"Thank you, Samantha."

Milad tapped on the door frame. "Miss Lena? Anything to be needing?"

"Do you have any wine?" said Lena. "My friends look a little parched."

Milad smiled. "No wine today, Miss Lena. Juice, yes?"

Sam nodded. So did Lisa. Lena looked at each of the nods. She looked at Milad. "Make it three, Milad. Three juice, straight up."

Milad left the room. Sam and Lisa helped along with the puzzle. A few minutes passed. Lena looked at the doorway. "I suppose he must be squeezing the fruit by hand today. He might need an extra set."

Sam thought about how much fun it was for one person to carry three full cups of any liquid. "I'll go see if he needs any help."

The walker pilots had disappeared from the hallway. Sam didn't see Milad. She went past the rooms of the residents to the kitchen. It was really more of a warming station for the food service trays that came in. There was a fridge, a commercial microwave, and a toaster oven on the counter. Two of the juice cups had been poured. The third cup was empty. Sam lifted the oversized juice box next to the cups. *Empty.* Milad must have gone to fetch more juice.

A coiled pocket notebook was next to the juice cups. It was open to some recent notes. *Probably keeping track of the feedings,*

Sam thought. She glanced at the book. The glance became a look. She picked up the notebook and read the notes.

> 8:10 AM: Breakfast, no singing. TV off.

> 10:42 AM: Napping. Slight singing, same song. Audio capture, search. Not identified.

> 11:42 AM: Lunch, no singing. TV on.

> 3:49 PM: Daughter visit with friend, puzzle, something about pie. Is pie important? Blueberry?

Sam flipped through the other pages. The notebook chronicled the moments within her mother's room at the Whispering Pines. A lot of notes about her singing, asking what it meant, what the song was. More important, the notes sounded nothing like the fractured English of Milad's speech. Sam flipped through the book. She stopped. The reflection in the toaster on the counter had changed. She turned to see Milad. He had his hands forward in a calming state. The voice was new. "Samantha don't panic. Let me ex—"

Sam panicked. She grabbed a full glass of juice and threw it in Milad's face. There was a slight reaction. His hands were still in a calming state. The juice was dripping off his face. He looked down at the mess on his uniform. He looked at Sam. "OK. I'm not going to hurt you. I'm not the bad guy here."

Sam looked at the counter. A plastic bread knife was resting on top of a paper plate. She grabbed it. "Don't come any fucking closer." She kept an eye on Milad as she grabbed the notebook. She motioned him to kneel on the floor. "On your knees, hands where I can see them."

Milad obliged, slowly, as though he wanted to make sure that he didn't startle Sam on the way down to the floor. His hands remained in a calming state. "I can explain every—"

"Why are you spying on my mom?"

"She might know something."

"She might know something about *what*?"

"About the Whiskey Jack. About Peale."

Sam moved forward. She could feel her heart pounding. She kept a firm grip on the plastic knife. She had heard once that plastic cutlery could kill, probably on an episode of *Orange Is the New Black*. Milad must have seen the same episode. *Milad*. "Who are you, really? Who do you work for?"

"My name is Aaron. Aaron Sen. I'm with CSIS."

"Where's your badge?"

"I'm undercover."

"You don't sound like you're from Syria."

"I'm not. I'm from Surrey."

"What the hell is CSIS doing in an old folks' home?"

It looked like Aaron wasn't sure if what he said next would diffuse or ignite the situation in front of him. He went for broke. "We think Peale had your dad killed. And Van Cleef. And the Peeters family. And a guy named Koshelanyk. Plus a whole lot of other bad stuff."

The words hit Sam like a Mack truck. She felt the tears welling up. She punctuated her points with the knife. "My dad died in a forest fire on July 29, 1989. At Eastland Lake."

Aaron looked at Sam. Calm, cool, collected. The scare of the knife had left the room. He slowly rose from the floor. Sam still had the knife. He reached for it and gently took it from her. He put the knife on the counter, looking at Sam.

"Do you still think that's true?"

Sam's tears flowed heavy and hard. Aaron held her wrists gently. She pounded her fists on his chest. It felt like hitting a brick wall. It was bad enough that her father was dead. The possibility that someone had done it to him made it a thousand times worse. She felt the mourning reactivate for Mr. Van Cleef, Zach's family. *Koshelanyk?* Wasn't that the last name of the girl Megan worked with? *Megan!* Sam lost it. She looked at Aaron wide-eyed. "My daughter. My daughter's at the lodge! He's got my daughter!"

Aaron continued to hold onto Sam's wrists. He tried his best to calm her. "He couldn't possibly suspect—"

"Blackbird!"

"What? Is that the song?"

"Yes. I mean, no."

"Sam, what are you trying to tell me?"

"Blackbird," said Sam. "I think I know what it means!"

"Sam, we should—"

Aaron didn't get a chance to finish his sentence. Lisa clocked him from behind with a bedpan. He fell to the floor in a heap. Sam looked at her lake bud. Lisa returned an equally confused look. She looked at the bedpan.

"What? It was clean."

CHAPTER
FORTY-SEVEN

Norman Peale had navigated his way to the
GC Surplus website. He had plenty of time to
input the winning bids for the auction items at
the Whiteshell Laboratories. Something was
nagging at him. He was ninety-five percent sure
it was nothing. *The smallest truth demands accuracy.* Ninety-five percent wasn't a hundred.

Peale clicked on the Manitoba listings. There
were three items up for bid that Peale needed
to acquire. Within those items were the other
items—ones that he had received payment
for from his American guests. He wanted to

place the bids before he joined his guests for dinner. *T-Bone Tuesday*. Just thinking of the evening fare kickstarted a Pavlovian response in Peale's salivary glands. At least he was high enough up the evolutionary chain to not drool on his button-down shirt.

The first item was a large steel cabinet, a specialized bright yellow unit designed to hold flammable liquids. The second sale lot was comprised of three purple filing cabinets. *It must have been a thing*, Peale thought. The last item was a mid-eighties model Chevrolet panel van that had a laundry list of mechanical problems. The faded blue paint had been peeling off the bodywork for years. The van had a specific caveat for the auction listing in block letters: VEHICLE MUST BE TOWED FROM SITE. Peale had already arranged for a towing company to retrieve the van from the lab on Wednesday after the auction had closed. The other items would already be inside the van.

Winning the bids had all the drama of a sunrise: it was going to happen. The GC Surplus website provided interested parties with information on winning bids from across the country. The location was also a factor. The locals might be interested in tools, bicycles, or a vehicle that was actually drivable. The items would have to be very special for someone to make the trek from Winnipeg to pick it up. Peale would typically do a thirty percent markup, based on the historical bid information. There were probably plenty of headshakes after an area local had checked on the winning bid and found out they'd lost to someone who was willing to pay much more. If only they knew what was inside.

The five percent. The nagging was getting the better of Peale. He placed the three bids, then closed out his session on the website. He made his way through the lodge. He was almost at the front door when Jake Kinsey intercepted him. "Afternoon, Norman."

"And a pleasant afternoon to you, Mr. Kinsey."

"Jake, Norman. After all these years, you of all people can call me Jake."

"The curse of the courteous innkeeper. How was the fishing today?"

Jake gave Peale a polite direction change on his shoulder. "Walk with me, Norman." He motioned him over to the largest of the couches near the fireplace. The two men sat. Jake waited until two of the staffers had finished their cleaning chores in the vicinity. He turned to Peale. "I believe tomorrow is Hump Day, isn't it?"

Peale nodded. "One of many references for a Wednesday, Jake. One of many."

"And speaking of humpin', I do hope that it will be only a consideration of the missus, Norman. Catching my drift?"

Peale shook his head. "There's nothing to worry about, Jake. I've already made the necessary arrangements. The items that we have promised to you and the other members will be ready upon your departure."

"In secure packaging?" Jake asked.

"Undetectable," said Peale. "You might say that we do have it down to something approaching art after more than forty years, Jake."

"I'd say Rembrandt," said Jake. He scratched his chin, somehow warming up the next thought by doing so. "You ever wonder about history, Norman?"

"I try not to think about the past, Jake. It serves little purpose."

"Not history-history," said Jake. "What I mean is, how will

history remember us? How will history describe what we are doing? What we have done?"

Peale leaned forward and spoke quietly. "Jake, my friend, I have done everything in my power to ensure that history will never know us. It serves no purpose. If history did stumble upon us, what would it discover? Top secret. Eyes only. Classified. History does not understand, nor does it appreciate the amount of maintenance involved in keeping the world as we know it, or, as John Q. Public knows it, on an even keel. History is just another form of media. The only ones who can tell this story are you and me. It stays with us. It dies with us."

Peale adjusted his position in the well-worn leather. He continued. "Your history will not include our dealings, Jake. You'll be laid to rest at Arlington, three-volley salute, a rousing burst of 'Taps,' and a folded flag. That is all that history can afford you, Jake. I truly hope that is enough."

"It'll have to do, Norman," said Jake. "It'll have to do."

The two men rose from the couch. They shook hands. Peale motioned towards the door. "Now if you'll excuse me, Jake, I just need to tend to one of the cabins."

Jake gave a quick and casual salute. "As you were, Norman. As you were."

Peale smiled. He exited the lodge and headed down the gravel path towards the bird cabins. He walked up the steps of the Blackbird and opened the door with his key card. The cabin was still empty. He walked around it slowly. *Something is not quite right.* He checked the drawers, looked under the bed, and checked the light fixtures. He walked to the bathroom. He checked behind the shower curtain and looked in the medicine cabinet. He tapped his key card against his chin. He was almost out of the bathroom when he dropped it. *Damned arthritis.* He bent down in front of the vanity. He saw what was wrong. He went to the phone next to the bed and keyed in a three-digit number. The phone connected on the third ring. "Yes?"

"McMasters."

"Yes, Mr. Peale? Is there a problem at Blackbird?"

"The new girl."

"Megan?"

"Yes, Megan. The legacy."

"What about her?"

"What time does her shift end tonight?"

"Around ten-thirty, maybe eleven. All depends on T-Bone Tuesday. Is there a problem?"

Peale looked back at the vanity in the bathroom. "Yes, McMasters. I'm afraid there is."

JULY 29, 1989
SOMEWHERE NEAR EASTLAND LAKE

Gerry Hutchings looked up at the thunderhead. He looked down at the forest floor. *Dry as a bone.* The forecast had been calling for thunderstorms for the weekend. The fire risk was as red as the signs would allow.

Gerry checked his backpack. He had enough provisions for the trek out of the area, as long as the wind kept moving in the direction of the forecast. He had been marking the trail for the last month, using the tops of old soup cans, a hammer, and nails that weren't straight enough to use for carpentry. He checked his watch. It was coming up on 5 p.m. He hadn't heard a rumble yet.

He heard the footsteps before he saw Jarrod Mulaney. His gait sounded as signature through pine needles and leaves as it did on pavement or gravel, even with the heavy backpack. As dry as it was, the shelter of the trees was still enough to invite plenty of mosquitoes to the party. Gerry reapplied the pungent Muskol. He tossed the bottle over to Jarrod. He fumbled but was able to control and catch it before it hit the ground. "I guess the Blue Bombers won't be calling anytime soon."

"Well, it's still technically a catch," said Gerry. "Besides, with your bum leg, I'll bet you're a shoo-in for the Roughriders."

Jarrod laughed. "Ottawa or Saskatchewan?"

Gerry didn't miss a beat. "Does it matter?"

The two men shared the laugh. Gerry ended his laugh first. Jarrod closed it out. Forced. Nervous. He removed his backpack. He removed the portable television, a battery-powered unit that included a cassette player and an AM/FM radio. Gerry gave him his wallet, his dental partial, his watch, and his keys. Jarrod would find them, as discussed. He would wait until nightfall to set the Hutchings' canoe adrift. Like Gerry, Jarrod had his cabin to himself this weekend.

There was a slight clearing near the rendezvous. It had been used for a campsite at one point, the remnants of a hastily constructed firepit, with chunks of rock that looked like complete failures at becoming puzzle pieces. Gerry brought the TV unit over to the site. He extended the antenna to the fullest height. He switched the unit on. A snowstorm eventually appeared on the screen. He turned the volume down to zero. He looked at Jarrod. "You honestly think this will work?"

"We've got a severe weather warning till eleven tonight," said Jarrod. He pointed skywards. "When those clouds start getting angry, they're going to be looking to lob a few bolts. Anything metal takes priority, especially something that's buzzing away like this."

"Did you get the good batteries?"

"Radio Shack," said Jarrod. "The gold ones."

Gerry smiled. "Gold. How appropriate."

"So, six months, right?"

Gerry nodded. "That's what I told him. And hey, sorry I couldn't be up front about it. I had to—"

"Make sure," said Jarrod, completing the thought. "I get it. Peale has friendlies everywhere."

"Thought at all about what's next?"

Jarrod chuckled. "Federal prison?"

Gerry returned the chuckle. *Federal prison.* Gerry had teetered that scale of justice back and forth. The one thing he knew for sure was that Consolidated would be dead as disco when the truth came out. The Canadian government and the American State Department would be all over it. *Middle managers, that's all we were.* Peale, his current military players, they were the bad guys. The immediate downside would be unemployment. *Maybe a book deal.* He started swapping the needed items from his smaller pack into the larger pack that Jarrod had brought. He checked the side pockets. Something was missing. He looked at Jarrod. "Where's the gun?"

Jarrod removed the small automatic from the side pocket of his windbreaker. He removed the clip, then reinserted it. He handed it to Gerry. "You sure a twenty-two is big enough? I think some bears might disagree with you."

Gerry put the gun into his pack. "Then I guess I better agree with everything that bear has to say." He hoisted the pack onto his back and adjusted the straps. "How do I look?"

Jarrod smiled. "Like one of those assholes from B.C. who drives one of those slow-ass Volkswagen campers."

Gerry extended his hand. "Keep an eye on Lena and the kids, OK?" Jarrod ignored the hand, going in for the awkward hug. Gerry wasn't expecting it, but he did his best not to add to the awkwardness. Gerry pushed off after fifteen seconds. "I'll see you in six months." He headed towards the path. "Don't forget," said Gerry.

"Forget what?" said Jarrod.

"The canoe," said Gerry.

"I won't," said Jarrod.

Gerry looked back only once and saw Jarrod arranging the items he had brought around the staged campsite.

CHAPTER FORTY-NINE

The man who Sam had first known as Milad had yet to come to. The same was true of the man she now knew as Aaron Sen, an undercover something in the employ of the Canadian Security Intelligence Service. The clunky English, the accent, all an act. Lisa had done an impressive job of employing the fireman's carry to get him into the backseat of her Jeep. "Don't they let these guys eat?" she had said, during the initial scoop off the floor.

"Are you sure you don't need any help?" Sam asked.

"Not until he discovers Whopper Wednesday," said Lisa.

Sam had rolled her eyes at that. She had told Lena that she had to go to work, as politely as she could under the circumstances. The type of work that Lena decided was accurate for her daughter didn't matter. Sam did have to go to work: the work of getting her daughter out of harm's way. Steve Mulaney had texted with the news that Jarrod was stable, and that he could use a ride back. He was taken aback when he opened the passenger door on Lisa's Jeep at the Pinawa Hospital. She didn't wait for him to question the existence of an unconscious stranger in the back seat, the one that Sam was keeping an eye on. Lisa threw the Jeep into reverse and mashed the gas.

"Jesus," said Steve, as he braced himself. "What the hell is going on? Who the hell is that?"

"CSIS spy guy," said Sam. "We've got to get back. Megan, she might be in trouble!"

"What's CSIS got to do with Megan?" said Steve. He slid into the door hard as Lisa cranked the wheel. He looked at Lisa. "You got more than one speed in this thing? Other than *Dukes of Hazzard*?"

Lisa was of the generation. "Folks in Pinawa hadn't seen a Jeep get driven like that in a long time."

"Ungh," said Aaron. He was starting to stir.

"He's waking up!" said Sam.

Aaron's eyes started to flutter. He saw Sam. He saw the friend of hers who must have bopped him on the head driving hard. He saw a rather large gentleman in the front seat who screamed ex-cop with fries, looking back at him with a Don't Try Anything look. "Wha . . . why did you . . . my head . . ."

"Lisa would like to apologize," said Sam, as she helped Aaron into a seated position. "Wouldn't you, Lisa?"

"Yeah, sorry, busy driving here." She slowed briefly as the Jeep made the transition from Pinawa town to the highway. Very briefly.

"My, my notebook," said Aaron.

Sam produced it. She flipped through the most recent pages. *Singing.* She pointed to the entries as she found them, showing them to Aaron. "You keep pointing this out, my mom singing." She read some more. "Audio capture?"

Aaron explained. "The song she was singing. It sounded familiar, but I couldn't place it. I couldn't—"

"Why did you need to place it?"

Aaron held the back of his head. "I thought, I thought it was important, you know? Like she was remembering something. I recorded it." He fumbled through his pockets and produced a small digital recorder. He handed it to Sam. "This was this morning. I *know* I've heard it before!"

Sam pressed Play. The song that Lena Hutchings had been singing had found the right notes. She hit Rewind. She looked at Steve. They had heard the song on the Mulaney hi-fi, right before Steve's father had his stroke.

Lisa added the lyrics, sort of. "Something-something-something learn to fly."

"'Blackbird,'" said Sam.

"'Blackbird,'" said Steve.

Lisa added. "Something-something-something for this moment to arrive."

"The dildo," said Sam.

Steve's eyebrows shot up. "The what-doh?"

"The dildo," said Sam. "The black dildo plane! Blackbird!"

No one knew quite what to say. The rumble of the Jeep filled the void for a few more seconds. Then Sam remembered.

"The Whiskey Jack. There was a Blackbird cabin!"

"What cabin?" said Lisa.

"Yeah, what cabin?" said Steve.

Sam explained to the group about the naming of the cabins at the lodge. "There was a cul-de-sac, at the back of the property, near the fence. There were three cabins. They were all named after birds. One was named Blackbird, I'm sure of it!"

"What were the other two called?" Lisa asked.

"Donald and Daffy Duck," said Sam. "How the fuck should I know?"

"Geez, sensitive," said Lisa.

"What about Blackbird?" said Aaron. "Was there anything special about it?"

"I, I don't remember," said Sam. "It must have been what Mom was trying to sing. Mr., I mean, Uncle Jarrod knew it too. He played it on the hi-fi."

"Is something hidden there?" said Steve.

"Something's there," said Aaron. "Something's going to be there. Tomorrow. There are people waiting for it."

"Who's waiting for it? What is it?" said Sam.

Aaron gave his best 101 explanation of the dark web to his Jeepmates. "We don't know what it is, or the quantity. The messages we've been able to intercept point to Wednesday. Whatever it is, it can't be good."

"Why not?" said Lisa.

"The countries they're coming from," said Aaron. "Plenty of terror cells. Militias, cartels, you name it. Even some domestic terror threats in the States."

"What do you CSIS guys think it is?" said Steve. "And don't try to tell us its classified."

"Well, it *is* classified," said Aaron. "We think it's nuclear."

"Nuclear. What, like a bomb?" said Sam.

"It wouldn't be an actual device," said Aaron. "But it could be the pieces to make a bomb, most likely a dirty bomb."

"Wow," said Lisa. "This is next-level James Bond shit."

Aaron continued. "All we know for sure is that we've had a few flags come up in the region for chatter. Then we dug into the history. And Sam's dad."

"What about my dad?" Sam didn't like the tone. She also didn't like what she was hearing. *Don't shoot the messenger.* Sam wasn't sure how she felt about Aaron's telling of her father's history. One thing she knew for sure: there was more to her father than she ever knew, maybe more than she would ever want to know. Like it or not, she was about to find out.

"Your dad had reached out in '89," said Aaron. "All we know is that there was an initial meeting, then nothing. The dark web chatter started up this year in the spring in a big way. That's when I was assigned to the whole thing."

"Big hill," said Lisa. The Jeep grabbed a smidge of air.

"You tried to tell me something about my dad before Lisa knocked you out," said Sam. "What was it?"

"It was—"

Steve screamed. "DEER!"

The buck didn't have a chance. Lisa didn't have time to brake. The lifted Jeep hit the buck, knocked it down, and went over it. The right front tire sunk into the soft shoulder. It pulled the Jeep into the ditch. Cattails, water, and mud flew through the air. Steam rose from the front of the Jeep. The occupants checked themselves for injuries. Lisa let the entire Jeep know what she was thinking. "You better be dead, you stupid assclown buck!"

"Is everybody OK?" Sam asked.

"I think my head hit the roof," said Steve.

"I really don't want to hit my head anymore today," said Aaron. He had a cut from the impact; not a gusher, but noticeable.

The Jeepmates made their way out. The buck had been killed on impact. About half of its rack had broken off, now lodged in the radiator of the Jeep. Lisa looked around. "Aren't we near Peeters's place?"

Sam mimicked the look. "Yeah, I think it's right over the next hill."

The Jeepmates started walking.

Megan knew that she had found parts of a much larger puzzle in the front seat of Norman Peale's Rolls. *The padlock.* The only way she would know for sure would be to try the key her mother had found in the lock that secured the metal box. *Mr. Peale.* Why was he bidding on those junky things at the Whiteshell Laboratories? *The Blackbird cabin. The gold ball in Peale's room. Her grandfather in the photo.* Megan knew one thing for sure: she had to get out of the Whiskey Jack as fast as she could. *Mom!* She had to let her know. She turned to Rhiannon. "Is there another way out of here?"

Rhiannon blinked. "Why would you need another way out of here?"

Megan looked closely at Rhiannon's eyes. *Great. She's half-baked.* Her new friend wasn't going to be much help. She looked out the side window of the garage. She knew she had seen them before, during her duties around the Whiskey Jack. *Cameras.* The entire property was under surveillance. Now was not the time to panic. It also wasn't the time to draw attention to herself. *Could she get a message out?* Megan thought of how to do it. She looked at Rhiannon. "Rhee, gimme your phone." She did a couple of quick searches, finding the links she needed. She composed a text, sending it to her mother. "I hope she figures this out."

"Figures what out?" said Rhiannon.

"Nothing," said Megan. "Let's load up these life jackets. I'll take them down to the dock."

McMasters tapped politely on Peale's office door. He heard a muffled "Come in." He entered. Peale was sitting at his desk. On the desk was an olive drab ammunition box. Next to it was a piece of wooden trim. The trim had shiny metal tabs on the smooth side. The box had been opened, a padlock nearby. A large blue three-ring binder sat next to the padlock. McMasters looked at the items, perplexed. "Mr. Peale?"

"I don't think you've had a chance to see this collection of our records," said Peale.

"Records?" McMasters asked. "I thought everything we had was digitized."

"Our most recent records, yes," said Peale. He pointed at the binder. "Some of what is in this binder is part of those records, some of it isn't. The only problem is that this exists.

It's my fault that it exists. And now, I think someone else knows it exists."

"Someone else?" said McMasters. "Who?"

"Our newest hire, Miss Goodman."

"How did she find it?"

Peale lifted the piece of wooden trim off the table. "These metal tabs attach to magnets on the bottom of the vanity in the Blackbird cabin. Miss Goodman had been cleaning the cabin when I interrupted her. She helped me hang the refinished sign."

"OK," said McMasters. He wasn't sure where Peale was going with this.

Peale continued. "If I hadn't dropped my key card, I wouldn't have seen it. Do you see it, McMasters?"

McMasters looked at the wood. "Uhm, oak?"

Peale exhaled. "The profile, McMasters. The *side* profile."

McMasters looked at the side profile. "Mr. Peale, what am I supposed to be looking at?"

"It was upside down."

"What was upside down?"

"The profile."

McMasters looked again. That's when he saw it. "I see it now."

"Unfortunately, I believe Miss Goodman had stumbled upon the hiding place while cleaning the cabin. When she put the molding back in place, it clicked into the magnets. I tested the fit. The molding could be installed right side up or upside down."

McMasters looked at the box. "Was the box open?"

"Thankfully, no," said Peale. "Unfortunately, knowledge of the box isn't particularly helpful at this juncture, not with the completion of the pending transaction so close at hand."

"I understand," said McMasters.

"Perhaps containment first, then an unfortunate accident. The summertime variety will do."

McMasters bit his lower lip. Peale saw the bite. "Is there a problem, McMasters?"

McMasters released his lip. "You know that it could be nothing."

Peale locked eyes with McMaster. "Could be nothing."

"Yes, Mr. Peale. It could be nothing."

"Nothing at all."

McMasters nodded. Peale turned in his chair. He looked at the cove. He answered to the water and the trees. "I wish we could take that chance." He turned back to McMasters. No words needed to be said. McMasters headed for the door. Peale turned back to the cove.

The Jeepmates walked single file on the left-hand side of 315. The road's soft shoulder wasn't a hit with Lisa's flip-flops. She looked at Aaron's nurse-style sneakers. "Hey, Secret Agent Man. You don't have an extra pair of those sneaks on you, do yah?"

Aaron was a little punchy after his recent head injuries. "Why don't you just hit me on the head again and take mine?"

"We're almost there," said Sam. "I just hope he's home."

Steve wiped the sweat from his brow. "It's been one hell of a day. I hope he's got beer."

Sam hoped the same, maybe something stronger. She put her hand on his back as they walked. She thought about asking him about his father's prognosis. She decided that her hand was saying what she needed to say for now.

The Jeepmates made their way down the steps to the

Peeters' family cabin. Something was cooking, a good sign. Zach was on the deck, attending to consistent flames from a box of Keg burgers. He saw the group. He looked at the grill. "Uh, anybody want a burger?"

"And a phonebook," said Lisa. "Put Mongo in the ditch."

"Shit," said Zach. "Don't know if Buckmaster's tow truck has the balls for that yank. That's gonna cost Lac du Bonnet money."

"Got any beer?" Steve asked.

"And a computer," said Sam. "I gotta look something up that isn't squinty phone-sized."

"Phone won't work up here," said Zach. He scooped the burgers onto a nearby plate. "Sometimes it'll bounce, but it's mostly at the dock. Let me get my laptop."

It took a couple of minutes to boot up the ten-year-old Compaq. Sam told the tale of the day as she knew it. She introduced Aaron. "There's something going on at the lodge."

Zach looked at Sam. "Really? No shit, Sherlock."

"Excuse me?" Sam asked.

"I could have told you that," said Zach. "The plane, those antique boats, shutting down for the winter. If that place were legit, they would have been out of business years ago."

Lisa was impressed, though in a Lisa kind of way. "Not bad for a guy who hasn't seen an office in like, what, ever?"

"Don't let the beach bum attire fool you," said Zach. "There's an Asper biz-school degree around here somewhere. Probably under a pizza box."

Aaron had found a blue gel cold pack for his head. "We've had our forensic accountant looking into it. They're still trying to figure out how they do it without raising any red flags on the tax side. Then there's the guests."

"What about them?" Sam asked.

Aaron explained CSIS's tracking efforts. "If you're crossing an international border, you have to key in your destination address. We've been watching the lodge for almost a year. There wasn't anybody who was a red flag. Then we dug deeper. That's when it got weird."

The group was fixed on Aaron's revelations. He continued. "All of the guys who have been coming in since we started looking are American ex-military. All of them high-ranking before they retired. Medals, commendations, the works. And it doesn't look like they're here for the fishing."

"How do you know?" Steve asked.

"The dark web traffic spikes whenever these guys come to visit," said Aaron. "These guys come in, and something goes out. Then, the traffic goes quiet until they come back."

"What are they smuggling?" Lisa asked. "Black flies and fish heads?"

"We think its nuclear," said Aaron. "Out of Whiteshell Labs."

"The dirty bombs theory," said Steve.

Sam looked at her cousin from another mother. "You've heard about this?"

"We'd hear whiffs of it when I was riding a desk," said Steve. "It would all get sent up the chain to CSIS. I don't remember them being too concerned, though."

"Why not?" Sam asked.

"Whiteshell doesn't have that kind of nuclear garbage," said Steve. "I'm sure other places do, maybe Chalk River. Moving it would be almost impossible, and pretty dangerous." He looked at Aaron. "Sorry, junior spy, but I think your intel is off."

"Then explain the dark web traffic," said Aaron. "And the timing."

"I'll give you that," said Steve. "But I gots a fiver that says it's something else."

"I don't really give a shit what it is," said Sam. "All I know is that right now my daughter is fluffing their goddamn pillows. And I've got to—"

A double-chime alert interrupted Sam's concern. She pulled her phone out of her pocket. She looked at Zach. "I thought you said phones don't work up here."

"Must have bounced," said Zach. "I guess you got lucky."

Sam looked at her phone. The message was from Megan's friend, Rhiannon. "Wait a minute," said Sam. "I think I got something." Sam looked at the message.

> Hi Mom. It's Megs. Here's that link
> I told you about for the university.
> https://eeb.yale.edu/courses/ornithology
> I really think it's what I want to do.
> You said Lisa needed a cabinet for
> the shed. Check this out.
> https://www.gcsurplus.ca/MBauctions
> They got other cool stuff too, closes
> tomorrow. TTYL.

"She's trying to tell us something," said Sam. She clicked on the first link. "University? We haven't talked about anything to do with . . . holy shit!"

"What?" Lisa asked. "What is it?"

"Yale," said Sam. "Yale University. She must have found something."

"The key!" said Zach. "Maybe the lock?"

"Ornithology," said Sam. "What would birds have to do with it?"

"*Blackbird!*" Steve said. "It must be Blackbird!"

Sam clicked on the other link. She showed the phone to Lisa. "Megan says you need one of these?"

"I do?" Lisa looked at the image, a steel cabinet in bright Safety Yellow. "I don't remember needing anything like that. What is that, an auction site?"

"An auction?" Aaron was back in the game. "Where is it? The auction?"

"Lemme check." Lisa scrolled down through the description. "Says Pinawa."

Aaron smacked his forehead. He instantly regretted it. "OW! So that's how they're doing it!"

"Doing what?" Steve asked.

"Whiteshell Labs," said Aaron. "The nuclear—"

"It's NOT nuclear!" Steve bellowed.

"When does the auction close?" Zach asked.

"Tomorrow, nine in the morning," said Lisa. "Ugh, that's early at the lake."

Sam felt the gears in her head. She grabbed the laptop and keyed in the surplus site. She chose the Manitoba/Nunavut region and scrolled through the items. "I got another Pinawa," she said. "Purple filing cabinets."

"Wow," said Lisa. "That was a thing?"

"It closes at nine in the morning too," said Sam. She kept scrolling. "There's a boogie van."

"A what van?" Aaron had never heard the reference.

"A panel van," said Steve. "Looks like an old Chevy. Did surveillance in one of those."

"What time," said Lisa.

"Huh?" said Sam.

"What time does it close?"

Sam looked at the auction information. "It's at nine too."

"And anyone can bid on this shit, right?" Lisa asked.

"Right," said Aaron. "And no one sees your bid. Highest bid wins."

Sam looked at the laptop, then at Zach. She smiled.

What? What are you smiling about?"

"Your credit card," said Sam. "Whichever one has the big fat limit."

CHAPTER
FIFTY-ONE

Megan put the life jackets into the service cart. She positioned the fishing rods between the seats to keep them from rolling out. She drove down to the water's edge. The path had been greatly improved since the untimely death of the Whiskey Jack's founder. She did notice the strange scars on one of the trees as she slowly rolled past. She wondered how they got there.

The guests who had been enjoying the warm summer waters had made their way back up to the lodge. The protected waters of the cove slapped lazily against the dock, the Norseman, and the Chris-Craft duo. The instructions were to place the gear in the storage benches closest to the Norseman. Megan was just about ready to head back up the hill when she heard a strange ringing sound. It was coming from a cabinet near the middle of the dock. Megan opened the cabinet door. A black rotary phone looked back at her. She picked up the receiver. "Hello?"

"Hi Megan, it's Vance," said McMasters. "I'm glad I caught you down there. I need your help with Mr. Peale's hardtop. I'll be right down."

"Uhm, sure. OK." Megan heard the phone click. It took about a minute until she saw him coming down the path. He gave a friendly wave along with his smile. Megan felt at least one of her knees go weak.

"Forecast is calling for rain tonight," said McMasters, as he walked towards Megan. "Need to batten down the hatches."

Megan had no idea what that meant. *Must be a boat thing.* "Uh, sure. What do you need me to do?"

"We've got to fasten the covers onto the hardtop," said McMasters. "It's a two-person operation. Need to make sure everything snaps into place just right. I did it once years ago by myself, tore one of the panels. Mr. Peale was none too happy."

Megan was starting to wonder when she would actually see the upset Mr. Peale that everyone had warned her about, including her mother. "Got it. Just tell me what you need me to do."

McMasters pointed at the cushions. "The panels are under there. You just have to lift up the cushions."

Megan got into the boat. The panels were folded neatly under the leather cushions. She lifted them out one by one. "OK, is that it?"

"There's one more," said McMasters. "Underneath the dashboard."

Megan made her way under the hardtop. She shimmied between the front seats. The space was tight and dark. She looked under the dash. "Uhm, Mr. uh, I mean Vance? I don't see anything."

"That's strange," said McMasters. "Let me take a closer look."

Yeah, sure. You can take a closer look. Megan continued to poke around in the space, a hint of a smile forming as she felt the void being filled by McMasters. She tried to snap herself out of the dreamy feelings. *Think of something else, think of something else.* Megan studied the space in front of her. There wasn't a rack or netting of any kind to keep something from rolling around. She turned around to say as much. She didn't get to. Vance McMasters jabbed a small hypodermic needle into her neck and depressed the plunger. Megan wanted to lunge. She saw her hands move in front of her like slow motion extras. She looked up at McMasters. His face had gone from striking to fuzzy. She felt herself falling—to the floor and away from every warm feeling she ever had about Vance McMasters. She was unconscious before she reached the bottom of the Chris-Craft.

CHAPTER FIFTY-TWO

The GC Surplus site proved to be a wealth of information. Aaron Sen had been conscripted into keyboard duty. He quickly found the previous sales at Pinawa. "OK, what are we looking for?"

Sam looked at the screen. "Well, prices have to be part of it. If you want to make sure you're going to win something—"

"You overbid the living shit out of it," said Zach.

Aaron scrolled and clicked. "There's definitely some weird prices. Take a look at this."

Sam, Steve, Zach, and Lisa squeezed together to get a view of the laptop. "What are we looking at?" Lisa asked.

"These bikes," said Aaron. "Not an uncommon thing to have around in a big facility. A lot of warehouses use them. Cheaper than a Segway and keeps your employees' heart rates up. Keeps health costs down."

"You sound more like an accountant than a spy," said Zach. "Ever consider the logistics industry?"

Aaron continued. "These aren't expensive bikes. They're beach cruisers. Fat tires, big seats, one speed. They're heavy too. You wouldn't get far on a mountain bike trail with one of these."

"So?" said Lisa.

Aaron picked up a pad he had been scrawling on. "So, the average price of these things new is between two and four hundred dollars, depending on the manufacturer. A lot of these old ones need work, like tires, ripped seats. Most of them are scratched up pretty good too."

"What are they selling for?" Sam asked.

"That's where it gets weird," said Aaron. "Not a lot, anywhere from fifty-ish dollars to a hundred for most of them. Then this."

The group looked at the screen. A green and cream Supercycle Classic Cruiser had been on offer. It had an oversized basket on the front, more about practicality than aesthetics. The rear tire didn't match the front. It looked well-used.

Aaron turned to the observers. "This thing went for over two hundred dollars."

"Is that a lot?" Sam asked.

Aaron clicked on a tab at the top of the screen. "They're $189 at Canadian Tire. Brand new, with no scrapes, no scratches, and matching tires."

"So that's how they're getting it out," said Zach. "Whatever *that* is."

"It's not just bikes," said Aaron. "There's all sorts of things that have been sold lately for at or close to market value new. I checked the records that I've been keeping on the dark web. All of these high prices correspond with elevated activity."

"So, whatever it is, it's going right out the front door," said Steve.

"Exactly," said Aaron.

"So, all we have to do is put in bids on this stuff," said Sam. "If we're the highest bid, we get it?"

"Right," said Aaron. "But there's got to be someone on the inside. Someone stashing whatever it is inside the auction items. I'm just trying to figure out the bicycles."

"What about them?" Steve asked.

"The voids are too small," said Aaron. "At least for anything nuclear."

Steve smirked. "You really want to lose that fiver, don't you?"

Aaron looked annoyed. "Then what is it?"

Steve went to answer. He stopped. He smiled. "It's a red herring."

Aaron had heard that one. "Maybe. Just maybe."

Sam leaned in. "So, it just looks like someone who doesn't know how to bid."

"Exactly," said Steve.

Zach placed his credit card next to the laptop. "Truth be told, I've bought way dumber shit than this."

"Megan," said Sam. The message, obviously coded. *Maybe they know.* She looked at Steve, the closest thing to a traditional cop in the Peeters' cabin. "We've got to get her out of there!"

CHAPTER
FIFTY-THREE

Rhiannon hadn't seen Megan for a while. She had gone back to tidying up in the main lodge after Megan had left for the dock. No one had told her to do it. All she knew was that cameras were everywhere at the Whiskey Jack. She had never seen it herself, but the rumour going around amongst the staff was that Mr. Peale had a sixty-inch flat screen in his main office, with sixteen live HD camera feeds that he'd watch like a hawk. He could zoom in, zoom out, and pan to the left and to the right. It was best not to tempt fate.

The area around the fireplace couldn't get any cleaner. Rhiannon moved her compact vacuum into the dining area. She pushed the vacuum along the windows looking out towards the water. *Where is she?* The window screens were open. She removed the dusting attachment for the vacuum. The screens didn't need it, but it would be impossible for anyone looking at her through a video camera to tell.

Don't tell. That was definitely implied, Rhiannon thought, when Megan asked her to delete the messages that she had just sent to her mother. There hadn't been any time to get into detail. Rhiannon didn't need the details. She knew that something did not quite wash when it came to her own dishwasher salary, a whopping twenty-two dollars an hour in a region where local businesses were still pissed about paying twelve. She had thought about school, maybe learning a trade at Red River College if she could stay off the kush. *Mom.* Rhiannon helped her out with the little extra that she managed to save. Most of it went straight to the liquor store. The Boler at Bird Lake Campground may have been small, but it had a lot less drama than the winter months back home.

Rhiannon gave the screens the best dusting they had ever seen. She almost missed the service cart coming up the path. What she didn't miss was the driver: Megan had taken it out, but it wasn't Megan coming back. Vance McMasters went slowly and cautiously up the path. Rhiannon lost sight of him as he rounded the corner. She looked back at the dock. There was no sign of her summer friend.

Everything looked normal, except for one thing: Mr. Peale's Chris-Craft hardtop. Rhiannon had been tasked on occasion to help with attaching the covers to keep the weather out. *Strange.* Her weather app on her phone hadn't said boo about bad weather. She was about to question it further when she felt a tap on her shoulder. She turned around. It was McMasters. He said something. Rhiannon couldn't hear it. He pointed to the switch on the running vacuum cleaner. "Can you turn that off for a second?"

Rhiannon obliged. "Yes, Vance. Anything else for tonight?"

"Nothing pressing," said Vance. "Just a reminder about tomorrow evening. Most of the guests will be leaving by four, so we won't be doing a dinner."

"What about the staff?"

"We're going to be shutting down for a few days," said McMasters. "Mr. Peale has some business to attend to in Winnipeg, which I'll be assisting with. Everything will be locked down till the following Wednesday. We'll be paying out as per usual, so no interruptions for earnings."

Weird. Rhiannon felt the gears turning in her head. Megan finding the old models in the garage, the auction papers in Peale's car. *Peale's gold balls.* And now, Megan seemed to be missing. *Something isn't right.* She smiled at McMasters.

"Getting paid to stay home?" Rhiannon did her best to make it sound like she had never heard of such a concept. "Sweet!"

"Compliments of Mr. Peale," said McMasters. Rhiannon thought about asking where Megan was. She looked back at the hardtop bobbing in the water.

She had an idea as to where she could be.

McMasters made his way down the hallway to Peale's office. He tapped lightly on the door. A muffled "Come in" followed. McMasters opened the door to see his employer surrounded by a colourful selection of gel freezer mugs. The mugs had recently arrived from a corporate branding outfitter in

Winnipeg. The Whiskey Jack logo had been applied to the mugs, in the colours of the mugs' respective hues. McMasters stated the obvious. "Those are truly hideous, Mr. Peale."

"No argument there," said Peale. He was using a heat gun to release the bottom of the cups from the inner cavity. "Luckily, our friends in customs have yet to make anyone prove that their Whiskey Jack freezer cup can actually be frozen."

McMasters picked up one of the cups that was awaiting its turn at the heat gun. At a glance, the cup appeared to be full of crushed ice. It was a clever illusion, a clear outer cavity that held a gel material that looked like small ice chunks. Once frozen, the gel never contacted the drink inside, but it did keep it frosty from first sip to last. Peale had a makeshift assembly line around his office. The bottoms of the freezer cups that had been removed by the heat gun sat on a dish rack. Gravity was forcing the gel pieces onto the tray below.

Next to the dish rack was a Pelican case. It was open, revealing the item that would replace the freezer gel nodules. Upon inspection, there would be no way for a customs agent to know that the new nodules were rough-cut diamonds. The Underground Research Laboratory's greatest secret wasn't the gold: it was the diamonds. They weren't of the Lac du Bonnet batholith. They came in the Pelican cases of equipment that accompanied scientists from all over the world, the kind that carried all manner of sensitive equipment for experiments. The kind of equipment that never saw the manhandling of a CBSA agent.

The diamonds had been treated to a clear lacquer coating, a practice that had been in place since the late eighties, when Peale realized the opportunity that the laboratory presented for the kind of international banking that didn't have pens chained to the desk. The scientists were easy prey. Most of them were easy to buy off in their respective countries and/or intimidate into cooperation. Dollars and gold were still bulky items to move without detection. Transferring funds in the digital age was as simple as a click, though it still left a trail as sticky as a common slug. Peale had even dabbled in turning the diamonds into cheap-looking costume jewelry, in between his penchant for carving signs for the Whiskey Jack cabins. The wives of the Pinetree line seemed to enjoy the eye-rolls they would get as they sashayed through customs wearing tacky millions.

Peale didn't look up from the task at hand. "Did you take care of the Goodman girl?"

"Sleeping like a baby," said McMasters. "Did you want me to sink the boat tonight or in the morning?"

"We'll see how the evening goes," said Peale. He pointed to a small tube on the credenza. "Can you hand me the glue?"

McMasters fetched the glue. "Her mother will be looking for her. I think she expects to pick her up after her shift."

"That is unfortunate," said Peale.

"Unfortunate?"

Peale scooped the diamonds into the cavity of the cup. "There's nothing more tragic than a mother and a daughter dying in a boating accident in the summertime."

CHAPTER
FIFTY-FOUR

The next few hours would be a new kind of agony for Sam. She wanted to scale the motorized gate to the Whiskey Jack, scoop up her daughter, and get as far away from Bird Lake as the old Chevy would take them. That's what she would have done, if she didn't have a sizable group in front of her advising her not to. Aaron and Steve were the level-headed voices of reason, even if they couldn't decide on what was hiding in the auction items that Zach had just dented his credit card with, items that wouldn't be available until tomorrow morning if the bids were successful. Lisa stayed close, offering her sisterhood as comfort, as well as a few over-the-top ideas. "Why don't we just ram the gate and go for it?"

"I think that ditch took care of your battering ram for you," said Zach. "And even I've watched enough bad TV to know there's probably something big, bad, and better-equipped than we are on the other side."

"He's right," said Steve. "And we can't let our minds get the better of us. Megan sent us a message, that's a good start. We have to assume she's OK."

"She can't be *that* OK," said Sam. "If everything was fine, why was it so cryptic?"

The group tried to come up with an answer for that. They couldn't.

Sam continued. "Megan knew she had to say something. She doesn't have a phone, so she borrowed her friend's." Sam realized something else. The message was cryptic, but it wasn't *too* cryptic. It wasn't even Nancy Drew. If Peale or McMasters saw the message that went out, the math would be simpler than two plus two. Then Rhiannon would be in the same trouble as Megan. Sam felt her mind going to all the horrible places where that trouble could be. She looked at her Odd Squad. "How can we get in without getting caught? It doesn't get dark for another five hours?"

"I think I know," said Zach. He disappeared into one of the bedrooms. He returned with a large cardboard box with the Amazon grin. He opened the flaps to reveal the contents. The group looked inside. "What the hell is that?" Lisa asked.

Zach smiled. "Boredom, Amazon, a credit card, and the ultimate lake toy all rolled into one."

The group helped with the unboxing of something called

a PowerVision PowerDolphin. "So, it's like a drone subma-rine?" Lisa asked.

"It runs on the surface," said Zach, as he went through the set-up guide. "The camera can sit above the water or tilt down to look underwater. Thought it might help find some Master Anglers."

Steve held the PowerDolphin, looking at it from all angles. "Self-righting?"

"Yup," said Zach. "The controller syncs with your phone. Heads right back to you when the battery gets low."

Sam was getting annoyed with the boys and the toy. "And how exactly can this help us get Megan back?"

"It beats an aerial drone," said Aaron. "A fly-by would draw too much attention. They're also way too loud."

"The range is almost a full klick," said Zach. "We could take it right into the Whiskey Jack cove from the camp-ground."

Sam looked closer at the strange soon-to-be-aquatic remote control creature. "There's only one problem."

"What is it?" Zach asked.

Sam picked up the PowerDolphin. "Look at it. It looks like a baby beluga escaped from some aquarium."

"Yeah," said Lisa. "He is kinda cute."

"And he'll stand out like a sore thumb," said Steve. "Even I could see this thing coming from a mile away." He pointed at his replacement orb to drive home his point.

Sam looked around the room as the Odd Squad debated what to do next. She stopped. "Hey, Zach. Is that couch a family heirloom?"

Zach looked at the couch. "Why? Is shit brown making a comeback?"

"Today it is," said Sam. "Get me some scissors."

Megan knew she had slept, but it was not a sleep she had ever known. She had a throbbing headache. It was hard to focus. *Where am I?* She tried to move. Her limbs were not responding. She could hear a strange sloshing noise. *Water!* She started to piece together her surroundings. Mr. Peale's boat. The side curtains. Prince Harry, or possibly Vance McMasters. *Vance McMasters.* In that moment, Megan lost all interest in gingers.

She felt her neck. She remembered the needle going in. There was a bit of a welt at the point of entry. No real pain to speak of. *Hot.* The side curtains were anything but a tight fit, but the temperature was a good ten degrees higher inside the boat than the exterior. *Air.* She needed some. It was close. She just needed to figure out how to get there, with a body that wasn't ready to obey her commands. The one thing that she could do was think about her current situation. She had been found out. She went back through the chain of events as she knew them. The sparkling orb in Mr. Peale's office. The hiding place in the Blackbird cabin. The Whiskey Jack float plane model kits in the garage. The text to her mother on Rhee's phone. *Rhee!* Had she been found out? Would she be joining her? *Mom!* Did she understand the text? If she didn't, she could be driving straight into a trap when she came to pick her up.

Air. Megan did her best to focus. Her head was closest to the boat's controls. It took a good fifteen minutes to get her chin on the seat cushion. It took another fifteen to get onto the seat in a position that was neither comfortable nor natural. *Air.* She pushed out the side curtain just enough to let in the breeze. She was sweating bullets. She couldn't see the lodge, but she could hear it. *Dinner.* The clinking of cutlery on plates, the steady drone of conversation. A few laughs. She looked over the side of the boat. The water of the Whiskey Jack cove lapped lazily against the hull. She wondered if the shock of entering the water would be enough to erase the effects of the sedative that currently commanded her motor skills.

She decided it was time to find out.

CHAPTER FIFTY-FIVE

Zach's Lincoln Navigator hadn't seen passenger use for some time. He pitched the floor garbage into the rear cargo hold as the Odd Squad waited. Five minutes later, they arrived at the Bird Lake Campground, drawing a few curious looks from the handful of campers present. No one exited a folding chair to investigate further.

Aaron had mounted his smartphone to the controller of the camouflaged aquatic drone. The Odd Squad peered at the screen as they watched the journey across the bay. "I've gotta get me one of those," said Lisa.

"Whatever the hell for?" Sam asked.

"Cool spy shit," said Lisa.

"Who you going to spy on?" Zach asked.

"I could tell you, but then I'd have to kill you."

"Shhh," said Sam, immediately embarrassed as to why shushing the group was even required. "It's almost at the lodge." The Odd Squad peered at the screen. Even with a few water droplets on the lens, the clarity of the surroundings was remarkable. Aaron adjusted the angle of the camera as the dolphin drone approached the Whiskey Jack dock. "How fast does a beaver go?" he said.

Lisa couldn't help herself. "Well, this one time, at band camp . . ."

"Slower," said Steve. "And Lisa, gross."

The screen showed the drone's journey as it passed by the Chris-Craft, the Norseman, and the fishing boats for the guests. Aaron steered the drone past the newer building where the fish-gutting shack had once stood. As expensive as Zach's latest boredom purchase had been, there was a noticeable omission to the video stream that was being viewed: it was as silent as a tomb. From the drone's perspective, the cove appeared to be deserted. Sam knew that the time of day would also be a factor, the usual supper hour. The lodge was just out of reach of the drone's camera.

As high-definition as the journey had been, the float-by of the drone hadn't offered any new information as to Megan's whereabouts. Sam's gut knew that something was horribly off. *Mother's intuition.* She was about to say as much when she stopped. "Aaron, go back."

"Where?" Aaron asked. "Did you see something?"

"What?" said Steve. "What is it?"

"Go into the cove and go past the dock again," said Sam.

"What did you see?" asked Lisa. "Is it Megan?"

Sam didn't answer. She watched as the drone made a second pass through the cove. She watched as it turned. It went past the fishing boats, past the Norseman. It passed the first Chris-Craft, the open runabout. It came to the second boat, the hardtop. "Aaron, can you turn the drone to look at the side of the boat?"

"Sure," said Aaron. "What are we looking at?"

Sam looked. "Can you back up?"

"Backing up," said Aaron.

"Slowly," said Sam.

"Backing up slowly."

Sam had moved as close to the screen as she could. Maybe it was mother's intuition. Maybe it was a sixth sense that every mother gets when the doctor cuts the umbilical cord and hands you a screaming boy or girl bundle. Whatever it was, it had brought Sam here, with a group of curious onlookers and a boatload of technology. She said nothing.

Lisa said it for her. "Oh my fucking God."

The group squinted at the fingernails poking out from the bottom of the side curtain. Periwinkle. Megan's favourite colour.

CHAPTER FIFTY-SIX

Norman Peale did what most people did when achieving the immediate attention of a group of boisterous drinkers and eaters is required: he tapped his wine glass repeatedly with a knife. The principals of the Pinetree line calmed. He put down his noisemaker and began his speech.

"Thank you all for joining me tonight and let me start by offering a hearty thank you to the fine staff at the Whiskey Jack Lodge." Peale started clapping. The rest of the group joined in. The wait staff along the walls returned smiles and nods to the patrons.

Peale continued. "It has always been a pleasure to host military men and their families at the Whiskey Jack Lodge." He raised his glass. "Thank you for your service." Peale sipped as other glasses were raised, clinked, and in a few cases, gulped clean. The wait staff swooped in quickly with refills.

Peale moved out from his centre position at the head table. "And it has been my distinct pleasure to have worked with you all for over forty years. It may not have been the kind of work that commands a front-page honour, but it is important work just the same. History will always be the final judge of the efforts of man, the results, and the consequences. But let it be known to all of you that history will judge us well."

Proper applause followed the end of Peale's statement. He smiled as it rolled towards him. He returned to his chair. He raised his glass to the room. "To the Pinetree line." The group responded in kind. The wait staff swooped in with more supplies. Through the screens, the sounds of pleasure craft and their users. They would be quieting down soon as the night drew near. It was always hard for Peale to tell how close any of the craft were to the Whiskey Jack, thanks to the natural acoustics of the cove.

He had no way to know that something was headed right for him.

Sam had been on the debate team back in high school. She had enjoyed the structure, the subjects chosen, and the strict time limits imposed for pleading one's case. But the Odd Squad's current exchanges at the water's edge of Bird Lake Campground were not a debate: they were a melee.

"I can call the detachment in Powerview," said Steve. "They could send in an ERT."

"Really?" Lisa asked. "Like a SWAT team?"

"We call it ERT," said Steve.

Zach motioned to Aaron. "Does CSIS have anything like that?"

"Not really," said Aaron. "Well, not *officially*."

"What the fuck is that supposed to mean?" Lisa asked.

"Depends on the threat," said Aaron.

"So where do kidnapped seventeen-year-old girls figure into the threat level?"

Aaron looked down at the gravel of the boat launch. "Pretty low, I'm afraid."

Steve perked up first at the sound of the footsteps approaching quickly from one of the lakeside campsites. A middle-aged man with salt and pepper camping stubble was pointing at the lake with his can of Kokanee. "Is she with you guys?"

Lisa looked around. "Where's Sam?"

Zach parroted. "Where's Sam?"

The Odd Squad looked towards the lake. Any chance of getting Sam's attention was gone. She was already halfway across the bay that separated the campground from the Whiskey Jack Lodge, riding an older Sea-Doo. As they watched the teal and purple craft speed away, the man asked a strange question.

"Which one of you is the agent in charge?"

Can I take your Sea-Doo out for a burn? Sam wondered how many times that question had been asked of the popular watercraft as she throttled across the bay. She didn't exactly *ask* to use the one she was riding now, more like a quick "National security, talk to my handler over there!" It sounded official enough. The camper she had stolen the Sea-Doo from didn't have time to protest. He might have spilled his beer.

The light was still strong on the bay, though very west. The foam vest she had donned from the seat was about three sizes too big. *At least they'll find the body.* Sam thought about Megan's body, how she hoped it was still a live one, that her rescue mission wasn't in vain. Her concerns turned to anger. *Mr. Peale.* She twisted the throttle to full.

Sam slowed the Sea-Doo as she approached the Whiskey Jack. Dinner was underway, judging from the lights in the dining room, the banter and laughter emanating from the open screens. She cruised slowly past the lodge. *Nothing to see here. Just a middle-aged woman riding an aquatic Chip and Pepper T-shirt.* She cruised into the cove. The water was calmer. She approached the Chris-Craft. Megan had graduated from poking her hand out of the curtain to her head. She didn't look good. Sam kept looking up at the lodge while trying to keep an eye on her daughter. She whispered as forceful as she could. *"Megan! Are you all right?"*

"Mom?" Megan's voice was different, a little like the typical teenager being roused for a school day. "Is that you?"

They must have drugged her. Sam felt her anger climb another click and grabbed the side of the Chris-Craft. She pulled herself up to her daughter. She killed the engine on the Sea-Doo. She held Megan's cheeks as she tried to fuse their foreheads together, to assure her through some form of mother-daughter mind meld that everything was going to be OK. Megan felt it. "Mom, I wanna go home."

"Can you move?" Sam asked.

"I, I think so." Megan's voice was anything but reassuring.

"Let's get you out of there," said Sam. She snapped off the portion of the side curtain and reached inside to help Megan onto the Sea-Doo. The transfer was anything but graceful. Sam grasped Megan's left arm. She rested her head against her mother's back. Sam felt relief.

"Now let's get the hell out of here," said Sam. She pressed the starter button. The Sea-Doo kicked over but didn't catch. She tried again. No combustion. *Oh shit.* She tried a third time, convinced that the entire lodge had heard her and were watching the pitiful escape attempt from the open screens. She knew what it was. Any lake girl did. She opened the gas cap. The tank was empty. *Oh double shit.* Sam looked around the dock. The tanks for the fishing boats would have already been removed for the night. The canoes were at the water's edge, locked with a long chain and a padlock. *A pedal boat?* Those were never locked, probably because no one ever really liked them. That meant getting to the shore, with a half-drugged daughter approaching dead weight, who would contribute little to the peddling needed to cross the water to the campground.

Sam had a plan.

CHAPTER
FIFTY-SEVEN

Rhiannon knew she had to make a move. Quickly. Purposefully. *Now.* She had her choice of three. First move: the dock. A quick reconnaissance run to yay/nay that her friend Megan was in serious trouble. She could do it in the time of a bathroom break. The silver foxes in the next room were more interested in booze and bullshit by this point of the evening. Second move: wash and stack. When did it become her place to intervene? She had just met the girl. Mr. Peale paid the bills, might even front some of the costs for future education if she made the right pitch. She didn't even know with certainty that Megan was in trouble. Third move: run like hell.

Before she could choose, Chef Henri shattered her train of thought like a lowball glass hitting the tile floor. "Rhiannon! Are you entered in a Grand Prix for food scraps?" He pointed at the bin next to her. It was getting close to the brim. She apologized. "Sorry, Chef Henri. I'll empty it right now." He made a noise of disgust as he made his way back to the grill. She could hear the abuse of the sous chefs continue as she carried the bin down the side of the lodge.

There were plenty of local animals that would have been extremely interested in the contents of the bin. The garbage shack eliminated that possibility. A sturdy shed with a critter-proof door, it wasn't large by any means. It was emptied on a daily basis, the refuse trucked to the area transfer station. Rhiannon tied the bag knot a second time out of habit. She exited the shed and looked towards the dock. The sheltered cove was without ripples. The boats hardly bobbed at all. That's when she heard the grunting. It wasn't a bear. She looked towards the sound. She recognized Megan's mom. She was trying to drag one of the yellow pedal boats off the shore. Megan was in the back seat of the pedal boat, half sitting, half lying down. Something was definitely wrong.

Rhiannon ran to the water's edge.

Sam had been gone too long. Lisa paced the shore hoping for a glimpse of her friend speeding towards them on the vintage Sea-Doo. Zach had forgotten his sunglasses. He shielded his eyes from the setting sun as he looked towards the lodge. Steve and Aaron were busy discussing tactics. Steve wanted to make a move. "You've got to call this in," said Steve. "This is taking too long."

"If we call this in, the whole investigation will be dead in the water," said Aaron. "Done. Over."

Steve pointed at the lodge. "It'll be over for Sam and Megan if we don't move now!"

"Look!" said Lisa.

The Odd Squad looked towards the lodge. Something slow, aquatic, and very yellow was making its way out of the cove.

Norman Peale was doing something he seldom did at the lodge: a second two-fingered evening scotch. He was relaxed. He was rested. He was ready for the next chapter.

Everything was in place. The overbids were sure to acquire the surplus items that held the remaining diamond cache at the Whiteshell Laboratories. The diamonds to be smuggled out by the members of the Pinetree line had been stowed in plain sight, in the freezer cups that bore the Whiskey Jack logo. Peale knew they were probably blood diamonds at minimum. These diamonds were currency, the kind of currency that had been transacting all sorts of clandestine operations for decades. *The greater good*. Peale caught himself wondering about that, who decided the greater good. That was easy: the Pinetree line did. What had started out as a cover-up centred on an experimental radar system gone haywire in November of '53 had grown into a vast array of holdings, all cleverly hidden within such shell companies as Consolidated Industries. Every member of the Pinetree line, both original members and recruits, had proven their mettle. All except for one. All except for Gerry Hutchings.

Peale thought back to the day that Hutchings was "retired" from the Pinetree line. It had nothing to do with the fire at Eastland Lake. Hutchings was a vocal opponent of the blood diamonds as the new finance arm for the Pinetree operations. "I'd rather be legally bankrupt than morally bankrupt," Hutchings had said at one of the last meetings he had attended at the Whiteshell Laboratories. Peale saw how the dissent had ruffled the feathers of Mulaney and Peeters. *The domino effect.* If it worked for communism, it could definitely topple an operation like Consolidated Industries.

The tip. Peale knew that the Koshelanyk kid hadn't meant it to be a tip, but that's what it had become. "I saw Mr. Hutchings in Lac du Bonnet today," he had said. Peale had asked him where. At first it was at the lumber yard. "Then, I saw him over at MacLeod's. He was stuffing the trunk on his Grand National with enough camping gear for a month." *A month.* "I honked at him. He said he was going up to Eastland Lake to disappear for a while." *Disappear. No one walks away from Consolidated Industries.*

And yet, there he was, Gerry Hutchings, July 1989, trudging through the brush near Eastland Lake like it was going to happen. The first shot hit him in the shoulder. Gerry looked in the direction of the shot. He saw Peale. Gerry ran as fast as he could into the trees. The second shot missed, shattering a tree branch above Gerry's head. Peale saw it then, the small automatic in Hutchings's right hand. The third shot hit Gerry in his lower hip. He cried out. Peale watched him fall, the gun Hutchings had held flying away from him. He saw the blood. He fired a fourth shot. He saw Hutchings's head jerk. He panicked. He ran.

It got easier after that. Van Cleef was up close and personal. Donald Peeters required an operative, one that would eventually become a victim himself. Peale could still hear the thud of the boat as it ran over Koshelanyk's corpse, over and over.

The Hutchings. Things were different now. McMasters had proven a cool and steady accomplice, beginning with his quick and struggle-free dispatch of Koshelanyk before staging the boating accident. His ex-military résumé had an impressive body count, the majority in black ops that never earned an official commendation. The end of the Hutchings would be clean, quick, and without question. *Too bad about the boat.*

Peale took a healthy sip. He saw McMasters approaching out of the corner of his eye. McMasters knelt down and whispered into his ear. He looked at McMasters. He rose from the table calmly. He followed McMasters out of the lodge to the dock, purposeful pace, not panicked. He looked inside the empty Chris-Craft. Megan Goodman was missing. He scanned the rest of the cove.

So was one of the Whiskey Jack's pedal boats.

CHAPTER
FIFTY-EIGHT

Three steps forward, two steps back. That's what the motion of the pedal boat felt like as Sam and Rhiannon made their way across the water—away from the lodge and towards the campground. Megan was still in and out of consciousness. Sam knew her left arm would hurt tomorrow from keeping her daughter from falling in. She didn't care.

"We're almost there," said Rhiannon. "I can see my Boler from here."

Sam saw the trailer, all by itself on a slight rise overlooking the water. "They still look like an egg."

"Yup, sure does," said Rhiannon. She pointed towards the shore. "Are those your friends?"

Sam saw the Odd Squad. She smiled. "Very much so."

Norman Peale felt a chuckle leave his mouth as he watched the stolen pedal boat moving across the water. McMasters had retrieved a rifle with a scope from a secret compartment in one of the Norseman floats. When Peale saw it, his demeanor changed from amused to angry. "Put that back where it came from."

"But Mr. Peale! I can hit—"

Peale grabbed the barrel and pointed it downwards. "It would not be advisable to start pumping bullets into a pedal boat in front of our distinguished guests, would you agree?"

"But the girl," said McMasters. "And her mother. They know too much!"

Peale walked over to the Riviera. He reached inside and retrieved a fine leather case which held even finer binoculars. He trained his eyes on the pedal boat. "Well, McMasters, it looks as though we can add our dishwasher to that list." He handed the binoculars to his henchman. "And I'm sure a few more friends and well-wishers waiting for her at the campground."

McMasters looked at the escaping pedal boat. He handed the binoculars back to his employer. He was dumbstruck. "Am I missing something here? Why are we letting them get away?"

"The double drowning would have been more convenient," said Peale. He returned the binoculars to the case as he continued. "The advantage here is that there are too many players involved. A consensus will not be reached. They'll elect to wait till morning. And by morning, we'll have received the items that will make Bird Lake a distant memory. Have you received your new credentials?"

"Yes," said McMasters. "Expertly done. But why did you have to make my last name Ringling?"

"Life is a circus," said Peale. "Tomorrow, a new one begins. In Belize."

Megan was getting better. Sam checked her temperature as she lay on the couch at the Mulaney cabin. Steve had retrieved his Glock from the gun case, just in case. Lisa had found an ancient bottle of Black Velvet hidden behind the glue traps under the sink. "This should sting like stepping on a hornet's nest," she said. She put the bottle on the kitchen table. She started pulling the available vessels from the cupboard.

Aaron explained why he couldn't call it in. "There's been a strict protocol since I started this: no digital communication. No phone calls, not even landline. Just me, a Bic pen, and this." He pulled his well-used coiled pocket memo pad out of his pocket. "I head into the field office in Winnipeg for updates every week."

Zach poured a shot of the whisky into a floral juice glass. He gulped. "But isn't this, like, a kidnapping or something?"

"Not anymore," said Steve. He pointed to the couch that held Megan and her mother. "Not when the alleged victim of said kidnapping is lying in front of us."

"But she's been drugged," said Lisa. "Can't we get them on that?"

"Doubtful," said Steve. He poured two fat fingers of the rye into an RCMP coffee cup. "She wasn't tied up. You'd need the syringe, toxicology, the trail of the drug, fingerprints, et cetera, et cetera. It's not like on TV. And she's a kid. Sometimes kids do dumb things."

"Sometimes adults too," said Sam. She had covered up her daughter with an afghan that must have been the work of the late Mrs. Mulaney. She took the last cup available, a green goblet that looked more like a parfait parking spot than a lowball. She poured. A lot. "If only I had never sent her there for a job."

"Like you could have known," said Lisa.

"Yeah, don't beat yourself up," said Zach.

Sam sipped. The burn wasn't the soul-cleansing solvent she had hoped for. Her legs were cramping up from the pedal boat escape. She massaged them. She stopped. "Where's Rhee?"

"She's on the deck," said Steve.

Sam left the table with her whisky. She saw Rhiannon in the subdued light from the interior windows. She was trying to spark the meagre scraps of a sorry blunt. The lighter was out of fuel. She looked up at Sam. "Maybe this is trying to tell me something."

"Doubt it," said Sam. "It's getting as legal as beer and blackjack anyway. You OK?"

"I guess," said Rhiannon. "Besides, I was going to be getting time off for a bit anyway."

"Off?" said Sam. "What's happening?"

"They said the lodge is closing down for about a week," said Rhiannon. "McMasters said that Pe— I mean Mr. Peale has business in Winnipeg or something. Said I will still get paid and all. But I guess there might be trouble now." She looked in the window at her lake bud. "Is she OK?"

"I think so," said Sam. She looked at the blunt between Rhiannon's fingers. "Rhee, I'm sorry I have to ask you this, but you guys weren't um, *experimenting* with anything stronger than that, were you?"

"Like, *injecting* stuff?" Rhiannon looked mortified. "That's like, so gross."

"Sorry," said Sam. "You know I had to ask."

"Yeah, I guess."

"So, you're going back to Lac du Bonnet?"

"I guess so. Gotta see my mom. She gets a little weird around this time of year."

"Weird? Weird how?"

"My dad, I guess."

"What about your dad?"

"This is the time of year when he drowned. And the boat cut him up."

"I'm sorry. What did your dad do?"

"He drove a logging truck for a while. Then he had that big accident."

"Accident?"

"On 315. That family?"

Sam knew which family. What was left of it was sipping cheap rye at the Mulaney kitchen table. She saw the chain of events. Her dad, then Donald Peeters, then Rhiannon's father. She looked at her daughter through the window. Drugging her might have been the first part. Now she was sure. *They were going to kill her.*

In a few hours when the auctions finished, Sam knew they would all find out what was worth killing for.

CHAPTER
FIFTY-NINE

Peale had pulled the Rolls-Royce out of the garage to let it warm up. He busied himself with the futility of a California Car Duster. He knew the Rolls would be covered in dust the minute that the tires turned a quarter of a mile down 315. It was more about the Zen, the way a Tibetan monk would create an exquisite sand mandala, then sweep it from existence.

His guests were making their way to the main lodge for checkout. Jake Kinsey gave his bride a quick buss on the cheek, then a slap to her backside that made her laugh. Peale thought he heard her throw in a "dirty old man" for good measure. He walked over to Peale with his right hand extended. "Another classic Canadian vacation in the books, Norman."

Peale shook the hand offered. "Glad you enjoyed it, Jake. Did you get your souvenir?"

"McMasters dropped it off this morning," said Kinsey. "I'm supposing we'll see the next one in the fall sometime?"

"We'll call you with the particulars," Peale lied. He was twenty-four hours away from putting the lodge behind him.

"Looking forward to it," said Kinsey. He looked at the Rolls-Royce. "That is one mighty fine automobile you've got there Norman."

"Part of the Van Cleef estate," said Norman. "Over two hundred thousand miles on it."

"I especially like that Manitoba licence plate of yours," Norman pointed at the personalized plate. "Why they make you spell it like that?"

"Seven character maximum," said Peale. "I think it gets the message across."

Kinsey looked at the plate that read PYNTREE. "In more ways than one," said Kinsey. He chuckled. "In more ways than one."

McMasters approached with an overnight bag. "Mr. Peale? We should really get going."

"Going?" Kinsey asked. "Where you headed, Norman?"

"Provincial zoning permits in Winnipeg," said Peale, another lie. "A larger boat house for next season."

Kinsey smiled. "Sounds like another place to put a bar, if you ask me."

"Fully stocked," said Peale. He extended his hand to a man he knew he'd never see again. "Till next time, Jake."

"Till next time," said Kinsey. He shook Peale's hand firm and proper. "Till next time."

The traffic on the way to Pinawa was light. Peale hadn't received the official notification yet from GC Surplus. It wasn't out of the ordinary. By the time the Rolls made the left turn up Ara Mooradian Way, the email would drop in his inbox. He had already arranged for the flatdeck tow truck that would haul away the derelict van, along with the file cabinets that he would be winning. There were enough rough-cut diamonds within the various nooks and crannies of the auction items to erase him and McMasters from Bird Lake history, diamonds that would never see the interior of a cheesy freezer mug with a Whiskey Jack logo. The cache was the last of the diamonds at Whiteshell Laboratories. The resort in Belize would operate much like the Whiskey Jack had. The visitors would be familiar, Jake Kinsey-esque in many respects, just from different countries with much busier revolutions. *The Pinetree line has been paid in full.* The new diamonds would be South American. There would be no elaborate auction schemes to contend with. Belize was much easier to bribe.

The tow truck was waiting at the entrance to the access road. It knew the Rolls. It pulled in behind it and followed as Peale headed towards the gate. The guard at the shack was a long-term employee. He recognized the driver of the Rolls. "Well, good morning, Mr. Peale. What brings you out to see us today?"

"Good morning, Earl," said Peale. "I believe you have a few surplus items ready for pickup?"

"Getting picked up right now," said Earl. "Though I think that tow truck they brought might need *your* tow truck."

Peale blinked. "I beg your pardon?"

"Here they come now." Earl pointed at the tow truck. He wasn't kidding about the condition. There was more rust than paint holding the body together. Only one of the two emergency beacons was working. The rust had yet to obscure the name of the proprietor. Peale knew the tow truck. He had passed it hundreds of times, at the Oiseau Garage. Stan Buckmaster was at the wheel. Samantha Hutchings occupied the middle position. On the right was someone who looked a lot like Peale's former associate Donald Peeters. Earl exited the guard shack to retrieve the paperwork. He waved at the trio as they headed down the access road. He fanned his nose as the truck pulled away. "I think that old girl needs a ring job."

Peale grabbed his phone. He checked the GC Surplus website. He checked his bids. He checked the recently awarded items. *Son of a bitch.* He hadn't won the items. Someone else had. Someone who obviously knew way too much.

"Was there something else you had won a bid on today, Mr. Peale?"

Peale didn't answer the guard. He slammed the Rolls into Drive and mashed the throttle to the floor while cranking the wheel hard to the right. Squealing and burning rubber filled the air in their respective ways. Earl looked at the tow truck driver that Peale had brought with him as he sped away. Judging by his gestures, he had no idea what was going on either.

Sam was concerned about two things at the moment: how quickly the Rolls would be on top of them, and if she had put Stan Buckmaster in the way of the most harm possible. She could see the sweat dripping down from his Oiseau Garage hat.

Sam looked behind her. The Rolls had just left the service road for the highway. It was gaining speed. "Slow down, Stan. Make sure they see us before you make the turn."

Stan backed off the throttle. "You know, Samantha, if your father knew what you were—"

"I know," said Sam. "It'll all be over soon."

Stan turned on his right blinker to head into Pinawa.

Peale was right behind the tow truck. The old van that it towed was tracking anything but straight. *Where the hell are they going?* Peale figured it was the RCMP detachment. It wasn't. The tow truck rumbled past. McMasters checked the clip on his Maxim 9. Peale thought the gun looked ridiculous. "That thing looks like a prop from *Blade Runner*."

"Built-in silencer," said McMasters. "Don't want to wake up the local constabulary."

"Sensible," said Peale. "Now, if we can just get this leisurely tour of Pinawa over with. We have a plane to catch."

The tow truck with the blood diamonds cache continued its meandering tour through the townsite. Friendly waves were exchanged by the townsfolk as they passed. *Smart*, Peale thought, as he returned a wave to a blue-hair with a blue tracksuit. *Plenty of witnesses.*

It drove past the Solo, past the hotel, past the hospital where Jarrod Mulaney was recovering from his stroke. Past the Whispering Pines Nursing Home, where Gerry Hutchings's wife was busy berating game-show contestants.

"This isn't good," said McMasters. "The whole town has seen us."

Peale gripped the wheel. "Patience, McMasters. I have a feeling we're almost at our destination."

The tow truck headed towards the outskirts of town.

CHAPTER
SIXTY

Sam cradled the stainless-steel canister as the
tow truck trio drove up 502. She cradled it like
some kind of infant, like a strange animal found
in a strange tale that involved an invisible magic
school or a bottomless wardrobe. There were
seven identical canisters inside the hulk of the
van that meandered behind Stan's tow truck.
She looked to the right, past Zach's concerned
face. She saw a sliver of Peale's Rolls in the side-
view mirror as it followed close behind.

The canister screw top came off easily. Sam
spun it open to take one last look. She closed it.

Zach looked at her with concern. "Are you sure you want to do this? You know you don't have to."

Sam stared at the canister. "I want to hear him say it."

"He will say it, Sam," said Zach. "He'll say it and more. They've got him dead to rights. Peale is going down."

Sam looked at Zach. "You realize what he's behind, right? What Rhee said? He killed your family, Zach. Rhee's Dad. And maybe—"

"Don't go there, Sam. You don't know that."

"He killed my dad!" Sam heard the words as they left her mouth. It was one thing to think them. It was something else entirely to say them. It seemed real now. All of it was very real now.

Stan clicked the blinker for the right turn into the Pinawa Dam Provincial Park. The dam started supplying power to a fledgling Winnipeg in 1906. It had been abandoned in 1951 when the Seven Sisters dam went live, along with the adjacent townsite that first bore the Pinawa name. The decommissioned dam had been used for artillery practice by the military, though legend had it that even the big guns couldn't make it fall. It was a popular day camping site, with natural rapids and the architectural feel of an ancient Roman ruin. It wasn't crowded for a Thursday morning. *At least it had people,* Sam thought. *Witnesses.*

The tow truck and the catch on its hook drew a few strange looks from the other visitors as it rolled into the parking area, almost as strange as the looks that followed the Rolls. Sam pointed to a spot that the visiting cars hadn't reached. "Pull over there, Stan."

Stan turned the wheel. "I just hope to God you know what you're doing."

"I don't," said Sam. "I really don't."

The tow truck came to a gentle stop. Stan switched off the beacon. Sam clutched the canister. She looked at Stan. She looked at Zach. Her lips were parched. Her throat was dry. Her resolve pushed through. "OK, boys. Showtime."

Peale watched as the doors to the tow truck opened. The driver seemed anything but threatening, heading quickly away from the tow truck towards the well-attended picnic area. The outboard passenger. *The Peeters boy*, Peale thought, an unkempt version of his late father. One occupant remained. *Hutchings*. He watched as Gerry's daughter slid out on the driver's side. In her hands was a familiar object. *A bargaining chip*. Peale opened his door. McMasters opened his, the Maxim 9 tucked in his waistband. Peale walked towards Sam. They met at the rear of the van. Peale looked at Gerry Hutchings's daughter. She wasn't the broken girl that he had remembered from her last day at the lodge. He could see the family resemblance. The eyes. *Gerry's eyes*. If she had any fear, she was doing an excellent job of concealing it.

Peale pointed at the canister. "I believe you have something that belongs to me."

Sam looked at the canister. She looked at Peale. "I think this belongs to a *lot* of people, Mr. Peale. Or may I call you Norman?"

"Call me whatever you like," said Peale. "I believe there are seven more of those containers, yes?"

"Bought and paid for," said Sam. "Did you want to send Zach Peeters an e-transfer? Better yet, why don't you bring back his family from the grave. I think that would be a fair trade."

She's a smart one, this Hutchings girl. "An unfortunate tragedy."

"That you arranged," said Sam. "Like Rhee's dad, and mine."

Peale wasn't interested in a dressing down of his conscience. He nodded at McMasters. McMasters raised his shirt to reveal the butt of the gun. Sam noted the oversized artillery. "Do you think he's compensating for something?"

Peale pointed at the canister. "The diamonds, Miss Hutchings. You can keep the van. And the file cabinets. And your life."

Sam looked at Peale. She looked at McMasters. She looked at the bargaining chip. She looked deep inside for the courage. She found it. "Let's take a walk," she said, pointing at McMasters. "Without the Goon Prince Harry." She turned away and started walking. She could hear her footsteps on the gravel. She didn't hear a gunshot, but she heard another set of footsteps. Peale had caught up to her. He was getting flustered. "Miss Hutchings, there is no need to prolong our exchange. Mr. McMasters and I have a pressing engagement."

Sam kept her focus on the walkway. "Yeah, I had a feeling about you two."

"You're putting your friends' lives in danger with this stroll. You do realize that."

"How many?"

"How many what?"

Sam turned to Peale as she continued to walk. She balanced the canister on her palm. "How many lives are in here?"

Peale rolled his eyes. "A touch of melancholy to add to this dramatic parting, Miss Hutchings?"

"How many?"

Peale looked at Sam. He said the words with casual coldness of a celluloid villain. "More than you can count, Miss Hutchings. More than you can possibly count."

Sam fixed her eyes forward. "Counting is important. My dad was an accountant. He used to say that even the smallest truth demands accuracy. Would you agree, *Norman*?"

"Sage advice," said Peale. "Your father was a fine man. I thought so right up to the moment I shot him."

Sam kept walking. *There it was.* The confirmation.

Peale continued. "Do you know why I shot him?"

"Something to do with the truth?"

"Your father was leaving you, Sam. He was leaving the company, your brother, and your mother. Like a common coward."

The pair had reached the end of the walkway, coming upon a large hexagon perched on a sloping chunk of Canadian Shield. The water from the lazy rapids swirled below. Sam leaned the canister on the edge of the railing. She did her best to keep her emotions in check. "My father wasn't a coward."

"He could have exposed us all," said Peale. He leaned on the railing with his arms crossed. "Instead, he ran into the woods like a scared yearling. You should thank me."

Sam gripped the canister between her hands. She looked at the freshly drilled hole in the cap. "It doesn't have to be big," Aaron had said, as Steve readied the cordless drill for the trip to pick up the auction items. Sam spoke to the canister. "I guess I should," she said. She turned to Peale. She bunted him square in the nose with the centre of the canister. He fell backwards against the rail. Sam looked long enough to see the blood start to flow. She leaned down as Peale tried to stop the bleeding. She locked eyes. She unscrewed the canister and removed the recorder.

"Thank you, Mr. Peale. Thank you very much."

She ran down the walkway. A few onlookers went over to assist Peale. That's when he pulled out his gun, the same one he had shot Gerry Hutchings with. The onlookers screamed. Peale pulled himself up. He squeezed off a shot. The bullet hit the railing just ahead of Sam, showering her with splinters. The second was wide and wild, a small puff of dust billowing from the mighty wall of the dam upon impact. She kept running. Another bullet kicked up enough of the dried plank behind her that the splinters hit her in the calf. The pain bolstered her speed.

She followed the curve of the walkway, which shielded her from Peale. She was almost at the parking lot. That's when she saw McMasters. He was running towards her with the Maxim drawn. He put on the brakes to achieve a firing stance. He would have hit Sam centre mass. Something distracted him. *Gravel*. He turned just in time to see the Oiseau Garage tow truck bearing down on him, still towing the derelict van. She watched as he aimed for the driver. He hesitated. It wasn't the old man: it was Steve Mulaney. He had squeezed into the bench seat of the tow truck for the ride in, hiding in the back of the van before they left the lab. "I think Dad would want me in the thick of it," he had told Sam. She hoped his one good eye was up for the task.

It wasn't a life-ending impact, but it was enough to send McMasters off for a nap. The Maxim landed at Sam's feet. She picked it up. She turned towards Peale. He was still approaching, gun raised. Sam had never fired anything more than a BB gun. She aimed. She squeezed the trigger.

It wasn't the loud report of Peale's gun, but it had the same effect. The bullet caught Peale in the right shoulder. The shock sent his gun into the water. He knelt down, bleeding, bloodied, defeated.

The approaching sirens grew louder.

SIXTY-ONE

Sam picked the splinters out of her jeans. She couldn't hear the rushing water anymore as she leaned against Peale's Rolls. The activity had overtaken it, and there was plenty of it. Plenty of RCMP, plenty of what Sam figured were CSIS members milling about. Aaron was getting a back pat and a handshake from someone who must have been his superior. Things were getting bagged, like Peale's waterlogged automatic and McMasters's ultra-gun. *Ultra-gun.* Sam thought she might use it in her Great Canadian Novel.

Zach made his way over to his lake bud. He leaned against the fender, taking in the goings-on. He spoke to the activity. "Kind of exciting for a Pinawa Thursday, doncha think?"

Sam nodded. "You think this is crazy, you should check out the farmer's market on Saturday."

Steve pointed over at the town ambulance. "Looks like the old man and his minion will need an Advil or two."

Sam looked over at the pair, still under heavy guard. Peale's shirt had been cut away for the bandages on his shoulder. McMasters had a large bandage wrapped around his head. She smirked. "I wouldn't give those pricks a generic Aspirin."

"Sam!" Aaron had finally pulled away from the law enforcement contingent. "Are you guys OK?"

Sam went to speak. Then she thought about the question. *Am I OK?* She knew she wouldn't be. There was an awful lot to process. She said as much. "I really don't know yet. It's going to take a little time, I guess."

"Lisa sent me a text," said Aaron. "They're waiting for you in town. We can give you guys a lift in."

"Lift in? What about Stan's tow truck?"

"Part of the scene," said Aaron. "We'll bring it back to him in one piece."

A few minutes later, the tow truck quartet were headed into Pinawa in a CSIS Suburban. Megan was the first to run up to them when they pulled into the parking lot of the RCMP detachment. The hug was more like a clench. Sam welcomed it. Lisa won for the bear hug category. "You're one crazy bitch, you know that?" The tears ran down Lisa's face like the trickle from a leaky garden hose.

"Takes one to know one," said Sam. Her tears had finally arrived.

Sam knew it was late in the morning. The floor tiles were anything but liquid nitrogen cold. *Coffee.* She let the smell of the percolated rounds guide her. Megan was attending to the Pyrex. She smiled as she extended her arms for the first hug of the day. "Morning, Mom."

"Morning," Sam yawned. "What time is it?"

"Pancake time," said Megan. She retrieved a foil pan from the oven. "I think they turned out OK."

Sam smelled the burnt pancakes. "They're perfect."

It was almost noon when the pair finally made their way to Pinawa. There was a little bit of a commotion at the RCMP detachment. Peale's Rolls was being off-loaded from a flat-deck tow truck, its PYNTREE vanity plate visible on the rear deck as it descended. A few media vehicles were present. Luckily, none of them knew that one of the principal members of the current events drove a faded silver Chevy.

At Whispering Pines, Lena was in good spirits, and in good recall. She called Sam *Sam*, she called Megan *Megan*. After a little light convincing, the trio made their way outside. Megan pushed her grandmother's wheelchair. The blackbirds were especially vocal. "Don't they sound lovely," said Lena.

"They sure do, Grandma," said Megan.

Lena reached up to grasp her granddaughter's hand. "They sure do."

The afternoon went quickly, as did the Solo blueberry pie that Sam had picked up on the way. She had decided to keep the news of the day quiet. The clock was rolling up on six. Sam gave her mother a hug and a kiss. "I love you, Mom."

"I love you too, Samantha," said Lena. "And it's time for me to get ready."

"Ready?"

"For your father of course. Isn't it Friday?"

"Uhm, yes, Mom. Today is Friday."

"And he's an accountant. Works in the city. Comes out every Friday."

The sundowning. Sam played along. "That's right, Mom. Every Friday. Just like clockwork."

"Can you tell the nurse that I'm ready to see him?"

Sam blinked. "Uhm, yeah, Mom. We'll go do that right now." She gave her mother another hug/kiss combo. Megan did the same. Megan looked at Sam as they exited Lena's room. Her look said it all. So did Sam's.

Sam walked up to the front desk. The attendant was different, around Sam's age, with too much red hair dye to be standard equipment. The name tag said JUDY. Sam did as she was asked. "Hi there, Judy? Lena, my mother. She says she's ready—"

"I know. Isn't it adorable?"

Sam was confused. "Her husband has been dead for over thirty years."

"It happens sometimes," said Judy. "Whether it's the dementia or the glaucoma, nobody knows for sure."

Megan leaned in. "So, what exactly is happening?"

"Here he comes," said Judy.

Sam turned. An orderly was pushing a white-haired man in a well-used wheelchair. He had seen much better days. He had also seen something that looked like a serious burn injury at some point in his life. His face, his hands, his neck. *That poor man.*

Judy continued. "That's John," she said. "Sounds better than John Doe, I guess."

Sam watched as the orderly pushed the man towards her mother's room. *He'll be here on Friday.* "John Doe?" Sam asked, her voice cracking.

"They found him after that fire at Eastland Lake in '89," said Judy. "No ID, third-degree burns over eighty percent of his body. Plus, he'd been shot too."

"Shot?" Megan asked.

"Three times," said Judy. "There's still a bullet in the back of his head apparently. Been in an institution most of his life, came here last year. Non-verbal, but every now and then . . ." Judy leaned closer. "When he does talk, he says weird shit."

"Weird how?" Sam asked.

"Weird random shit," said Judy. "Like it's the heat that's so hot. And something about Joey Heatherton's pants?"

Sam turned to her mother's room. The orderly was wheeling Gerry Hutchings through the door. There was no way that Aaron could have known. As far as he knew, Gerry Hutchings was dead and buried. *The truth I was told.* Sam turned to Judy. "Thank you, Judy. Thank you." She started walking towards the room. Judy stopped her. "Miss? I'm sorry but visiting hours are over."

Sam stopped. "Visiting hours? But you don't understand. I know who—"

"You can always see them tomorrow," said Judy. "And it's date night. Three's a crowd, you know?"

Sam's tears came quick and steady. Megan looked at her, confused. "Mom, what is it?"

"It's Dad," said Sam, her voice broken and elated at the same time. "Your grandfather. He's not—"

Megan moved in to hug her mother. They looked down the hallway. They could hear Monty Hall from Lena's room. Something about making a deal.

ACKNOWLEDGEMENTS

APRIL 16, 2021

Third time's a charm, and the thrice wouldn't be as nice if it weren't for the multiple assists. Let's start with Jack David at ECW Press, who continues to embrace what I truly believe, which is that Winnipeg and Manitoba-centric stories are worth telling. Emily Schultz, my primary editor of record who always gives the right nudges/kneecaps, and Laura Pastore on the copy edit side, with continued apologies for the grammatical minefields that make up my drafts. The rest of the ECW gang: Samantha Chin, Caroline Suzuki, Jessica Albert, David Caron, Susannah Ames, Alex Dunn, and Aymen Saidane. If I've missed anyone, I owe you a Coke.

Bird Lake is a very real place and I highly suggest that it become a road trip destination, since flying these days seems to be the equivalent of bathing in the shallow end of the Petri dish. While the Whiskey Jack Lodge is a pure conjuring, it has its beams in the memories of my former gig as an auto journalist. If you ever get to Tofino on Vancouver Island, swing by the Wickaninnish Inn for the feel I was going for. Closer to home was the Separation Lake Lodge north of Kenora. I worked a summer there in my youth and have fond memories of watching overloaded float planes struggling to take off.

I hope that I've done the right things in regard to the challenges faced by so many families that are dealing with a loved one in a cognitive decline. Be it Alzheimer's, dementia, or shrinking arteries, it is full of pain and illumination. Be gentle. Be supportive. And most importantly, be with them as much as you can.

While my dad is blessed with many a Dad joke and -ism, I need to tip the trucker cap to my late father-in-law, Emile Marshall, a.k.a. "It's the heat that's so hot." His daughter Carol, a.k.a. my bride, has been and continues to be my greatest cheerleader. Much love and thanks to you, my Sweet Baboo.

A salute to Curtis McRae, my go-to for anything military and aircraft-specific. The fly-by did occur at Bird Lake, though it was most likely a Canadair CT-133 Silver Star, if my blurry recollections of wing tanks hold true, or maybe a CT-114 Tutor. Sadly, no pictures exist. I've always liked the look of the Canuck, which explains the cameo.

The story of Pinawa is glossed over at best, though its importance in the development of atomic energy in Canada is one worth looking into, and it's nowhere near as hinky as I've made it out to be. (Except for the deer. Lots and lots of deer.) As things continue to wind down at Whiteshell Laboratories, one can only hope that it doesn't become like so many boom towns that have gone to dust, rust, and bust.

A slight technical note. The GC Surplus disposal website changed up their online auction protocols in 2020 to an eBay-style system. In 2018, it was still a sealed-bid system. I miss those sealed-bid days. No better surprise than checking your inbox and finding out that a well-used RCMP Crown

Victoria was heading to your driveway for the price of one new F-150 payment.

As for Manitoba Provincial Road 315, that hump in the road that makes your car jump to the other side has been smoothed out a bit. Hands at nine and three. Hit the horn hard and often.

See you on the lake,
Michael J. Clark

ENVIRONMENTAL BENEFITS STATEMENT

ECW Press Ltd saved the following resources by printing the pages of this book on chlorine free paper made with 100% post-consumer waste.

TREES	WATER	ENERGY	SOLID WASTE	GREENHOUSE GASES
9	**700**	**4**	**30**	**3,810**
FULLY GROWN	GALLONS	MILLION BTUs	POUNDS	POUNDS

Environmental impact estimates were made using the Environmental Paper Network Paper Calculator 4.0. For more information visit www.papercalculator.org

This book is also available as a Global Certified Accessible™ (GCA) ebook. ECW Press's ebooks are screen reader friendly and are built to meet the needs of those who are unable to read standard print due to blindness, low vision, dyslexia, or a physical disability.

Purchase the print edition and receive the eBook free! Just send an email to ebook@ecwpress.com and include:

• the book title
• the name of the store where you purchased it
• your receipt number
• your preference of file type: PDF or ePub

A real person will respond to your email with your eBook attached. And thanks for supporting an independently owned Canadian publisher with your purchase!